MANSFIELD PARK

THEORY IN PRACTICE SERIES

General Editor: Nigel Wood, School of English, University of Birmingham

Associate Editors: Tony Davies and Barbara Rasmussen, University of Birmingham

Current titles:

Don Juan
Mansfield Park
The Prelude

Forthcoming titles include:

A Passage to India
To the Lighthouse
The Waste Land
Antony and Cleopatra
Henry IV
Measure for Measure
The Merchant of Venice
The Tempest

MANSFIELD **PARK**

EDITED BY
NIGEL WOOD

OPEN UNIVERSITY PRESS
BUCKINGHAM · PHILADELPHIA

Open University Press
Celtic Court
22 Ballmoor
Buckingham
MK18 1XW

and
1900 Frost Road, Suite 101
Bristol, PA 19007, USA

First Published 1993

A catalogue record of this book is available from the British Library

ISBN 0 335 09628 X (pb)

Library of Congress Cataloging-in-Publication Data

Mansfield Park / Mary Evans . . . [et al.]; edited by Nigel Wood.
       p.   cm. — (Theory in practice series)
    Includes bibliographical references and index.
    ISBN 0–335–09628–X (pb)
    1. Austen, Jane, 1775–1817. Mansfield Park.   I. Evans, Mary,
1946–   .   II. Wood, Nigel, 1953–   .   III. Series: Theory in
practice series.
PR4034.M33M36   1993
823′.7—dc20   92–32423
                                                                   CIP

Typeset by Colset Pte Ltd, Singapore
Printed in Great Britain by St Edmundsbury Press Ltd,
Bury St Edmunds, Suffolk

Contents

The Editor and Contributors

MARY EVANS teaches sociology and women's studies at the University of Kent at Canterbury. She is the author of various books on literature, including *Jane Austen and the State* (1987) and *Reflecting on Anna Karenina* (1989), and is currently at work on the writing of biography and autobiography.

BREAN S. HAMMOND is Rendal Professor of English at University College of Wales at Aberystwyth. He was educated in Edinburgh and Oxford, and was thereafter lecturer and senior lecturer in English at the University of Liverpool. He has written books on Alexander Pope, on politics and satire in the eighteenth century and on Swift's *Gulliver's Travels*, as well as many articles on seventeenth- and eighteenth-century literature, and the odd foray into drama. This is his first attempt at Jane Austen.

CLAUDIA L. JOHNSON is an associate professor of English at Marquette University, and the author of *Jane Austen: Women, Politics, and the Novel* (1988), as well as articles on eighteenth-century literature and music. She is currently finishing her next book, *Equivocal Beings: Sex, Sentiment, and Ideology in the Fiction of Wollstonecraft, Radcliffe, and Burney*, which will be published by the University of Chicago Press.

BARBARA RASMUSSEN is lecturer in English at the University of Birmingham. Her research interests include the writings of Alice and

Henry James, and the interaction between psychoanalytic and literary texts.

NIGEL WOOD is a lecturer in the School of English at the University of Birmingham. He is the author of studies on Gay and Swift and of several essays on literary theory. He is also editor of Fanny Burney's diaries.

Editors' Preface

The object of this series is to help bridge the divide between the understanding of theory and the interpretation of individual texts. Students are therefore introduced to theory in practice. Although contemporary critical theory is now taught in many colleges and universities, it is often separated from the day-to-day consideration of literary texts that is the staple ingredient of most tuition in English. A thorough dialogue between theoretical and literary texts is thus avoided.

Each of these specially commissioned volumes of essays seeks by contrast to involve students of literature in the questions and debates that emerge when a variety of theoretical perspectives are brought to bear on a selection of 'canonical' literary texts. Contributors were not asked to provide a comprehensive survey of the arguments involved in a particular theoretical position, but rather to discuss in detail the implications for interpretation found in particular essays or studies, and then, taking these into account, to offer a reading of the literary text.

This rubric was designed to avoid two major difficulties which commonly arise in the interaction between literary and theoretical texts: the temptation to treat a theory as a bloc of formulaic rules that could be brought to bear on any text with roughly predictable results; and the circular argument that texts are constructed as such merely by the theoretical perspective from which we choose to regard them. The former usually leads to studies that are really just footnotes to the adopted theorists, whereas the latter is effortlessly self-fulfilling.

It would be disingenuous to claim that our interests in the teaching of theory were somehow neutral and not open to debate. The idea for this series arose from the teaching of theory in relation to specific texts. It is inevitable, however, that the practice of theory poses significant questions as to just what 'texts' might be and where the dividing lines between text and context may be drawn. Our hope is that this series will provide a forum for debate on just such issues as these which are continually posed when students of literature try to engage with theory in practice.

Tony Davies
Barbara Rasmussen
Nigel Wood

Preface

The idea for this series arose from the teaching of a course on Methods and Contexts at the University of Birmingham. I would like to express my gratitude to all there who supported the idea in the first place, especially Tony Davies, Tom Davis, Lynne Pearce, Martin Pumphrey and Barbara Rasmussen who supplied many essential and timely suggestions, as did Ray Cunningham and John Skelton at the Open University Press. The challenge set by the work of the late (and much missed) Raman Selden in this area will be obvious to all those versed in the difficulties and rewards of practising theory. Several of my present and former students will recognize here a few of my favourite topics repeated in the introduction, and those who signed up for my Jane Austen option might trace their own contributions. Alison probably regretted that I ever turned to Austen, but still helped in many ways.

My greatest debt is to the contributors who have made this a genuinely collaborative project, and who introduced me to the variety of ways that most worthwhile writing, today as in Austen's time, resists authority.

Nigel Wood

How to Use this Book

Each of these essays is composed of a theoretical and a practical element. Contributors were asked to identify the main features of their perspective on the text (exemplified by a single theoretical essay or book) and then to illustrate their own attempts to put this into practice.

We realize that many readers new to recent theory will find its specific vocabulary and leading concepts strange and difficult to relate to current critical traditions in most English courses.

The format of this book has been designed to help if this is your situation, and we would advise the following:

(i) Before reading the essays, glance at the editor's introduction where the literary text's critical history is discussed, and

(ii) also at the prefatory information immediately before the essays, where the editor attempts to supply a context for the adopted theoretical position.

(iii) If you would like to develop your reading in any of these areas, turn to the annotated further reading section at the end of the volume, where you will find brief descriptions of those texts that each contributor has considered of more advanced interest. There are also full citations of the texts to which the contributors have referred in the references. It is also possible that more local information will be contained in notes to the essays.

(iv) The contributors have often regarded the chosen theoretical texts as points of departure and it is also in the nature of theoretical discussion to apply and test ideas on a variety of texts. Turn, therefore, to the question and answer sections that follow each essay which are designed to allow contributors to comment and expand on their views in more general terms.

A Note on
the Text

All quotations from Austen's novels are taken from the Penguin editions (full publication details supplied in the references), and have been abbreviated in the text as follows:

E   *Emma*
LS   *Lady Susan/The Watsons/Sanditon*
MP   *Mansfield Park*
NA   *Northanger Abbey*
P   *Persuasion*
PP   *Pride and Prejudice*
SS   *Sense and Sensibility*

Introduction

NIGEL WOOD

When Jane Austen was only seven (1782), her family converted their dining parlour at Steventon rectory into a temporary theatre to stage *Matilda*, a tragedy written by Dr Thomas Francklin, a friend of Samuel Johnson's and also one of those 'fine' London preachers so distrusted by Edmund Bertram (*MP*, 121). This was no isolated rashness. Sheridan's *The Rivals* followed two years later, and by 1787 the barn was requisitioned for a Christmas production of Susannah Centlivre's *The Wonder! A Woman Keeps A Secret*. At about this time, probably until she was eighteen, Austen tried her hand at humorous dramatic writing. The texts of three short plays remain: 'The Visit, a Comedy in Two Acts', 'The Mystery, an Unfinished Comedy' and 'The First Act of a Comedy', as well as a full five-act play, 'Sir Charles Grandison, or the Happy Man' – as the title suggests, a free collage of episodes taken from Samuel Richardson's *History of Sir Charles Grandison*.[1]

The point to this biographical detail is to highlight an obvious mismatch between the young Austen's relish for acting and stagecraft, and Fanny Price's moral disapproval and self-imposed exile from the Mansfield bustle during the preparations for *Lovers' Vows*. Alternatively, we could consider the early letter to her sister, Cassandra (9 January 1796), where the previous night's ball had provoked Austen '*to be particular*' with her 'Irish friend', Tom Lefroy: 'Imagine to yourself everything most profligate and shocking in the way of dancing and sitting down together. I *can* expose myself, however, only *once more*, because he leaves the country soon after next Friday . . .'. The one fault Lefroy has is that 'his morning coat is a great deal too light' (Chapman 1932, I: 2–3). It is but a small inferential step to associate the social daring shown here with perhaps Emma Woodhouse's indiscretions with Frank Churchill (at Miss Bates's expense) during the Box Hill expedition in *Emma* (361–9), or the cheerful lack of proportion of Lydia Bennet when in sight of a red uniform in *Pride and Prejudice* with the noting of Tom Lefroy's sartorial blemish. Austen's biographical record cannot leave us with a secure prediction as to her moral outlook, and yet the literary and heritage myth that is Jane Austen is nurtured by many 'intentional fallacies' that are based on a settled England of the mind, and which need to be bracketed off from Revolutionary zeal as well as Gothic excess.

It would be a particularly partisan view, however, to ignore the biographical evidence in the construction of our own 'Jane Austen', even were we to find that necessary, just as it would be naive to read off her often ironic narratives as reliable documents on the Hampshire/ Bath life of her contemporaries. For example, one of the most attractive and persistent moving forces behind the 1787 Christmas festivities at Steventon was her frivolous paternal cousin, Eliza, comtesse de Feuillde, recently arrived from France in flight from the Terror. Once in the bosom of the family, she appears to have attracted the attentions of Jane's brothers, James and Henry. Her own husband was to be guillotined in 1794, freeing her to pay serious attention to Henry, whom she married in 1797. Hypothetical scene-setting at Steventon during the festivities conjures up a Jane of twelve years (Fanny Price?), noting with awe the forbidden fruit almost plucked by the exotic Comtesse (Mary Crawford?), and the struggle with virtue on her brother's part (Edmund Bertram?). So far so good – or at least, neat, but it should also be remembered that Austen was to dedicate her 'Love and Freindship' (*sic*) (composed *c*.1790) to Eliza Austen, an act most probably intended as a compliment – even given the tale's preoccupation with deception.[2]

Despite the family's belief, expressed by her nephew, J.E. Austen-Leigh, in his *Memoir* (1870) of her, that she based no fictional character on anyone living (*P*, 374), there are sufficient details in the biographical documents to supply certain interpretational patterns. Except for a relatively brief period, split between Bath and Southampton (1801–9), she lived in rural Hampshire. There were visits along the south coast of England and also several up to London, where Henry had rented a house in Sloane Square (up to 1813) and then taken an apartment in the City, but normality for her was provincial and apparently consistent with her fictional locations. Much like Catherine Morland visiting Northanger Abbey, or Elinor and Marianne Dashwood in *Sense and Sensibility* attempting to fathom London society, or Elizabeth Bennet, when faced with Darcy (and Pemberley) – and, most certainly, Fanny Price schooled in how to be grateful at Mansfield – Jane Austen felt herself constantly at an economic and social disadvantage. Her letters also help us believe in the spectating spinster of middle age, and the writer who gradually became aware both of her success and its limitations.[3] It is not long before students come across the letters to Anna Austen (9 September 1814: '3 or 4 Families in a Country Village is the very thing to work on') or to James Stanier Clarke (11 December 1815: 'I think I may boast myself to be . . . the most unlearned and uninformed female who ever dared to be an authoress') or, perhaps most commonly cited, the letter to her brother, J. Edward Austen (16 December 1816), in which she contrasts his 'strong, manly spirited [written] sketches, full of Variety and Glow' with her own 'little bit (two inches wide) of Ivory', full of miniaturist polish but devoid of bravura impact (Chapman 1932, II: 401, 443, 468–9). The most basic cause-and-effect critical commonplace relegates Austen to the role of patronizable *female* author, deploying a searching realism because she had no other imaginative resource.

I have taken the time to sketch this 'Jane Austen' for two reasons. First, it can be an appealing vision. Her novels can all be read as a guide to an England we have lost (and to which some would like to return) and so it would account for her continued (yet surprisingly contemporary) vogue in English literature syllabuses as well as with the reading public at large. Many careful revisions have to be made in order to keep this world intact, yet it has had a tenacious hold on critical judgement. Second, it should be clear that Austen can appear in her writing in unexpected passages – not just as the Fanny Prices or Elizabeth Bennets of her world, but also in the moral frailties of those we are encouraged to reject. The Jane Austen who wrote *Mansfield Park* is in any case significantly distant in years and views from the dancing partner for Tom Lefroy or the budding dramatist, and it is this later Austen, this 'other' author, that has preoccupied much recent criticism.

The Realism of Instruction

The earliest reviews of Austen's work are few in number and usually routine in inspiration. To a large extent this is due to the low esteem in which the novel form was regarded. I will return to this in the next section. However, from the earliest notices, it became clear that, when Austen's work *was* prized, it was largely because of its 'realism'. This did not quite carry the associations among her readership of, say, the late-century 'naturalism' of a Zola, namely, an obviously documentary representation that is advanced in a spirit of almost scientific experimentation (see Selden 1988: 51–6). For example, the anonymous reviewer for the *Critical Review* (February 1812) found *Sense and Sensibility* 'a genteel, well-written novel' which could be regarded 'as agreeable a lounge as a genteel comedy, from which both amusement and instruction may be derived'. Its 'excellent lesson' and 'useful moral' were 'essential requisites', so the 'naturally drawn' characters and 'probable' incidents were hardly a slice of life alone in that they served an educative function and were not merely freely available sets of empirical details (Southam 1968, 1: 35). Certainly, the critical landmarks in the growth of Austen's popularity all indicated how successfully unsurprising her plots were – that is, how they subordinated the excitement of individual events to the needs of a preconceived framework. The 1823 reader for the *Retrospective Review* noted this turn to probability in plotting as a 'revolution' in the evolution of the novel: 'Without any wish to surprise us into attention, by strangeness of incident, or complication of adventure . . . the stream of her Tale flows on in an easy, natural, but spring tide' (Southam 1968, 1: 109). Sir Walter Scott, when considering *Emma* (in the main) for the *Quarterly Review* (October 1815, issued March 1816), held Austen up as a model for those who believed that the novel as a form had weaned itself from the prose romance and those emulators that had indulged in sentimental excess. *Emma* belonged 'to a class of fictions which has arisen almost in our own times, and which draws the characters and incidents introduced more immediately from the current of ordinary life than was permitted by the former rules of the novel' (Southam 1968, 1: 59). The analogy with 'the Flemish school of painting' was not far-fetched, considering the unheroic subject-matter, which was, however, 'finished up to nature, and with a precision which delights the reader' (Southam 1968, 1: 67). It is not clear whether this 'precision' is a matter of the accurate detailing of reality, or something which appears identical, but which demonstrates a crucial step away from such an art of transparent representation: the conduct of a narrative 'with much neatness and point' (Southam 1968, 1: 68). If you believe that reality is neat and carries an implicit lesson, then you will observe no split between Scott's reverence for Austen as realist and as moralist.

This distinction between Austen and earlier novelists certainly placed the emphasis on where she departed from what had become the trademarks of the popular novel in the 1790s.[4] Sensation and sentiment suggested the possibility of individual freedoms amidst a society or wider political order that was open to sudden change (a corollary of the unexpected twists in the plot and sudden danger for the protagonists). As Gary Kelly, Margaret Kirkham and Marilyn Butler have made clear, the political debates of the time, including those centred on the role of women, attracted several novelists who exploited the wider scope of prose fiction (and some of its lack of generic self-definition) by including doctrinaire sermons and idealistic role models in their plots.[5] Austen's control in subduing her pedagogical impulses, by contrast, could be a sign of maturity and/or non-partisan transcendence of the local and contemporary. In the view of the Archbishop of Dublin (Richard Whately) in his *Quarterly Review* article (January 1821), the new seriousness with which readers could now safely take novels resulted from the 'solid sense' they contained (Southam 1968, 1: 87). In this, Austen was abundant and her works could

> safely be recommended, not only as among the most unexceptionable of their class, but as combining, in an eminent degree, instruction with amusement, though without the direct effort at the former, of which we have complained, as sometimes defeating its object.
>
> (Southam 1968, 1: 105)

Unlike Scott and others, Whately does not pass over *Mansfield Park* but rather appreciates Fanny's moral choices and her spirited rejection of Henry Crawford. He is also entertained by the implied criticism of the Bertram household. Sir Thomas is 'one of those men who always judge rightly, and act wisely, when a case is fairly put before them; but who are quite destitute of acuteness of discernment and adroitness of conduct' (Southam 1968, 1: 99). For Whately, Austen's artistic 'finish' aided her moral value, whereas Scott's emphasis falls on the artistic judgement that renders the motivating ideas palatable.

These two full-length studies should not be taken to indicate that Austen's work was commonly read or even widely available. The five-volume Bentley Collected Edition published in 1833 was surely no commercial risk but the fact that a full issue took so long to appear does not imply widespread acceptance. It is perhaps surprising to come across the divisions her work could cause in Victorian critical circles. Sometimes her 'realism' could be rated as merely plain and prosy, sometimes as so economically deployed that it was a sign of consummate mastery. The latter view was eloquently held by George Henry Lewes (the future companion of George Eliot) who in his *Fraser's Magazine* piece of 1847, confessed to envying the author of *Pride and Prejudice* (and *Tom Jones*) above Scott. This may not have been so decided an endorsement if he had not also held that the writing and reading of novels was 'a fine thing' and that the novel had risen 'to the first rank of literature' (Lewes 1847: 686). When given more scope for his opinions in 1852 for the *Westminster Review*, his tribute to 'The Lady Novelists' dwelt ostentatiously on Jane Austen. A reverence for her work was the acid test of the serious critic – not just of the novel, moreover, as she is dubbed the 'greatest artist that has ever written', exhibiting the 'most perfect mastery over the means to her end' (Southam 1968, 1: 140). Perception of this, though, could only be reserved for the gifted few. Those who looked for 'strong lights and shadows' found her 'tame and uninteresting' (Southam 1968, 1: 141).

It is likely that Lewes was responding in part to the puzzlement expressed by Charlotte Brontë at his *Fraser's* preferences. In her letter to Lewes of 12 January 1848, she finds *Pride and Prejudice* the fruit of a mind merely 'shrewd and observant', her nature 'a carefully fenced, highly cultivated garden, with neat borders and delicate flowers', and her characters accurately 'daguerrotyped' and 'commonplace' (Southam 1968, 1: 126). This opinion lived with her, for she elaborates on it two years later (12 April 1850) to her publisher, W.S. Williams. *Emma* comes across as superficial almost by design. With Scott's values as comparison, it is significant how rapidly such artistic control could be reassessed. Brontë finds 'a Chinese fidelity, a miniature delicacy in the painting', that soothes rather than excites: 'the Passions are perfectly unknown to her' (Southam 1968, 1: 128). Lewes's sustained regard for her work, on the other hand, kept Austen's art before the public. His *Blackwood's Edinburgh Magazine* article (July 1859), 'The Novels of Jane Austen', concedes that other novelists may be able to excite greater interest, but that 'interest-value' is bound to wane as it is linked to one set of historical conditions. Austen's art not only endures, apparently freed from such temporal conditions, but still carries its original 'life' for new generations. He regards it as proverbially true ('as probably few will dispute') that 'the art of the novelist be the representation of human life by means of a story; and if the *truest* representation, effected by the *least expenditure* of means, constitutes the highest claim of art' then we find it in her work (Southam 1968, 1: 152). However, Austen's 'classic' status was not ensured until the last third of the century, prompted in the main by the image of the writer provided by her nephew, Rev. J.E. Austen-Leigh, in his *Memoir*.

The *Memoir* is reproduced in the Penguin edition of *Persuasion* and now confirms most prejudices both for and against Jane Austen. For a seminar several years ago that had read novels by Fanny Burney and George Eliot as well as Austen I set a series of prose passages from the *Memoir* with the subject's name carefully removed. There was almost unanimous agreement on to whom the unknown writer was referring. This was the case despite the competition from deliberately chosen extracts from Burney's journals and J.W. Cross's 1884 *Life* of Eliot that might have dissolved otherwise evident biographical differences. The *Memoir*'s great use for late Victorian taste lay in its creation of Jane Austen as the dutiful family member, the amateur genius who could still help run a household. While we may now value it less, this Austen myth is potent. A new generation of readers discovered Austen in 1870, and, it could be argued, so did the Academy. In a series of reviews of the *Memoir* the first serious assessment of the artfulness of the works is attempted and is set against the love of a close rendition of provincial life.

It would be as well to pause at this point to enumerate the various *aesthetic* choices carried by that one term: 'realism'. Its utility in critical judgements can sometimes be due to its lack of specific reference. Does it denote an empirical or a psychological state of affairs? Does it reflect the choice of subject-matter ('kitchen-sink drama', the inclusion of non-fictional documentary evidence) or its stylistic treatment? Or does it describe the neutral observer, freed from polemical ranting or overinvolved empathizing? Commonly, it unites all those who feel that language can or should represent life faithfully. What we see emerge from Regency and Victorian readings of Austen's work is a preoccupation with her mimetic accuracy – in short, her ability to render the detail of a narrow, yet focused, version of social life. Her art was thus the talent of hiding art, which entailed a significant opposition between her artistic restraint, which signalled true judgement, and the overtly imaginative and highly metaphorical styles of some of her contemporaries' writing, which too much resembled the

Romantic forms that had emerged in the form's self-conscious infancy.[6]
Similarly, the value placed on 'realism' by Scott, Whately and Lewes
delivered her work from the didactic, conduct-book tradition that
exonerated the clumsy practitioner because her/his creed was in the
right place. If Austen's 'realism' is no longer quite the saving grace it
once was, then that is possibly because we no longer need to excuse
the novel form. Novelistic 'realism' is usually placed in quotation
marks because the term no longer meets with a simple definition and
also because critics wish to distance their judgements from the naive
belief that certain kinds of art embody a more empirical value than
others.

From 1870 onwards the reliance on a Jane Austen who embodied
ethical values so stealthily in her work is needed much less. The *Memoir*
supplies an attractive myth to take its place. Her nephew regards her
characters 'as familiar guests to the firesides of so many families, and
are known there as individually and intimately as if they were living
neighbours'. Her 'ideal characters' were known for their 'moral recti-
tude', 'correct taste' and 'warm affections' – all to be observed in the
real Jane Austen (*P*, 273). Fanny Price is therefore not just a *dramatis
persona* but even the *propria persona* of her author. While holding
'strong political opinions' as a girl (*P*, 331), it goes on record that she
'never touched upon politics, law, or medicine' (*P*, 282). She meets her
end as a 'humble, believing Christian', able to hold her life in review as
one long round of 'home duties, and the cultivation of domestic affections, without any self-seeking or craving after applause' (*P*, 387). This
homage could be infectious. Trollope, for example, could revere the
'excellent teaching' in her work, 'free from an idea or word that can
pollute'. Consistently, there was inculcated the 'sweet lesson of
homely household womanly virtue' (Trollope 1938: 104–5). It would
seem that this very artlessness helped her own ethics to shine through
more clearly.

The 'Other' Jane Austen

For contrast, it would be instructive to place the *Memoir* alongside
John Halperin's much less charitable *Life* (1984) or three studies that
have marked a sea change in Austen studies: D.W. Harding's essay,
'Regulated Hatred: An Aspect of the Work of Jane Austen', which
first appeared in *Scrutiny* in 1940, Marvin Mudrick's *Jane Austen: Irony
as Defense and Discovery* (1952; 1968) and Lionel Trilling's essay on the

novel in his *The Opposing Self* (1955; first printed in the *Partisan Review*, 1954). For Harding, to dwell on Austen's surface ease and poise involves a particularly one-eyed glance at her irony. There can be found in her novels a polite and submerged form of attack on her readers as 'her books are, as she meant them to be, read and enjoyed by precisely the sort of people whom she disliked; she is a literary classic of the society which attitudes like hers, held widely enough, would undermine' (Harding 1939–40: 347). This could account for the careful fragility of her manufactured endings. Lacking this subversion, *Mansfield Park* is a grave disappointment, Fanny Price (worthy, but dull) the standard-bearer for the whole novel. For Mudrick, Harding's essay was to open up several possibilities. Acknowledging the redis-covered review by Richard Simpson of the *Memoir* (first published anonymously in the *North British Review* in 1870), he proceeds to drive a wedge between the familiar quietist Aunt Jane and the writer more addicted to ironic detachment than a tidy hearth. Simpson had noted how disparate the desire for romantic love and its fulfilment was from the results Austen actually provided for her protagonists: 'She sat apart on her rocky tower, and watched the poor souls struggling in the waves beneath' (Southam 1968, 1: 246). Mudrick notes how the reader's sense of the authorial withdrawal from the mess of life is entwined with the critical need to discriminate between the overt sentiments of the Austen text and their defensive function. The Highbury/Mansfield/Kellynch regimes cannot sanction emotional display or imaginative indulgence because their *raison d'être* is stability and continuity, the *ancien régime* amidst curious and largely unwelcome change much like some encircled wagon train. Thus social convention redeems *and* immolates those who enjoy its material benefits:

> it is Jane Austen who has created Marianne [in *Sense and Sensibility*], the 'burning heart of passion' even if she buries her finally in the coffin of convention . . . Irony is her defense as an artist, the novelist who organizes her work so firmly and totally as to leave us without a sense of loss for the personal commit-ment she will not make; and convention is her defense as the genteel spinster when the artist is overcome, perhaps by some powerful social or domestic pressure . . .
>
> (Mudrick 1968: 91)[7]

Irony is thus a mode of withholding comment while making a statement.

Trilling's appreciation of Austen's irony stems from a similar source to that noted by Mudrick. *Mansfield Park* seems to affirm 'literalness . . . that there are no two ways about anything', and yet its ironies can be structural and interactive ones, where the participation of the reader is integral. However, Trilling is more aware of the positive elements that are introduced by Austen's often sardonic commentary. Irony is not just a matter of 'tone', for 'primarily, it is a method of comprehension'. 'Spirit' is given meaning by its struggle with the conditioning powers of 'circumstance'. Fanny's spiritual strength is perfectly meaningful even when it is undramatic and at rest: 'To deal with the world by condemning it, by withdrawing from it and shutting it out, by making oneself and one's mode and principles of life the very center of existence' (Trilling 1955: 206–8, 211) is a comprehensible strategy for dealing with life, and yet the offence offered by the novel to liberal tastes ensures its greatness. Another Jane Austen was discovered, one congenial to a reassessment of *Mansfield Park*.

In a sense these views anticipate many of the present critical concerns with this 'other' Jane Austen, but their virtues of close and always intelligent reading seem very much of its New Critical age. In 1963, when introducing his widely popular 'Twentieth-Century [Critical] Views' on Austen, Ian Watt looked for a time when the author's 'social and moral assumptions' might be the subject of analysis as well as the literary forms which embodied them:

> It is surely mistaken to assume that the affirmative elements in her morality and her humor are not as real as the subversive ironies which occasionally accompany them . . . for how one sees is surely not more important than what one makes a point of seeing, or not seeing.

Piling up yet more instances of her 'awareness and insight' obeys the law of diminishing returns (Watt 1963: 13).

It is not that recent criticism has attempted to render Austen's fiction as overrated or superfluous to modern concerns, but rather that much feminist, Marxist or post-structuralist attention has been drawn both to the specific form of 'realism' deployed by her, to how it was constructed and to what end. The works emerge as rhetorical acts, which can be assessed for both their subconscious disclosures and their ideological agenda. Mary Evans, for example, has recently placed more emphasis on the radical satirist, a figure familiar to those who have appreciated the Mudrick line on her irony. Alternatively, Evans's work makes distinct the central difference between novels of 'manners' and those of 'morality'. Austen's concern is with the survival of morality 'in a world which is increasingly hostile to all interests other than the purely economic' (Evans 1987: x). By observing the crucial differences that lie in definitions of socially acceptable conformity and those of personal morality, the irony has a thematic and so structural utility. Similarly, in studies by Marilyn Butler (1975), Alistair Duckworth (1971) and Margaret Kirkham (1983) social, gendered and even political discourses impinge on the Hampshire calm of Chawton House.[8] For Butler, in 1975, Austen's work was anti-Jacobin in its efforts to dramatize a distrust of individualism and innovation, yet in her Introduction to the second edition (1987) and her contribution to J. David Grey's *The Jane Austen Handbook* (1986) she is ready to admit the proto-feminist, if not feminist, Austen.[9] She may have 'kept women within the domestic sphere, from which feminists and liberals wished to release them', yet, by the way, she also renders 'the plight of women, within these confines, more tellingly than anyone else' and her letters 'suggest alienation and misanthropy' (Grey 1986: 195).

Historical or sociological analysis should take into account the limited validity of much of the biographical evidence we now have. It is not simply a matter of exploding belletristic opinions and ignoring the testimony of Austen's descendants; it is more a recognition that history can be constructed out of what could not be on the record directly. The present critical emphasis has fallen on answering the question 'How?', and this involves not merely a catalogue of *what* is 'seen', but rather a consideration of the cultural conditions that have rendered certain ways of seeing intelligible at certain times.

Feminist readings of Austen's work, for example, have often found little on which to work without contextualizing. Fanny Price's self-abnegation and painful awkwardness at Mansfield does not promise well – especially not when compared with the wit and poise of an Elizabeth Bennet. However, this was something Austen had contrived. She confesses to Francis Austen (3 July 1813) that her first impressions of the early drafts of *Mansfield Park* were that it would be not half so entertaining as *Pride and Prejudice*, although it might sell well on her past record (Chapman 1932, II: 317). Cassandra Austen was told on 2 March 1814 that Henry Austen's reading of the book had cheered her. In giving 'great praise to the drawing of the characters', he 'understands them all, likes Fanny, and foresees how it will all be' (Chapman 1932, II: 376) – a complacent view, as, on 5 March, Cassandra is told how he has changed his mind as to his powers of prediction, saying how 'he defied anybody to say whether H.C. [Henry Crawford] would be reformed, or would forget Fanny in a fortnight' (Chapman 1932, II: 381). Apparently, it is necessary to 'understand' the characters, and Austen relishes the narrative traps of the work. Back on 2 March, Henry (her favourite brother) was praised for his percipience in admiring Henry Crawford, 'I mean properly, as a clever, pleasant man' (Chapman 1932, II: 378). This may seem a perverse way of 'understanding' the disruptive and eventually denounced stranger from London. The evidence of the letters shows, at the very least, how self-conscious she had become about narrative method, especially the way individual characters could be embedded within her plots. *Pride and Prejudice* became a significant bench-mark. It provided her with the first reassuring sign that her fiction could be read enjoyably and with discernment. *The Critical Review* for March 1813 dubbed her as 'the fair author' and praised her subtle characters, not one of whom 'appears flat, or obtrudes itself upon the notice of the reader with troublesome impertinence' (Southam 1968, 1: 47). Fanny Price was to be an experiment.

In any case, the turn to the writing of *Mansfield Park* signalled a new beginning. *Northanger Abbey*, although published (posthumously) in 1818, derived from drafts entitled 'Susan' on which Austen had first worked in 1798–9. Similarly, *Elinor and Marianne*, cast in epistolary form, was a product of (probably) 1795 and November 1797, although heavily revised in 1809–11 as *Sense and Sensibility*. *Pride and Prejudice* had started life as *First Impressions* in 1796–7. In conception, if not eventual execution, Austen's first completed work was a product of the 1790s and the secure environment of Steventon. From 1799 to 1809 there is very little of her writing left. This is a divide that has proved difficult to explain. *The Watsons*, her unfinished novel of manners, was probably begun in late 1804 at Bath and provides some form of evidence for the silence. Emma Watson, the draft's heroine, 'was naturally cheerful' (*LS*, 151), which is just as well as she undergoes a rapid change of fortune from comfort and serene good taste as the adopted child of her rich and childless aunt and uncle to one of want and dependency when she is returned to her ailing father's house – small and culturally constricted – when her widowed aunt remarries. It is as if Fanny Price had been cast out from Mansfield indefinitely.

There is much that is being worked through in *The Watsons*. Weaker characters than Emma Watson's might have been 'plunged . . . in despondence' (*LS*, 151). There are at least three possible reasons for the blankness of these Bath/Southampton years: first, Jane Austen felt acutely that her father's decision to uproot the family from Steventon by resigning his living was wrong. Life now became a series of rented rooms and travel that quickly palled. It also marked a decline in status and economic security.

Second, she had met with disappointment when attempting to place her work with publishers. 'Susan' had been bought for £10 in 1803 by Crosby and Co. thanks to the efforts of Henry Austen. Its non-appearance touched Austen dearly. When reminding Crosby and Co., on 5 April 1809, of their promise of an 'early publication', she even offered to forward a fresh manuscript, the previous one having been lost 'by some carelessness'. The six years' delay was an 'extraordinary circumstance' (Chapman 1932, I: 263). Crosbys replied that it was no inadvertence, no one else would publish it, but they were not bound to do so and that she could buy the work back – for £10.

Third, the death of her father and her closest friend and confidante, Anne Lefroy (1804–5), forced self-reliance on her very rapidly.

It is about this time that her remaining letters are least communicative, for the very good reason that her sister destroyed more letters than she preserved for posterity. At source, there is family interest in the dutiful 'Jane Austen'[10] and it would certainly be easier to provide the world with a further endorsement of her natural conservatism than explore the more radical touches of her irony and the heterodox notions such analysis might reveal.

Reading Novels and Gender

To a great extent the early faintness of praise for Austen's work is due to the relative infancy of novel reading as a genteel taste. In 1775 Sheridan was not alone, in his play *The Rivals* (I.ii), in portraying the circulating library as a supplier of sentiment and romance for a predominantly female clientele.[11] Austen was quite clear about the low esteem in which the novel was traditionally held. She becomes the intrusive narrator in *Northanger Abbey* to defend the practice of novel reading:

> I will not adopt that ungenerous and impolitic custom so common with novel writers, of degrading by their contemptuous censure the very performances, to the number of which they are

> themselves adding – joining with their greatest enemies in bestowing the harshest epithets on such works . . . Let us leave it to the Reviewers to abuse such effusions of fancy at their leisure, and over every new novel to talk in threadbare strains of the trash with which the press now groans. Let us not desert one another; we are an injured body.
>
> (NA, 58)

The 'we' mentioned here seems rather vague, but, when, later in the same paragraph, examples of 'our' writing are cited in mock-dialogue, Fanny Burney's *Cecilia* (1782) and *Camilla* (1796) and Maria Edgeworth's *Belinda* (1801) make up her list. That the most successful novelists at this time were women is significant.[12] The theme that unites these three novels is a specific one: a solitary female's unsentimental education. Typically, Burney portrays heroines confronted by complex networks of patriarchal authority which can result in direct physical threat, and it is telling that Austen does not choose to include here Burney's most popular and comic work, *Evelina* (1778). Both *Cecilia* and *Camilla* search for their filial or personal identity and discover that the very process of the search has provided them with their destiny – in both cases, the loss of the hope and spontaneity with which they started their quest. Edgeworth's *Belinda* is no victim, but her independence of mind still shows up the predatory and manipulative nature of male 'mentors' (such as John Thorpe, from *Northanger Abbey*?). It is in novels like these that, Austen claims, we meet with the display of 'the greatest powers of the mind, in which the most thorough knowledge of human nature, the happiest delineation of its varieties, the liveliest effusions of wit and humour are conveyed to the world in the best chosen language' (NA, 58). The passage is too protracted to be ironic at the expense of the two young readers (Catherine and Isabella) and its sudden appearance is a reminder that there are more respectable experiences to be gained than those from Ann Radcliffe's exercise in Gothic sentiment and terror, *The Mysteries of Udolpho* (1794), the work explicitly burlesqued in Chapters 20 to 24 of the novel.[13]

'Female Virtue', according to James Fordyce as recently as 1766, was suborned by the reading of novels, which were

> in their nature so shameful, in their tendency so pestiferous, and contain such rank treason against the royalty of Virtue, such horrible violation of all decorum, that she who can bear to peruse them must in her soul be a prostitute.

She who touches pitch must be defiled, perhaps, and we can rest confident that the author has not read any of them *personally*. He is 'assured' that in them Love and Honour were no longer held up in the most advantageous light, as in the 'Old Romance' (Jones 1990: 176-7). It therefore should come as no surprise that the pompous dunce, Mr Collins, from *Pride and Prejudice*, should refuse to read aloud from a novel '(for every thing announced it to be from a circulating library)' and choose instead the improving and instructive 'Fordyce's Sermons' (*PP*, 113).[14]

When Burney and Austen are praised for their 'realism' by contemporaries, therefore, it is also a comment on the growing seriousness with which the hitherto 'low' form was treated.[15] Austen wrote to Cassandra on 18 December 1798, confessing that the family were 'great Novel-readers & not ashamed of being so' (Chapman 1932, I: 38). While our present syllabuses include several innovative novelistic styles from the eighteenth century, the vast majority of Regency readers still turned to 'improving' Fordycean tracts, religious homilies or conduct-books – or, at least, were supposed to. When the prose classics were encountered, it was as likely as not in an abbreviated form as a 'chapbook'.[16] Romances were widely read without being countenanced in the public sphere, although Clara Reeve, in her *The Progress of Romance* (1785), made much of their distinctiveness from the more realistic novels and advanced the proposition that the latter might give more cause for concern as they often provided the illusion of consistency and accuracy in their portrayal of moral dilemmas (Reeve 1785, II: 86-7). No one could be influenced by the obvious fantasies of the Romance for good or ill (see Browne 1987: 35-8). The frequent target for the moral majority was the novel that dealt with love and courtship, but it was not just the moral guardians who proclaimed against the dangers of a private reading experience. While sensibility could be said to possess a radical power, it was often mistaken for a mere provision of self-indulgent sentiment by those seriously committed to reassessing the role of women. Mary Wollstonecraft, in her first novel, *Mary, A Fiction* (1788), portrayed a heroine who was too much in love with her own philanthropy and therefore had inflated expectations of her fellow humans. She is made for martyrdom, not respect. Part of this skewed outlook derives from her mother's indolence and defensive 'chastity'. To compensate for the privations she feels in the larger world, she is an avid reader of 'sentimental novels', especially the 'love-scenes' (Wollstonecraft 1976: 3). On the same lines, Mary Hays, the fierce advocate for greater tolerance in politics and human relationships in her *Letters and Essays* (1793), has her self-destructive Emma Courtney (in the *Memoirs* (1796)) a chain-reader of circulating-library novels, devouring between ten and fourteen a week (Hays 1796, I: 26).

The textual references to reading novels (specifically) are thus heavily coded, and Austen's clarity and force of voice in favour of the genre in *Northanger Abbey* exhibit a partisan involvement in its support. She must thus demonstrate that the form is a serious one by attempting to deny its Romance ancestry, at the same time as escaping from the conduct-book formulae associated with the improving tracts that preached in effect that women needed to be advised – and therefore subdued. It is also necessary, for this specific requirement to be met, that novel reading is not the sanitized and approved reading aloud of improving fiction within the family circle. Fanny Price may read, and, even if we do not hear of her glancing specifically at novels, there is a specific liberation for her in the act of solitary attention to the written. The first moment of sisterly intimacy she enjoys with Susan in Portsmouth stems from the shared need to escape the turmoil of their home. Susan learns to be 'quietly employed'. Books are a necessary component of this spiritual comfort and growth to maturity. Remembering the books she had access to at Mansfield, its effect is 'so potent and stimulative' that Fanny joins a circulating library: 'She became a subscriber – amazed at being any thing in *propria persona*, amazed at her own doings in every way; to be a renter, a chuser of books! And to be having any one's improvement in view in her choice!' Susan is to be subjected to sharing Fanny's 'own first pleasures, . . . biography and poetry'. This is also a timely diversion from the concern at Edmund's stay in London: 'for even half an hour, it was something gained' (*MP*, 390–1). The enforced solitude of reading is an important resource. This is clear when Emma Watson withdraws to her sick father's chamber, to be 'at peace from the dreadful mortifications of an unequal society'. While tending him, she is 'at leisure, she could read and think'. The otherwise oppressive concern at her decline in fortune is diluted by a means 'which only reading could produce'. She turns 'thankfully . . . to a book' (*LS*, 151).

For Mudrick, Austen's irony could be at the same time defensive and a means of self-definition. The very act of reading shares something of this power to construct the self, for not only is it a solace, but also a means of resistance. Fanny's room at Mansfield is not just a bolt-hole, but a place for contemplation. When Edmund visits her there to tell her of his reluctant decision to act, the perturbation Fanny feels on his departure forbids even the relief of reading, which therefore means 'no composure' (*MP*, 177). However, the books Edmund finds on her table are not novels. They include George, Lord Macartney's *Journal* of his stay in China (1807), the poetic *Tales* of George Crabbe (1812) and a probably recent collection of Samuel Johnson's papers for *The Idler* (written 1758–60). As John Lucas has pointed out, Fanny's tastes in literature are not classic,[17] but at the same time they are not presumably the ones marked by the reading of *novels*, the choice already made by the actual reader of *Mansfield Park*, or perhaps we should say, the *normal* consumer of fiction.

Austen's sustained interest in how her works were read is not directly attributable to an investment in her own personality. After all, the title pages of her novels never disclosed her name.[18] It is more likely that the increased fascination in how her narratives were received testifies to an attention to her craft in using characters (*including Fanny Price*), not as role models, but rather as necessary contributions to more general comment on social organization.[19] Interpretation of her novels is hindered more than advanced by the fixation with her supposed 'realism' (or lack of it). Marilyn Butler, when concluding her study of Austen's place in the ideological debates of her time, sought to correct our received view of her as a provincial realist with no feel for a wider imaginative or intellectual life. First, 'the crucial action of her novels is in itself expressive of the conservative side in an active war of ideas' which is indicative also of her limited naturalism: 'the ideal accompanies the phenomenal. She can be tellingly objective, but this too is part of a campaign against subjectivity' (Butler 1975: 294). Without this supporting context it would be all but impossible to decide just what was part of the metonymic relay of apparently redundant details that spells realism and what can be metaphorical material, carrying quite specific codes.

I have approached Austen's depiction of gender differences from this angle because an appreciation of this might render certain objections to her fiction beside the point (or rather *my* point). Butler's valuable examination of Jacobin and anti-Jacobin ideas from the 1790s onwards certainly does place Austen in the reactionary camp.[20] Her plots, however, do not reward tradition uncritically, as Butler also points out. It has almost become a tenet of current critical belief to recognize that traditional patriarchal figures are in decline in her fiction: either the grander patriarchs (Sir Thomas Bertram, Lady Catherine de

Bourgh, Sir Walter Elliot) or fathers (living: Mrs Bennet, Woodhouse and Price, or dead: Mr Dashwood). For Sandra Gilbert and Susan Gubar, in 1979, this was part of Austen's covert opposition to patriarchy. What is, is sick; women have to be strong because male protection is rarely any such thing. This does not stop Austen developing her own 'cover story': that in deferring to male power she can dramatize 'how and why female survival depends on gaining male approval and protection'. Women have to submit to this forceful social organization, rather as Kate has to be mastered by Petruchio in Shakespeare's *The Taming of the Shrew*. The 'sensible man', through love, has the 'rebellious, imaginative girl' delivered to him – and society – by the dead hand of circumstance (Gilbert and Gubar 1979: 154). Austen was, consciously or not when writing *Mansfield Park*, committed in her own life to no such marriage or accommodation. As an increasingly self-conscious writer, she is portraying heroines who are exemplary in the sense that they educe our sympathetic support, but they are *not* Jane Austen. Would Fanny Price read one of Austen's works? What Gilbert and Gubar stress is the sense of contradiction between the 'decorous surfaces' that speak balance and acceptance and the 'explosive anger' concealed by them (Gilbert and Gubar 1979: 111).[21] As Gubar noted in her 1975 essay, 'Sane Jane and the Critics', the act of writing for Austen formed a means of escape from the 'restraints she imposes on her female characters' (Gubar 1975: 255).

This significant work of critical revision marks just as much a change of approach as that of Harding and Mudrick, but it has been influential in quite contrary directions. Butler's historical work returns us to an Austen whose social and even political preferences are better defined, and those are conservative ones. For Gilbert and Gubar, the split in her psyche between the necessity of acceptance and the perhaps unacknowledged desire for radical change in women's roles defies a clear location in a general historical context. It would be remarkable if either view had gone unchallenged since the 1970s. Butler's guiding distinctions between Jacobin and anti-Jacobin have provoked several alternative emphases. For example, Gary Kelly's detailed study of the Jacobin novel may commence from some initial clarities, yet, when dwelling on particular cases, it runs up against many items that are hybrid (see especially Kelly's 'Jane Austen and the English Novel of the 1790s', in Schofield and Macheski 1986: 285–306). In his survey of the fiction of the Romantic period in 1989 he is sceptical of the common litmus test applied to the immediate reactions to French Revolutionary events (1989: 24–42) Life had moved on, and the more pressing reality for Austen at Chawton would have emanated from reports of the war with France and the waves of extra-parliamentary popular protest at enclosure and electoral corruption.[22] Claudia L. Johnson, in her study of Austen in *Women, Politics, and the Novel* (1988), and also in her contribution to this volume, finds distinctions between novelists based on such extrinsic criteria as reactions to political events less than helpful (see Johnson 1988: xvii–xxv). Similarly, Gilbert and Gubar's recuperation of the antagonistic Austen has been regarded as merely a determination to find feminist sentiments somewhere in Austen's work. Jane Spencer's mapping of *The Rise of the Woman Novelist* (1986) refuses any of their help, for 'the underlying assumption that women's writing *must* have a feminist meaning . . . needs to be questioned', for 'the relation between women's writing and patriarchal society is not simply one of opposition'. As she attempts to establish, women's writing was often accepted on terms that did the general status of women no favours: 'women's writing is not the same thing as women's rights' (Spencer 1986: xi). Similarly, in the recent work of Nancy Armstrong and Leroy W. Smith, a crucial line has been drawn between the appropriation of Austen's texts to support our own cultural values and the continuing analysis of her historical location.[23]

The current debate on gender issues has in any case generated broad analyses that often involve wider social and cultural concerns. Johnson's work has embraced politics and sexual difference as interdependent spheres of influence and her reading of *Mansfield Park* is alive to Austen's pervasive irony that is often directed against conservative sacred cows. While reactionary ideologues 'have it their way, it is only to give them the chance to show how little, rather than how much, they can do, and so to oblige them to discredit themselves with their own voices' (Johnson 1988: 120). The character eminently qualified to be the passive recorder of this impotence is Fanny Price, and part of her power actually stems from her obdurate silences or physical immobility. By withholding applause an audience at a play, for example, can be swingeingly critical. Silence can signify a refusal to play the game by leaving open the infinite possibility that there are other paradigms.[24]

Shifting ground a little, it would be relevant to argue that the depiction of male and female novelistic characters at this time, given the recent debates on gender of the 1790s, would have to obey different ground-rules. 'Action' for a man is possible in a society where such opportunities for self-definition emerge from *choice* – of occupation, vocation or simply just physical movement. When surveying the grounds at Sotherton, the 'one wish for air and liberty' that the party forms, as if by some communal instinct, leads them to venture forth to taste the 'sweets of pleasure-grounds' (*MP*, 118). Julia Bertram is obliged to 'restrain her impatient feet' and keep pace with Mrs Rushworth and Mrs Norris. By a process of complex social negotiation, this same Julia has enjoyed the fruits of precedence during the journey out to Sotherton by occupying the barouche-box seat next to Henry Crawford. Her delight is due to the powers of male choice (Crawford's ready smile cast on her), not her own. Similarly, Maria's despondence at this is caused by factors quite outside her control. Her lift of spirits on nearing the 'capital freehold mansion' is palpable, wholly due to the consolation that 'Mr Rushworth's consequence was hers' (*MP*, 110) – or was about to be. This same appearance of autonomy surrounds Maria's betrothal to Rushworth in the first place. Matrimony comes to be seen as a 'duty', and the significance of this particular attachment, the reason why it can now become a 'prime object', is that it can be sanctioned by the 'rule' of 'moral obligation' that is so composed of elements of material advancement and the desperation of social survival that she can feel it 'her evident duty to marry Mr Rushworth if she could'. 'Personalities' are not freely chosen in these instances, and Austen's irony is never far removed from those aspects of social assumption that appropriate the discourse of ethical motivation for rhetorical apology.[25] On Rushworth's part, there is a poor substitute for moral enquiry behind his choices. When first 'struck' with Maria's beauty, 'and being inclined to marry', it is but a small step to the conclusion that he 'fancied himself in love' (*MP*, 72). This is not the strategy of a writer who would require of her/his readers the belief that Mansfield society is a protecting influence.

Whether this scepticism can be applied to all forms of social possibility described in the novel is a more complex question, as much of the social control exercised in the narrative is manifested in self-censorship. Julia's reluctant pace alongside Mrs Rushworth is outwardly conformist, a bowing to her hostess's claims of propriety (and property), but she lingers so long behind the others because of Mrs Norris's probably mercenary decision to commandeer conversation with the housekeeper (we later hear how she has come into possession of pheasant's eggs and a cream cheese (*MP*, 132)). Julia's predicament is described thus:

The politeness which she had been brought up to practise as a duty, made it impossible for her to escape; while the want of that higher species of self-command, that just consideration of others, that knowledge of her own heart, that principle of right which had not formed any essential part of her education, made her miserable under it.

(*MP*, 119)

The external guardians of this 'principle of right' are authoritarian ones known as Rushworth/Norris.

It is significant that the full resonance of that term, 'principle of right', might well be missed on first reading. Is it *individual* right, that might be codified in Bills or complaints? Or, more commonsensically, some notional ethical imperative that provides some impersonal yard-stick for human behaviour? We should also note the profound pun waiting in Julia's dissatisfaction with her 'lot' (*MP*, 119). Does it pick up the 'happy lot' that would fall to the inheritor of the barouche-box seat (*MP*, 109)? Then, as now, there was a semantic association between a 'lot' cast as an item used to determine destiny by a chance selection and its use to signify the actual destiny which you end up inheriting. Men are implicated in this social determinism, but it is women who are its potential victims. This leads Nina Auerbach to conclude that it is Fanny alone who can rise 'from being the prisoner of Mansfield to the status of its principal jailer' ('Jane Austen and Romantic Imprisonment', in Monaghan 1981: 25) – a reminder that there are narrative as well as verbal ironies in *Mansfield Park*.

Such irony does not allow us to regard the 'real' as an absolute. The net effect of the realism deployed in Austen's work, far from forging an identity between signifier and signified, departs from this homology to serve two associated, but certainly not identical, ends. First, it was a means of dissociating the work from the conduct-book tradition which belittled women as it offered them apparently well-meant advice. Crucially, however, it was also a counter to the myth-making that. allowed women the dubious privilege of being exquisitely sensitive. Both Catherine Morland (*NA*) and Marianne Dashwood (*SS*) read novels and indulge in art to give them a hold on life, a habit they have to subordinate to life's more immediate claims as a mark of maturity. As Janet Todd has recently made clear,[26] this necessary rejection of sentiment that characterizes the novel of education is a gesture of suppression. Marianne becomes a victim at the same time as she plays a full part in Austen's happy ending: the plot 'mocks and stifles the agony of the female victim' by socializing '[her] near scream . . . into sensible rational discourse' (Todd 1986: 145). To some, Austen's conclusions seem deliberately perfunctory, their necessary curtailing of irony, with its consistent distancing of the authorial self from endorsement or outright disapproval, a complex statement about the cost of social compromise, especially for women. To others, the reader's perception of the fabricated and sudden closing happiness a hallmark of comedic relief; the author ordains a comic providence and creates an ordered and just ending out of unpromising materials. The more unlikely this is, the more it works against the grain of the earlier narrative, the more it could advocate the inevitable success of society in moulding individuals for their own self-protection – or, at least, the urgent necessity that it in fact does so. Closure, the foreclosing on thematic and stylistic options, could be a failure in narrative probability, but also a deliberate one to demonstrate the primacy of ethical considerations.

According to Barbara Herrnstein Smith, poetic closure 'may be regarded as a modification of structure that makes *stasis*, or the absence of further continuation, the most probable event'. This 'absence' creates its own satisfaction, as it must accompany a reader's 'expectation of nothing' (Smith 1968: 34). Smith's helpful definition implies a delicately drawn-up contract with the reader on Austen's part. What happens if the reader is left expecting more? Could this lack of aesthetic satisfaction, or rather, this departure from satiric realism for the romance of marriage, be quite deliberate? Our receptiveness to Austen's conclusions is rarely an overt problem. The successful marriage is a convenient mark of maturity and lends itself to images of continuity, of change within stability. We may feel that the closing passages of Austen's novels are rather thinner in interest after the proposal scene, but are ready to accept the rush to conclusion as the dues she pays to propriety and Regency taste. The 'perverse' analytical reading will, however, refuse to be satisfied by the unitary discourse of common sense which is calculated to educe normative readings, and is probably not reassured by deliberations as to what the author may or may not have intended. It is all but impossible, for example, for contemporary productions of *The Merchant of Venice* to include a Shylock from the Elizabethan stage, complete with gaberdine and hooked nose both designed to render the stage Jew instantly ridiculous or unproblematically alien. Similarly, we are likely to find Katherine's final obedience to Petruchio an uncomfortable spectacle. It might render them explicable, but does a resort to placing such gestures 'in context' make them palatable today? We perhaps return to Harding's conclusion that the book's greatness lies in its power 'to offend'.

Analysis of *Mansfield Park* can only begin when mere description of the narrative events is no longer sufficient to account for its varied effects on generations of readers. There are few more divisive features in *Mansfield Park* than Fanny's 'heroism' and most of the discussion so far has indeed centred on Fanny's role in the novel. This is not accidental, as it is my experience that most initial impressions of the work on which more sophisticated readings are later elaborated are decisively coloured by how, or if, Fanny is deemed to act as Austen's moral *exemplum*. It is necessary to draw a clear distinction between the full semantic complexity of *Mansfield Park* and the excerpts from it that represent Fanny Price's declarations of belief. She is not silent; if frugal in assigning her direct discourse, the novel is persistent in telling the reader what she thinks.[27] When Austen confesses to her niece, Fanny Knight (23 March 1817), that 'pictures of perfection' make her 'sick & wicked' and that *Emma* will also contain a 'Heroine . . . almost too good for [her author]' (Chapman 1932, II: 487), there is every reason to believe that such goodness is didactic and not realistic. Fanny may become 'My Fanny' by the close of the novel, but this identification may be tempered for several readers by the immediate narrative context:

> Let other pens dwell on guilt and misery. I quit such odious subjects as soon as I can, impatient to restore every body, not greatly in fault themselves, to tolerable comfort, and to have done with all the rest.
>
> My Fanny indeed at this time, I have the satisfaction of knowing, must have been happy in spite of every thing. She must have been a happy creature in spite of all that she felt or thought she felt, for the distress of those around her.
>
> (MP, 446)

The question revolves around whether the sudden distance from the narrative events adds a closing climax, or whether the accustomed veil of irony extends even to this narratorial voice. Questions as to the perfunctoriness of the last chapter are a way of restating a desire for consistency and resolution. Textually speaking, the last chapter is significant and anything but an afterthought. The first paragraph is stridently evasive. Consequently, the 'happiness' found by turning one's back on 'odious subjects' resembles an effect of some novelistic sleight of hand. Fanny becomes the possession of the novelist as well as a locus for identification, but the 'knowledge' of the first-person voice is curiously indirect. Fanny 'must' have been happy (it is even worth restating – but with weaker returns), as if her life has taken on an autonomy that does not admit a creator's certainties. However, it is possible she may only have 'thought she felt' sympathy for those less fortunate. Presumably, the narrator's omniscience returns at this point to question Fanny's self-knowledge and, most surprisingly, her range of sympathies.

This passage is one of the clearest examples in *Mansfield Park* of how 'Fanny' can be a focus of careful narratorial calculation. Margaret Kirkham's comparison of Fanny with Jean-Jacques Rousseau's image of wifely (and sentimental) perfection in Sophie from his *Emile* (1762) elicits consistent parodic allusions to the submissive and childlike female of patriarchal myth (Kirkham 1983: 101–6).[28] Fanny Price is tougher than she looks – or rather than she is allowed to appear in Mansfield society. As Mary Evans notes in this volume (pp. 24), this particular role holds great attraction for Henry Crawford. Austen dwells on how Fanny is regarded less as a rational and independent being than as a 'wife'. The ball arranged for Fanny at Mansfield ends for her when Sir Thomas, 'with the advice of absolute power', despatches her to bed. While the act could have been motivated by concern for her health, 'he might [have meant] to recommend her as a wife by shewing her persuadableness' (*MP*, 285–6). This is a successful ploy, as Henry Crawford, two chapters later, is 'fairly caught' (*MP*, 296) and spends a whole evening's walk expatiating on her graces of principle and domestic economy, especially how she caters for Lady Bertram's every whim, 'so much as if it were a matter of course that she was not to have a moment at her own command' (*MP*, 300). His sister is ready to find Fanny 'a sweet little wife; all gratitude and devotion' (*MP*, 296).

Fanny's stand against such social assimilation can only be achieved by passive resistance. It would be fascinating to encounter a form of *female* heroism at this time constructed on radically different premises. It is not just Lady Bertram who learns of distant action from letters read on drawing-room sofas. When Lydia Bennet breaks free from Longbourn with Wickham in *Pride and Prejudice* this independence is hardly heroic in Austen's terms, as this self-assertion has not been sanctioned. Similarly, in *Emma*, Harriet Smith has only to stray a little way along the Richmond road ('apparently public enough for safety') from Highbury to encounter predatory gypsies and she has to be rescued by Frank Churchill. It is enough to engross the 'young and the low', to have Mr Woodhouse trembling in his chair, and have him prohibiting any stir 'beyond the shrubbery' (*E*, 330–2). Marianne Dashwood is near to the shelter of Barton Cottage and her own garden gate when she turns an ankle and is caught up by Willoughby and restored to a 'chair in the parlour' (*SS*, 74–5). Emma's first sight of Harriet and her rescuer comes when they are within twenty yards of the safety of 'iron gates and the front door' (*E*, 330). Gates and walls protect women in Austen's fiction and rarely imprison them.

However, with fine distinction, this great outdoors is not to be confused with the public sphere. Balls and more formal social gatherings evince freedom granted and even defined by social consent. Under attack from Henry Crawford's advances, Fanny's 'modest gentle nature' is not enough. She shakes her head 'involuntarily' and that is enough for Crawford to rejoin battle for her attention: ' "What did that shake of the head mean? . . . What was it meant to express?" ' Fanny wishes she had been 'as motionless as she was speechless' (*MP*, 339). Within herself she is chaste and *meaning* can be uncontested and so quite *impersonal*, part of the given decorum that is itself never expressed. Uttering your own version or interpretation of affairs renders you liable to judgement and even possession. John Gregory's *A Father's Legacy to his Daughters* (1774) is clear in advocating reserve even to the point of silence:

> modesty, which I think so essential to your sex, will naturally dispose you to be rather silent in company, especially in a large one. – People of sense and discernment will never mistake such silence for dullness. One may take a share in conversation without uttering a syllable. The expression in the countenance shews it, and this never escapes an observing eye . . .
>
> (Jones 1990: 46)

Henry Crawford was obviously not the sort who chose to notice such things.[29]

For the Londonized Mary Crawford this reserve provides a social dilemma, too. Whether Fanny is 'out' or not is a conventional short-cut to discovering the point of such silence and so placing Fanny in a metropolitan context: 'I begin now to understand you all, except Miss Price . . . I am puzzled'. Mary Crawford is not the only one who finds her 'unreadable'. The narrator poses the rhetorical enquiry as to 'what was *she* doing and thinking all this while? and what was *her* opinion of the new-comers?' Although this is answered briefly, it is a construction which only the narrator could possibly have put on her behaviour, she is so 'very little attended to'. Edmund's defence of Fanny stems from the force given to fact rather than interpretation. He even refuses to answer Mary's question, as Fanny 'is grown up. She has the age and sense of a woman, but the outs and not outs are beyond me' (MP, 81). Fanny should not mean but just be.

Here is one of the contradictions that teases criticism. Such 'heroism', activated by abstract 'principle' (MP, 271), is wedded to apparent stasis. Fanny distrusts 'improvement' and the mercurial mimickry of a Yates or Crawford, but her recalcitrance as a woman provides a stubborn (because largely tacit) answer to the patriarchal and traditional assumptions about not just gender roles but also ownership. Neither Sir Thomas nor Henry Crawford can own her affections; there are certain 'duties' that cannot be squared with the self-possession that Fanny seeks to maintain.[30]

It is crucial, therefore, whether this heroic 'principle' can be arrived at by a reliance on tradition and precept or rational examination. Under the pressure of gathering jealousy at Mary Crawford's influence with Edmund and just before the passage on 'principle', Fanny is striving to be 'rational, and to deserve the right of judging' her (MP, 271). When stressing the centrality of education in emancipating women, Mary Wollstonecraft reduces the argument not to one of deciding what women need to know, but rather, what people require:

> the inquiry is whether she have reason or not. If she have, which, for a moment, I will take for granted, she was not created merely to be the solace of man, and the sexual should not destroy the human character.
>
> Into this error men have, probably, been led by viewing education in a false light; not considering it as the first step to form a being advancing gradually towards perfection; but only as a preparation for life.
>
> (Wollstonecraft 1989, V: 122)

Reason involves the power to escape the male gaze and its determining influence. 'Life', when set against the ascent towards 'perfection', is no arena for female self-improvement.

Wollstonecraft's Vindication (1792) has recently been regarded as kin to Austen's sympathetic portrayal of rational self-improving women.[31] Fanny, newly introduced to Mansfield, would have been sustained by Wollstonecraft's distrust of 'the education of the rich'. They are rendered 'vain and helpless' because the 'unfolding mind' is not 'strengthened by the practice of those duties which dignify the human character'. It is those in the middle class who appear to be in 'the most natural state' and free from the corruption that attends those primed only for pleasure or 'susceptibility of heart' (Wollstonecraft, 1989, V: 75). This would also have consoled Austen in Bath and Southampton. However, Austen is never content to ignore the claims of 'Life' for those of a purely personal vocation. Fanny is finally released from Crawford's attentions by the 'sound of approaching relief, the very sound which she had been long watching for, and long thinking strangely delayed', namely, a 'solemn procession, headed by Baddely, of tea-board, urn, and cake-bearers'. It is by this means that she is delivered from 'a grievous imprisonment of body and mind. She was at liberty, she was busy, she was protected' (MP, 341). The daily social round consoles in its regularity and decorum. Far from circumscribing the individual, it protects her/his liberty.

Just what do we join, therefore, when we embrace the rituals of middle-class life? From Portsmouth, the view of Mansfield is sharpened, but it could also be selective. The 'consideration of times and seasons', the 'regulation of subject' and 'propriety' that life in 'her uncle's house' apparently provides seems a rather partial construction, given the full reason for Fanny's appearance again at her first home. It is of great relief to Fanny at Portsmouth too to find this reverie cut short by not only her three younger brothers but also 'the tea-things, which she had begun almost to despair of seeing that evening', and Susan's efficiency in this task is a rite of passage that will end at the Park (MP, 376-7). Mansfield is described as *owned* by Sir Thomas and this is no idle detail. According to the entry in Samuel Johnson's *Dictionary* (1st edn 1755), 'propriety' can mean both 'peculiarity of possession; exclusive right' and 'accuracy; justness'. A time for every purpose under heaven is allowed by those who own and so ordain opportunity. Human subjects as well as those of conversation are well regulated. For a woman to leave this care would be to surrender to a wilderness both figurative and perhaps literal. This aspect of Austen's feminist individualism should not be shirked because we have now begun to perceive its links with more recent forms of resistance to patriarchal authority.

There are powerful trains of association at work here. While there are several moral objections to the almost Portsmouth level of bustle surrounding *Lovers' Vows* with its loosening of established social roles, it should not be overlooked that there is almost as much sin in usurping the space owned by Sir Thomas. When Edmund is dubious about the expanding scope of the production, he laments the 'end of all the privacy and propriety' that had safeguarded the application of the idea at first (*MP*, 175). The project looks like involving some who are barely acquainted with Mansfield and its ways. The gates are opening. With Sir Thomas's return, there is a conversion of the green room back to its habitual use (his private chamber), and a general current of revision takes hold – the house is 'restored to its proper state' (*MP*, 203), Mrs Norris is confounded at her discovery that the activity possessed an 'impropriety which was so glaring to Sir Thomas' (*MP*, 204), Mr Yates is vanquished in leaving the house 'in all the soberness of its general character' (*MP*, 209) and Mansfield becomes an 'altered place' under his 'government' (*MP*, 211). This rule is still in place at the close of the novel, and although the ties of blood are looser then (Fanny becomes the daughter Sir Thomas always wanted (*MP*, 456) and Portsmouth has to be renounced), the cluster of ideologically compacted symbols that is Mansfield is still in place. An improbably reformed Tom will succeed Sir Thomas and, much like the East Room allowed Fanny, the living at Mansfield provides her with a haven of ownership within the greater unit, as perfect 'as every thing else, within the view and patronage of Mansfield Park, had long been' (*MP*, 457).

This seems reassuring and provides the climactic power that the 'happy ending' ensures, but the suddenly synoptic 'view' of the new Mansfield still marks a sacrifice of the personal voice. There is also a deliberate abstention 'from dates' in its description so that we might be better able to fix our own (*MP*, 454), but also, we could argue, so that the act of closure is not as exposed as it might have been if greater detail had been needed. In any case, Sir Thomas's *moral* authority is hardly still intact; he has proved a spectacularly bad educator and Austen has to resort to the radical powers of potent illness to produce a successful continuity of Bertram power. A veil is even drawn over the usually climactic proposal scene that ensures Fanny her greatest happiness; in the more detailed perspective of Chapter 47 we read of an Edmund still in shock at Mary Crawford's true self, a woman he had regarded as one 'whom nature had so richly endowed' (*MP*, 441).

As Brean S. Hammond and Claudia S. Johnson both emphasize in this volume (see especially pp. 71–2, 110–12), Austen's irony unsettles the realist mode. To use Pierre Macherey's terms, we could say that this is more than just 'style', but rather the means by which 'fiction' challenges 'illusion', by which a '*determinate representation*' of ideologically produced dreams and images gradually undermines their power, and resists a reductive interpretation (Macherey 1978: 61–5).

Furthermore, to search for a key meaning just in the closing chapters of a novel is to fetishize the closure of the text, to remain prey to the narrative ordering and remain blind to those 'palimpsestic' qualities of Austen's work where 'surface designs' *obscure* socially unacceptable meanings (Gilbert and Gubar 1979: 73). 'Nature', 'community' or even 'government' and 'propriety' could therefore emerge as social institutions, when irony stresses an attention to context at the expense of text,[32] but to attempt this critique would be to stand clear of 'realist' assumptions and hear what the language is trying not to say.

CHAPTER 1

Henry Crawford and the 'Sphere of Love' in *Mansfield Park*

MARY EVANS

[Psychoanalytic criticism of literature forms no consistent pattern. In broad outline it concerns itself with the origin of desires and even self-identity: the unconscious. Freud's essays on art and literature relate art to the dream, where the artist is kin to the neurotic, 'oppressed by excessively powerful instinctual needs', but without the 'means of achieving these satisfactions' (Freud 1953–74, 16: 376). Art, therefore, is an activity to 'allay ungratified wishes', both in the artist and also in her/his audience or readers (Freud 1953–74, 13: 187). Strategies of creation (*and* of reading) may be studied for·their attempt to resist full acknowledgement of the unconscious. Primitive wishes have to be transformed into the culturally palatable or 'traditional'.

Analysis of art has therefore to scrutinize the text of the 'dream'. It appears rather as an archaeological site, with significant layers that need to be unearthed and reconstructed. The goal is to re-form, out of these fragments, an intelligible order. Freud's case histories usually result in 'cure', whereby the patient can be reabsorbed into 'normal' life, *but* the process of analysis is hardly a simple process of reconstruction. The analyst's imposition of order involves an imaginative linkage between dislocated items. Just as a text can never be exhaustively (and so be totally accurately) interpreted, the analysand does not return to the past through analysis, but rather achieves a new understanding of it in the *present*. Far from recovering the past, it is reassessed according to a current perspective. Freud describes this goal of analysis in his case-study of 'Little Hans':

> Therapeutic success . . . is not our primary aim; we endeavour rather to enable the patient to obtain a conscious grasp of his unconscious

wishes. And this we achieve by working on the basis of the hints he throws out, and so, with the help of our interpretative technique, presenting the unconscious complex to his unconsciousness *in our own words*. There will be a certain degree of similarity between that which he hears from us and that which he is looking for, and which, in spite of all resistances, is trying to force its way through to consciousness; and it is this similarity that will enable him to discover the unconscious material.

(Freud 1953–74, 10: 120–1)

Just as the analyst involves her/himself in the process, we should not keep ourselves fenced off from the creative potentialities for association and even 'play' in our reading of the text. If the psyche is radically divided by the need for self-protection or self-delusion, the view of reality will be a *constructed* one and related to hidden wishes or fears – in short, the unconscious. The 'past' is always revised by a present-day need to colonize it and this process addresses the need to 'tell stories' about ourselves (to ourselves) in order that we attain a shape or 'character' (in time and space), when we are confronted by the alien mystery of formlessness and the unknowable.

Mary Evans's understanding of Henry Crawford derives from a reading of his early sexual development. Freud's concentration on infantile sexuality as a key to the adult's growth to 'maturity' earned him his early notoriety, yet this is due to an elision of the sexual with the sex act itself. For Freud, in *An Outline of Psycho-analysis* (published in 1940), 'sexual life includes the function of obtaining pleasure from zones of the body – a function which is subsequently brought into the service of reproduction. The two functions often fail to coincide completely' (Freud 1953–74, 23: 152). In Henry Crawford's case, his inability to resolve his early Oedipal conflicts structures his view of women. The initial close relationship with one's nurturing mother has to be replaced by a growing consciousness of one's separate identity. For the boy there is, according to Freud, a perception of the father as a rival which leads to infantile impulses to kill him in order to possess the mother without interruption. This Oedipal complex can be supplanted by a fear of castration, that is, where the father's authority threatens the growing boy, who directs his maturing desires towards him so as to take his own authoritative place in time. The Oedipus complex forms a nucleus of desire that eventually has to be subject to the repressions of the healthy society. This eventually was to lead to a rather pessimistic view of the political order in Freud's *Civilisation and its Discontents* (1930), which stressed the individual's instinctive resistance to the acknowledged restraints of civilized society.

The inability to co-ordinate one's desire with one's sense of adult responsibility can, in extreme cases, lead to impotence. Every civilization needs to find some cultural check on its libidinal opportunities, and so, through Crawford's case study, Evans discovers the particular psychic checks and balances that maintain the social economy of Mansfield Park, and also how the new order ushered in by Fanny and Edmund can be seen to improve on it.]

NIGEL WOOD

Jane Austen does not, in any of her novels, invite her readers to speculate about the potency – or otherwise – of her male characters. It may therefore seem inappropriate to suggest that an essay by Freud, *On the Universal Tendency to Debasement in the Sphere of Love* (Freud 1953–74, 11: 177–90), first published in 1912, has anything to offer readers of *Mansfield Park*. After all, the essay begins with a discussion of psychical impotence and continues to outline the circumstances in which 'the executive organs of sexuality', as Freud describes them, refuse to carry out the sexual act. Such problems do not form part of the manifest narrative of *Mansfield Park*, in which the usual preoccupations of Austen's novels (marriage, property and self-education) are dominant.

Yet despite this apparent distance between Mansfield Park, late eighteenth-century Northamptonshire, and the concerns of early twentieth-century Vienna, much is similar in the two works. Freud can illuminate our understanding of Austen; equally, I would argue, Austen can illuminate Freud. Therefore it is not my intention here to suggest that only the more recently published work is the explanatory text; on the contrary, there seems to me to be much in Austen which enhances and enriches the arguments of Freud. What I shall argue here, then, is that Jane Austen gave us, in Henry Crawford, a central character in Freud's account of male sexuality, the man who cannot resolve his Oedipal conflicts in a way which allows him to fuse sexual desire and emotional commitment. In his case histories Freud described male fears of castration and of ambivalence, while in his other essays he pursued the issue of the different paths which women and men must take to adult sexuality. For men, Freud always maintained, a satisfactory negotiation of infant and childhood emotional relationships demanded an identification with the father. The male child – to become the satisfactory adult – is allowed to maintain his love for his mother, but has to accept the limits of that love. The human person who might illustrate the unsatisfactory transition to adult male sexual identity is absent from Freud: we are told about Little Hans, the Rat Man and homosexuals, but we do not have a person to demonstrate the living reality of the incomplete resolution of the Oedipal drama. But in Henry Crawford we arguably have exactly that person, the man who has significantly failed to abandon the infantile state of both love and sexual desire for his mother and direct his affections and his desire towards an adult woman.

In nominating Henry Crawford as a 'missing person' in Freud's account of male sexuality, it is implicitly accepted that fiction can be read in terms of the 'hidden' narrative. The demonstration of these 'hidden' narratives, like the hidden agendas of social life, have become an accepted part of literary criticism in the last twenty years, as the impact of psychoanalysis has become more considerable. The force of organizing structures, of latent rather than manifest ideas and the psychic order of the text have all become commonplace issues on the agenda of the reading of fiction. As this stance has become more widely accepted, so has the tacit assumption of Freud's prioritization of the sexual in the construction of human emotional existence and the increasing questioning of rigid lines between different forms of text. For Freud, the centrality of the sexual lay, as Peter Gay has suggested, in his view that the early experiences of all human beings are the key to the understanding of adult life. Gay writes:

> Pushing the origins of sexual feelings back to the earliest years had enabled him to explain, on wholly naturalistic and psychological grounds, the emergence of such powerful emotional brakes as shame and disgust, of norms in matters of taste and morality, of such cultural activities as art and scientific research – including psychoanalysis. It also laid bare the tangled roots of adult love.
>
> (Gay 1988: 148)

The 'tangled roots of adult love' have formed the substance of fiction for generations. The 'great' themes of the novel – sexual desire and jealousy in particular – are as central to Freud as they are to novelists. The emphases are different in terms of the novel and Freud's case histories, but the basic issues are similar: that human beings, as adults, live out the emotional relationships which have reached only partial resolution in infancy and childhood. Freud, like the writers of fiction, does not assume a *stable* self. As much as the bourgeois world would like clearly defined human beings, whose emotional behaviour is entirely congruent with their social role, Freud was able to show – like the major novelists – that the social world cannot assume human emotional life as fixed.

Freud's essay *On the Universal Tendency to Debasement in the Sphere of Love* is initially concerned with impotence. The substance of the paper, however, is Freud's interest in the origin, and the maintenance, of sexual desire. (It is, of course, the case that in this essay, as in much of his work, Freud takes for granted the existence of sexual desire as heterosexual desire.) The men are those who, in his words, 'seek objects which they do not need to love, in order to keep their sensuality away from the objects they love' (Freud 1953–74, 11: 183). In this brief remark Freud sums up a tradition in Western sexuality which has been widely remarked upon by historians. Numerous writers have pointed to the emergence of an articulate body of nineteenth-century Western opinion which advocated precisely the kind of 'split' which Freud describes.[1] Men were advised to channel their sexual desire towards prostitutes and the professional sexual 'servants' of the nineteenth century, in order to keep themselves 'pure' for their wives. Even though such advice did not escape criticism, there nevertheless remained a powerful tradition which saw the separation of love (and marriage) and sexual desire as essential for social stability and social survival.

Like many others of his time, Freud recognized that there was a powerful explanation (in an age of imperfect contraception and hazardous childbirth) for the disjunction of marriage and sexuality. If male heterosexuality was expressed outside marriage, then wives could be left free of pregnancy and its manifestly debilitating effects. The obviously exploitative features of the arrangement are clear: working-class women become the means through which bourgeois and petit bourgeois men meet their sexual desires. In the last twenty years it has become commonplace to question the assumption which took for granted male sexual desire for women as 'natural'. Feminism and the gay movement have both offered powerful critiques of the construction of desire, and the supposed 'naturalness' of the desire of men for women. Moreover, it has become part of the late twentieth-century discourse on sexuality to view with suspicion any account or practice of sexuality which fails to see the existence of sexual desire in women.

However, these critiques of conventional thinking about sexuality did not emerge until long after Freud's essay on impotence. For Freud, as for others of his generation, there remained an implicit assumption that sexual desire – if 'normal' – was heterosexual. It was not that Freud did not recognize impotence, frigidity in women or homosexuality, but all these possibilities were to be analysed and understood as aberrations, as departures from normality. Significantly, though, all were to be understood in terms of an individual's biography. Freud did not believe that people 'chose' homosexuality or heterosexuality in any existential sense; on the contrary, the circumstances and the experiences of childhood dictated what kind of sexual person would emerge in adult life.

In the case histories in Freud's work which have become famous and much studied (in particular Dora, the Wolf Man and Little Hans) we see Freud relating events in childhood to adult behaviour. (Even more directly, in the case of Little Hans, we see Freud relating childhood to childhood.) But in the essay on *The Tendency to Debasement* we do not have a character, an individual, to illustrate Freud's analysis or to give human substance to a theoretical account of individual development. Here, then, I would like to introduce Henry Crawford as the missing human person in Freud's essay. The reason for this introduction is not, as suggested earlier, to demonstrate that we can 'use' Freud to illuminate literature. That point has already been made in a considerable range of writing in the last twenty or thirty years. The linking of Henry Crawford and Freud is to develop Freud's essay (rather than Jane Austen's novel) and to propose that theory – as Freud himself recognized – can often emerge after the human recognition of an event or a process. When Freud wrote about the Oedipus myth and the riddle of the Sphinx he was acknowledging that cultures can represent ideas long before they can understand them.[2]

The secondary literature on Jane Austen generally includes Henry Crawford among the morally flawed characters of Austen's fiction.[3] It would be difficult to do otherwise, since Crawford – unlike some of the other silly, shiftless, deceitful characters – crosses a social and moral line which is unique in Austen. Other characters are unkind, selfish and less than honest in their dealings with others, but Crawford enters into an adulterous relationship with Maria Bertram. Whereas Willoughby in *Sense and Sensibility* is guilty of ordinary greed and Captain Wickham in *Price and Prejudice* is both greedy and dishonourable, they are both saved (largely by the efforts of others) from committing acts of blatant social transgression. Crawford, far more sophisticated and worldly than either of these men, attempts to manipulate the social world for his own purposes, only to find that he has taken on forces that are larger than his own. In attempting to make Fanny Price love him, in the equally calculated seduction of Julia and Maria Bertram and in the final determination to recapture his hold over Maria Bertram, Henry Crawford sees himself as in *control* of the emotional destiny of the others. He has – at least initially – little sense of the possible fusion of morality and emotion, and he represents, quite outstandingly in English fiction, an almost European character created out of ideas about 'the game' of love. Crawford, with his sister Mary, arrives at a quiet English village, and then begins to play a part, and a game, that would not be out of place in Laclos's *Les Liaisons Dangereuses* (1782) or Mozart's *Cosi fan Tutte* (1790). Notions of the integrity, the commitment, the honesty of love are given short shrift by a character who regards the adult emotional world as a game to be played and enjoyed.

What is so striking about Henry Crawford in *Mansfield Park* is that he challenges, in his attitudes to emotional life, the absolute fusion of the emotional and social order which is represented by Sir Thomas Bertram. In a very real sense, *Mansfield Park* is a novel which is preoccupied with moral law, and patriarchal moral law at that. We are presented at the beginning of the novel with the most conventionally patriarchal figure in Austen's fiction in the shape of Sir Thomas Bertram. A man of absolute integrity, he is deeply concerned with doing what he perceives as 'right', a definition which includes a considerable emphasis on the maintenance of social order. As he says of Fanny's place at Mansfield Park in the early pages of the novel:

> There will be some difficulty . . . as to . . . how, without depressing her spirits too far, to make her remember that she is not a *Miss Bertram* . . . It is a point of great delicacy, and you must assist us in our endeavours to choose exactly the right line of conduct.
>
> (*MP*, 47)

Unfortunately for Sir Thomas, and his family, his notion of 'right' is largely formal and legalistic, and contains little that suggests an understanding of the possible internal moral capacities of human beings. Morality, and moral behaviour, in the person of Sir Thomas Bertram is about 'doing the right thing' and 'taking the honourable course'. As guides to human behaviour these conventional expectations are often useful, and often suggestive. Unfortunately, as Sir Thomas is to discover to his cost, they are meaningless if not accompanied by a recognition of the more diffuse, and less legalistic, ideas about morality. To all his children (with the possible exception of Edmund) Sir Thomas represents an iron code, the patriarchal law, the governor of hearth and home who hands down the tablets of the social and moral order with the certainty and the authority of a latter-day Moses.

Faced with this moralistic figure, Henry Crawford can hardly fail to see that absent from the moral understanding at Mansfield Park is an integration of human need and desire into morality. Significantly, however, Henry Crawford does not, at least initially, meet Sir Thomas. In the opening paragraphs of Chapter 4 we are reminded of Sir Thomas's absence from home (business has taken him to Antigua and the care of his overseas investments) and during this absence Maria Bertram becomes engaged to Mr Rushworth. No sooner has this happened than

Mr Crawford arrives at Mansfield. Readers must put their own gold stars by these pages; Jane Austen does her best to remind us that patriarchal authority is absent and that in this vacuum it is possible that its limitations will be tested. The people to test what is in this case quite literally the law of the father (since the mother, in the shape of Lady Bertram, is as absent a moral figure as it is possible to be) are Henry and Mary Crawford, 'the brother and sister of Mrs Grant' (*MP*, 73). We already know that Dr and Mrs Grant are a couple deeply committed to pleasure and indulgence (particularly the indulgence of the stomach in the case of Dr Grant) (*MP*, 59) and so we are somewhat prepared for further characters for whom pleasure is not a foreign or unknown experience.

What readers could not, however, predict about Mary and Henry Crawford is that their own biographies should contain so little experience of patriarchy in the form of parental authority. We are given (as is the general pattern in Jane Austen) precise information about the material assets of brother and sister. From this we learn that Henry owns a considerable estate in Norfolk and that Mary has capital assets of some £20,000. But we are also left to deduce that their father has played little part in their lives. To quote Jane Austen's account of their family history:

> the society of the village received an addition in the brother and sister of Mrs Grant, a Mr and Miss Crawford, the children of her mother by a second marriage. They were young people of fortune. The son had a good estate in Norfolk, the daughter twenty thousand pounds. As children, their sister had been always very fond of them; but, as her own marriage had been soon followed by the death of their common parent, which left them to the care of a brother of their father, of whom Miss Grant knew nothing, she had scarcely seen them since. In their uncle's house they had found a kind home. Admiral and Mrs Crawford, though agreeing in nothing else, were united in affection for these children, or at least were no further adverse in their feelings than that each had their favourite, to whom they showed the greatest fondness of the two. The Admiral delighted in the boy, Mrs Crawford doated on the girl . . .
>
> (*MP*, 73–4)

So far, reasonably good – or 'good enough' – surrogate parenting for the young Crawfords. Then Jane Austen introduces the substantial blot on the emotional history of the young Crawfords:

> Admiral Crawford was a man of vicious conduct, who chose, instead of retaining his niece [on his wife's death], to bring his mistress under his own roof.
>
> (*MP*, 74)

Illicit desire is not just known to the young Crawfords, it is actually brought into the household in which they have spent their childhood and adolescence. It is an extraordinary history for characters in Austen's fiction, most of whom are brought up by their natural parents in circumstances which may fall short of domestic harmony and respect (as at the Bennets) but never fall short of conventional propriety. Thus introduced into Mansfield Park, where parenting has been conventional in every way, are two characters who have experienced in their short lives the loss of a mother, the disappearance of a father and the complications of long-term adultery. The death of a mother in the late eighteenth century was hardly novel (and Jane Austen's own family contained instances of young women – young mothers – who died at early ages) but what is more exceptional about the Crawfords' family history is the reason for the absence of their father, and the clearly explicit adulterous relationship between Admiral Crawford and his mistress. We are never told why Henry and Mary Crawford's father vanished from their lives so soon after his wife's death. Widowers – particularly those as relatively affluent as the Crawfords' father must have been – did remain with their children, and gave their everyday care to women such as the excellent Mrs Weston in *Emma*. These surrogate mothers, whether employees or close family friends (such as Lady Elliot in *Persuasion*) allowed widowed fathers to continue to live with their children. We are given no information as to why the Crawfords' father should have so apparently precipitously handed over the care of his children to his brother: a curious family history, and yet one stated by Jane Austen with no apparent curiosity or condemnation. Indeed, she writes of the matter with complete lack of concern and interest.

To the reader, however, a mystery has been introduced. We have to ask if there is not some clear authorial intention at work here, some concealed purpose in terms of the kind of characters that she wishes to construct for the Crawfords and their world. One similarity is already made by the account of the Crawfords' early days: that between Fanny Price and Mary and Henry Crawford. Fanny Price has been farmed out, at the tender age of nine, to Mansfield Park and the care of her uncle and aunt, in much the same way (although for different reasons) as Mary and Henry Crawford. In both cases the failings and/or inadequacies of the parental home have to be made good by an uncle. Long before Fanny and Henry meet as adults, and share any other kind of experience, they have already known, in childhood, the vicissitudes that attend the failings and absences of fathers. The homes to which Fanny, Henry and Mary go as children are, of course, markedly different. Henry and Mary go to a home in which – as we are tersely informed by Jane Austen – domestic disagreement is explicit. Fanny, on the other hand, travels from domestic disorder to domestic order of the most developed kind. Mansfield Park, as ruled by Sir Thomas, is a model of conventional behaviour. The father provides more than adequately for his children, the mother and father never appear disunited or in disagreement and there is no interruption in the expectation, and provision, of patriarchal authority.

So what we are provided with, by Chapter 4 of *Mansfield Park*, is an outline of some fascinating similarities and differences between the central characters of the novel. More particularly, we learn that Henry Crawford and Fanny Price, characters from very different social strata, have shared the experience of a disrupted childhood, and have both known discontinuity in their contacts with adults. Emotionally, the worlds of these characters have much in common – and far more than the apparent differences between them would suggest. The similarities in their early experiences might even, it is not, perhaps, too fanciful to suppose, account for the attraction that develops between them in the second half of the novel. Even when we are repeatedly told that Fanny Price is wary of Henry Crawford we are also given hints that her initial dislike is diminishing on closer acquaintance (see *MP*, 81 and 241). Given the character of Fanny's father, it is possible to see how resonant a person Henry Crawford would be. Urbane, sophisticated and charming as Henry is (and loud and ill mannered as is Fanny's father) they both communicate a vivid masculinity that is absent from many of the other male characters. When Fanny (and the Bertram sisters) first meet Henry Crawford he is described as 'absolutely plain, black and plain' (*MP*, 77). Subsequent meetings radically alter the views of Maria and Julia Bertram about Henry Crawford; what changes their view is Henry's ability to engage with women, to cross the conventional barriers that restrict conversation between women and men. Fanny's father has no such talent (indeed, part of his lack of gentility, at least as far as Jane Austen sees it, is his inability to hold a sensible conversation with anyone) but what he does have is an energy in his responses to the world which he shares with Henry Crawford. One set of responses are those of tutored English gentlemen, the others those of a virtually uneducated sailor, but what unites them – the identity of response – is the vigour and indeed the passion with which they are offered.

In Austen's work character is frequently revealed through the stage-set exchange of opinions and views around the dinner or card table. This convention is followed as much in *Mansfield Park* as elsewhere, as is the pattern of conversation in Austen. This pattern dictates that conversation is largely, although not exclusively, heterosexual. Men and women talk to each other, as do female members of the same family, but conversations between men are unknown. For whatever reason, Jane Austen includes no conversations between men in her novels; conversations between male friends, and between fathers and sons, are reported but we are not allowed to overhear the specifics of the exchange. It might well be that Jane Austen felt that she did not know *how* men talked to each other, and thus had no confidence in manufacturing their conversations. Whatever the reason, the literary result is that men's characters have to be constructed in Austen's fiction from their actions or from their conversations with women. An account of the relations between men, and the extent to which men compete or collude verbally, is excluded from the text. The significance of this absence is that men are given little opportunity in Austen to reveal themselves as anything other than different from women. The similarities between men – and most particularly, of course, the similarity of being male in a patriarchal culture – are little explored. Thus when men are given opportunities to play different roles from those which formal convention demands of them, some – and Henry Crawford is a case in point – seize the opportunity with relish. As Jane Austen tells us – without enthusiasm or praise – Henry Crawford can act, in a literal, rather than a conventional, sense.

So, too, it becomes clear in the concluding chapters of *Mansfield Park*, can Mr Price. He does not act in a play, or in the role Crawford chooses for himself of the determined lover, but he does put on more than one reasonably convincing performance as a man in command of a situation. Two examples demonstrate this: when reading to Fanny the account of the upheaval in the Rushworths' home he remarks that 'a little flogging for man and woman too, would be the best way of preventing such things' (*MP*, 428). The primitive desire to control and punish is apparent here, as is the equally primitive desire to establish a sense of power. Mr Price is not just telling Fanny, and the world, what he thinks of Maria's behaviour, he is also setting himself up against Sir Thomas. As he says:

> I don't know what Sir Thomas may think of such matters: he may be too much of the courtier and fine gentleman to like his daughter

the less. But by G— if she belonged to me, I'd give her the rope's end as long as I could stand over her.

(MP, 428)

It is a classic speech of a powerless patriarch, a speech which contains an almost poignant display of the fear, envy and suspicion not just of women, but also of those assumed to have more social significance. But it is an act. As Mr Price almost certainly knows, he has no chance of intervening in Maria's affairs, still less of being regarded as of importance. Indeed, contradicted by Fanny about the truth of the report, he immediately retracts his remark and contents himself with a general mutter about the state of the moral universe.

This role playing – and its rapid abandonment – occurs within the space of two pages of *Mansfield Park*. Henry Crawford's assumption of the role of Fanny's lover lasts much longer, and is far more elaborate, but it is just as much (as Crawford well knows) an act. In Henry's case it is an act which takes over the actor, at least for a short time and until confronted by a real challenge to his vanity. The psychological parallels are striking: two men acting parts and abandoning them with almost indecent haste when thwarted. All the more credit is due, then, to Sir Thomas Bertram for noticing that Fanny and Henry Crawford have quite a lot in common. Sir Thomas does not make the point that Fanny and Henry Crawford share a somewhat similar emotional history, or a similar experience of absent/problematic fathers. But what he does suggest to Fanny (in the face of her fervent – and therefore revealing – denials) is that she and Crawford are more alike than she cares to admit. As he says:

> You are mistaken, Fanny. The dissimilarity is not so strong. You are quite enough alike. You *have* tastes in common. You have moral and literary tastes in common. You have both warm hearts and benevolent feelings; and Fanny, who that heard him read, and saw you listen to Shakespeare the other night, will think you unfitted as companions? You forget yourself: there is a decided difference in your tempers, I allow. He is lively, you are serious; but so much the better; his spirits will support yours.

And he adds, in a sentence that includes much of both the emotional narrative of the novel and Freud's later essay on love:

> I am perfectly persuaded that the tempers had better be unlike; I mean unlike in the flow of the spirits, in the manners, in the inclination for much or little company, in the propensity to talk or to be

silent, to be grave or to be gay. Some opposition here is, I am
thoroughly convinced, friendly to matrimonial happiness.

(MP, 345)

It is Fanny's opposition to Crawford that, as we know, provides her
major attraction for him. Used to the immediate conquest of women, a
woman who remains aloof from his charms is both interesting and
engaging. Yet common-sense lore and parlance have often suggested
that refusal is an endlessly successful strategy of romantic negotiation.
'Playing hard to get' has been a known aspect of the culture of romance
since at least the sixteenth century. Fanny Price, rather than being the
straightforward innocent pursued by Henry Crawford, could well be the
subtle, devious seductress intimated by her critics. Fanny comes to
represent to Henry Crawford what Freud described as 'frustration in
reality' (Freud 1953–74, 11: 181). She denies him access to her and with
every denial and refusal she increases the hold that she has over him.
Maria and Julia Bertram offer themselves to Henry Crawford without
hesitation. There is no refusal on their part; on the contrary, they are at
pains to point out to Crawford that they see no barriers to his total
possession of them. They – as separate people – would be all too happy
to disappear as separate beings and merge with Henry Crawford.

However, the offer of unrestrained access is one which Henry
Crawford absolutely refuses. He did not want, let alone desire, the available. His interest is in the unavailable. To Freud, this pattern is entirely
characteristic of many Western men, and the conduct of Western heterosexual relationships. In On the Universal Tendency he argues that the
currents of affection and sensuality are seldom fused in our culture. The
general pattern of the development of men's sexuality includes the denial
of access to the mother: the father intervenes to prevent the boy's fulfilment of his fantasy desire. But in Henry Crawford's case not only did
the mother die, but also the father vanished. The infant – or child –
Henry Crawford was left with no female figure to desire, and no male
figure to deny desire. What Henry became as a result of the disruption of
his childhood was one half of the Crawfords, brother and sister. Circumstances created a particularly close alliance between Henry and Mary
Crawford and it was a collusive alliance that was to continue well into
adult life. Henry – again, just like Fanny – had a particularly close relationship with a sibling, and a sibling who was prepared to tolerate, even
encourage, a brother's whims and romantic escapades. When Henry and
Mary arrive at Mansfield Park Mary Crawford tells Mrs Grant that
Henry is hotly pursued by young women:

I have three particular friends who have been all dying for him in their turn; and the pains which they, their mothers, (very clever women,) as well as my dear aunt and myself, have taken to reason, coax, or trick him into marrying, is inconceivable!

(*MP*, 75)

The insincerity of the speech is evident; Mary Crawford is evidently only too pleased that her engaging, amusing brother remains hers.

The collusion between brother and sister on the subject of Henry's relations with women remains throughout the novel. It is to Mary that Henry outlines his scheme for making the Bertram sisters admire him, it is to Mary that Henry confides his determination to make Fanny love him and it is Mary, in the concluding chapters of the novel, who defends Henry's actions to an amazed Fanny (see *MP*, 426). The relationship between Mary and Henry is more than close, it is quasi-incestuous, in that it is the relationship through which Henry Crawford mediates his relations with other women. Through, and with, his sister, Henry befriends the Bertram sisters, *not* the brothers, and has endless access to social occasions at which Maria and Julia will be present. 'Love', 'court-ship' and 'marriage' are the terms in which Jane Austen constructs rela-tionships between the sexes, but if we cross these out and substitute Freud's terms of 'sexual activity' and 'sensuality' then it is possible to see more clearly the dynamic underlying Henry's attitude to women. Above all else, we can see that Henry Crawford's attitude to women is far from *rational*. Why should a handsome, apparently heterosexual, man not marry, especially when presented with women who are rich, beautiful and available? What makes him hesitate? And what makes him refuse to seek women for himself, but all the while take the position of the pursued? The answer, Freud might argue, is that Henry Crawford is suffering from a bad case of psychical impotence. In these cases, Freud argues, affection and sensuality are not – as they should be – united, but are disunited. Because the child has never resolved his desire for his original love object (the mother) she remains implacably fixed in the unconscious. But she remains implacably fixed as the person who is deeply desired, but has never become loved. Given this history, what emerges is people whose sexual activity 'is capricious, easily disturbed, often not properly carried out, and not accompanied by much pleasure. But above all it is forced to avoid the affectionate current' (Freud 1953–74, 11: 182). And it is in that sense that Henry Crawford does not act rationally: he does not seek to find a person with whom he might create a relationship that meets both his sexual and emotional needs and thus achieve the affectionate relations that end the isolation of the single state. He seeks people to love him, but (at least until he meets Fanny) he does not seek to love. To quote Freud:

> The whole sphere of love in such people remains divided in the two directions personified in art as sacred and profane (or animal) love. Where they love they do not desire and where they desire they cannot love. They seek objects which they do not need to love, in order to keep their sensuality away from the objects they love . . .
>
> (Freud 1953–74, 11: 183)

The passage could have been written about Henry Crawford, and indicates precisely the ability of Jane Austen – and indeed literature in general – to encapsulate patterns of human behaviour that only subsequently have received formal analysis. Crawford's emotional history, and his relations with women, illustrate the causes and consequences of certain kinds of experiences in childhood and infancy. Most particularly, in Crawford's case, what is significant is the disappearance of his father, and the childhood and adolescence spent in an environment which was indulgent but morally flawed. Jane Austen cannot help but point out that 'education' and 'principle' are essential for the nurture of the young. Yet at the same time she is too sceptical a social analyst to accept the easy premise that paternal authority equals moral excellence. As she recognizes, Sir Thomas Bertram's presence throughout his children's childhood and adolescence did not make them good in any internal sense; it made them obedient and conventional and taught them all the necessary rules of social behaviour but it did not teach them moral discipline or knowledge of themselves. Henry and Mary Crawford, brought up in the far more pluralistic and worldly environment of their uncle's home, were never subjected to paternalistic authority. Most of all, and what they brought to Mansfield Park, was a belief that the world, both socially and morally, was endlessly a matter of negotiation. From the episode of Mary Crawford's harp – in which she demonstrated a profound belief in the ability of money to buy convenience (*MP*, 89–93) – to the conversation at the novel's conclusion in which Mary blithely suggests buying back Maria and Henry's good names (*MP*, 442–4), Jane Austen shows us a view of the world which assumes the absence of a fixed order.

This question of the merit – or otherwise – of the fixed order of patriarchy runs as a central theme through *Mansfield Park*, as much as it does throughout Freud. In one sense we can read *Mansfield Park* as an essay on the failings of unthinking patriarchy, in another we can read it as a discussion of how to be properly patriarchal. We have to explain the moral failings of Maria Bertram and Henry Crawford (as Jane Austen well knows) and as readers we have also to decide if Jane Austen's explanation is adequate. What we are given is that Henry Crawford was 'ruined by early independence and bad domestic example' (*MP*, 451) and that Maria Bertram (like her sister) 'had never been properly taught to govern their inclinations and tempers, by that sense of duty which can alone suffice' (*MP*, 448). The concluding chapter of *Mansfield Park* thunders with the call for rational, disciplined education of the young and dire warnings of the consequences of its absence.[4] Jane Austen, just as much as Freud, has no sympathy with the idea that desire and passion are to be allowed as explanations, let alone justifications, for human action. Both, however, recognize that the conditions of sexual desire and erotic attraction exist and that some way of integrating them into social life has to be achieved. Both – in different ways – suggest that no real adult satisfaction of sexuality is possible; whether restricted or allowed, sexual satisfaction is endlessly elusive.

In Jane Austen's fiction, as much as in Freud's essays and case histories, we are allowed a view of characters who indulge, and follow, their sexual instincts. Lydia Bennet (like her father) in *Pride and Prejudice* allows physical attraction to determine her choice of spouse, and numerous other characters enter marriage on the basis of mutual sexual appeal. Jane Austen then observes, either explicitly or metaphorically, that sexual passion seldom lasts. More directly, Freud remarks that 'freedom later given to that pleasure in marriage does not bring full satisfaction'. As the covers on the furniture fade in the sitting room of Charles and Mary Musgrove's home in *Persuasion* we know that the characters are living out all the disappointments of marital sexuality that Freud predicted. The fact that marriage actually demands sexual activity (indeed, without it marriage is deemed not to exist) is, of course, largely the reason for the sexual disappointments endemic to the marital state. As Freud writes:

It can easily be shown that the psychical value of erotic needs is reduced as soon as their satisfaction becomes easy. An obstacle is required in order to heighten libido; and where natural resistances to satisfaction have not been sufficient men have at all times erected conventional ones so as to be able to enjoy love.

(Freud 1953–74, 11: 187)

Therein is contained the sexual history of Henry Crawford, Fanny Price and Maria Bertram.

But literature does not summarize in the same way as psychoanalysis does. On the contrary, it sets out to elaborate and to illustrate themes and issues. So Jane Austen explores the development of Henry Crawford's passion for Fanny Price and finds that it lies (as Freud was to claim) in Fanny's resistance to Henry. Given that Fanny's emotional history is close to Henry's (absent father/surrogate father and close relationship with a sibling) it is inevitable that Fanny herself is a resonant person for Henry, and indeed his unconscious. As Jane Austen says (in one of her many moments of unerring prediction of the themes of psychoanalysis), Fanny Price was 'the woman whom he [Henry Crawford] had rationally, as well as passionately loved' (*MP*, 453). When Fanny refuses Henry's proposal of marriage she encourages his ardour, but long before that she had refused to enter the erotic world of the play *Lovers' Vows* and the equally sexually charged world of every-day, drawing-room conversation. She almost literally refuses to talk to Henry Crawford; she denies him access to herself in a way that is entirely unknown in his experience.

Access to the person, the self, through conversation was, as Jane Austen well knew, the most deeply erotic form of everyday exchange between the sexes. From *Clarissa* onwards, the eighteenth- and early nineteenth-century novel had developed and extended the possibilities of literary and verbal exchange between the sexes. Conversation in the novel, in much narrative fiction, thus has a status not unlike that of conversation in psychoanalysis. The power relation in psychoanalysis is of a different order, but in both cases individuals discourse (and the word is used deliberately) on the subjects that currently preoccupy them. Psychoanalysis recognizes that words conceal meanings as much as they reveal them; Jane Austen – writing almost a hundred years before Freud – knew that words were the medium through which individuals constructed and concealed themselves. That this should occur in ordinary, domestic, conversation was part and parcel of the social world. When Fanny and Edmund discuss Mary Crawford, immediately after her arrival at Mansfield Park, it is to what Mary *said* that the pair turn their attention. Their ensuing analysis is both determined and rigorous; no excuses are allowed, no concessions to wit or beauty. As Edward remarks: 'But was there nothing in her conversation that struck you Fanny, as not quite right?' And Fanny is quick to take up the point:

'Oh! yes, she ought not to have spoken of her uncle as she did. I

was quite astonished. An uncle with whom she has been living so
many years, and who, whatever his faults may be, is so very fond
of her brother, treating him, they say, quite like a son. I could not
have believed it!'

'I thought you would be struck. It was very wrong – very
indecorous.'

(*MP*, 94)

So here, only a few days after her arrival, is the beginning of the
unmasking of Mary Crawford that is to continue throughout the novel.
It is an unmasking, moreover, which occurs almost entirely through
conversation. Nobody (apart from Henry Crawford and Maria Bertram)
actually does anything in *Mansfield Park*. As Charlotte Brontë was later
to complain about Jane Austen, Austen's fiction is singularly lacking in
decisive action, deliberate choice and other indications of heroic and
determined purpose.[5] *In Persuasion* we see – in the final, amended,
chapters – not only Captain Wentworth's declaration of love, but also a
growing irritation on Jane Austen's part at how slow social development could be (*P*, 218–49).

The singularity of the incident in *Persuasion* arises, however, less from
Jane Austen's lack of imagination than from what we can see in her
work as the definitive understanding in English fiction of the ways in
which human beings construct their own fate, through an endlessly
complex fusion of circumstance and intent. In *Mansfield Park* she
suggests to us that it is impossible to alter the essential reality of the
individual: Mary and Henry Crawford might try to be good, just as
Maria Bertram might try to play the dutiful wife, but sooner or later the
'real' characters of these individuals will reveal themselves. In part – as
the assiduous students Edmund and Fanny know – the person is
revealed through words and conversation. But as Jane Austen also
recognized, occasionally human beings are tested by involvement in
particular situations. In an idea which is as old as the testing of Hercules
in Greek mythology, Jane Austen presents her characters with the tests
of an outing in the English countryside and participation in amateur
dramatics.

In both these central incidents in the novel, the Crawfords do rather
badly in moral terms, as do the Bertram sisters. During the expedition to
Sotherton, Mr Rushworth's country estate (in Chapters 9 and 10),
Maria and Julia Bertram make explicit their affection for Henry
Crawford, Mary Crawford reveals her contempt for the church and the
extent of her worldly ambitions, while Henry Crawford demonstrates

an impressive command of innuendo, hidden agendas and subtexts. Most transparently, all the characters demonstrate Freud's assertion that 'an obstacle is required in order to heighten libido' (Freud 1953–74, 11: 187). Confronted by a locked garden gate at Sotherton, Maria Bertram and Henry Crawford are determined to find a way around the barrier, a determination paralleled by the immediate decision by Mary Crawford to avoid conventional barriers: 'Here is a nice little wood, if one can get into it. What happiness if the door should not be locked!' (*MP*, 119).

The family outing to Sotherton reveals, as many family outings do, the extensive rivalries and tensions within society's smallest, and most intimate, group. The locked gate at Sotherton immediately provokes characters into revealing actions, actions which of course prefigure later developments in the novel. But the outing only lasts for a day, and there is little opportunity once the party returns to Mansfield Park to act out fantasies and desires – until, that is, the prospect of performing the play *Lovers' Vows* arises, accompanied by the Honourable John Yates. Performing the play, quite as much as the content of the play itself (which includes suggestion of incest and illegitimacy), immediately provokes moral reservations in Edmund and Fanny. Performing other people's emotions is not something Edmund regards lightly. Yet for his brother, that is precisely the appeal of the play: 'I can conceive no greater harm or danger to any of us in conversing in the elegant written language of some respectable author than in chattering in words of our own' (*MP*, 151).

Other people's words are, to Tom Bertram, entirely harmless. A literal-minded, and largely unreflective man, he cannot see, as his brother certainly can, the inherent complexities of the language of fiction. For Tom Bertram, his brothers and sisters will simply speak words written by other people. What Edmund sees is that he – and the other actors – will use the semblance of distance that is an essential part of acting to voice ideas, desires and fantasies that they themselves might have and yet cannot voice in conventional society. The public voicing and articulation of feelings that otherwise remain concealed is a part of drama; the play *Lovers' Vows* posed particular problems which Edmund Bertram was well aware of. The play revolves around unnatural and inappropriate relationships. Specifically, the mother in the play (the character called Agatha that was played by Maria Bertram) establishes a close, if not actually incestuous, relationship with her son (the character named Frederick played by Henry Crawford). The play affords Maria and Henry numerous occasions on which to be alone together, and to embrace in public. Henry Crawford emerges as an excellent actor, a person who enters with consummate skill into the pretence of being another person. Playing a role comes as naturally to Henry Crawford on the stage as it has in the drawing room.

What enables Henry Crawford to act so well is that he is clearly able to understand fantasy. He knows, in a way which the characters do not, that he is in a play, that he is engaging in an alternative make-believe world. The relationship which he would like with Maria, and is not allowed by the social world, is his for the asking on stage. Part of the attraction of the fictional relationship is that because mothers and sons are allowed a degree of intimacy anyway, Henry and Maria can experiment with the expression of love and affection in ways that are otherwise denied. However, for both characters the parts offer opportunities to return to desires and fantasies that are deeper and of longer duration than those of immediate adult attraction. In finding a fictional mother, played by a real woman who attracts him, Henry Crawford can bring together his desire for his real mother (lost in early childhood, and never outgrown through a relationship with his real father) and his desire for Maria. But Maria, who is *not* his real mother, in a sense betrays Henry by not fulfilling the demands of the role. She – the real-life Maria – does not love Henry as a son, but as an adult, sexual partner. Thus what ironically, and paradoxically, confronts Henry Crawford in *Lovers' Vows* is the creation of the fantasy situation that he must long have wanted, namely the reappearance of his mother. But he finds himself let down by the very fact that what appears to be an emotionally rewarding situation is not fantasy made real, but fantasy distorted by another person's reality, and the reality of the situation for Maria is that she loves Henry Crawford not as a son, but as a potential husband.

Access to the mother is, as Freud repeatedly reminds us, a complex negotiation in which the refusal of the mother to enter into an incestuous relationship with the son is a crucial part in the development of adult male sexuality.[6] In playing out his erotic fantasies in *Lovers' Vows*, Henry can return to the erotic fantasies of childhood at the same time as expressing adult desire. The situation is one of enormous attraction and psychic reward. As Henry himself most significantly remarks of the period of rehearsing *Lovers' Vows*: 'We were all alive . . . I never was happier.' Brought to emotional life by the appearance of a mother, Henry becomes within a hair's breadth of uniting fact and fiction (*MP*, 236).

At that moment, Sir Thomas Bertram returns and, like the majority of fathers, takes away Henry's recently refound mother. In a dramatic entrance, Sir Thomas severs the bond that has developed between mother and son, and returns Henry to reality. Maria is no longer Agatha, but Miss Maria Bertram, already engaged to another man, and a creature of the real world. Henry has no desire for this woman. She is obviously accessible, no father stands between her and Henry, and she offers Henry no opportunity to return to a world of infantile desire. Only when she meets him as a married woman – and refuses his attentions – does she again become desirable. As Jane Austen describes the meeting:

> He saw Mrs Rushworth, was received by her with a coldness which ought to have been repulsive, and have established apparent indifference between them for ever; but he was mortified, he could not bear to be thrown off by the woman whose smiles had been so wholly at his command; he must exert himself to subdue so proud a display of resentment; it was anger on Fanny's account; he must get the better of it, and make Mrs Rushworth Maria Bertram again in her treatment of himself.
>
> (*MP*, 452)

Here, then, is the refusal in reality that Freud saw as so important (indeed essential) a condition for the development of erotic attachment between women and men. Maria – by the conclusion of *Mansfield Park* – refuses Henry as a fantasy mother and now as a real-life woman. Little wonder that Henry Crawford becomes literally driven to possess her; or, as Jane Austen describes it, 'he went off with her at last, because he could not help it' (*MP*, 452).

The understanding implicit in that last sentence unites Jane Austen and Freud. Jane Austen, quite as much as Freud, understood that human beings are often powerless in the face of their emotions. Both Austen and Freud saw that whatever the rules and sanctions of society, human beings would generally only be able to offer an approximation to ideals of individual behaviour. The conclusion of *Mansfield Park* is in itself a brief treatise on the principle of accommodation in human affairs. The fine, ideal principles and the promise of the Bertram children with which the novel opens are finally resolved and moulded into the relationships of compromise with which the novel concludes. The personal compromises which Jane Austen describes are the human reality of the incompatibility which Freud recognized of sexual instincts and civilization. Nevertheless, as he writes:

> The very incapacity of the sexual instinct to yield complete satisfaction as soon as it submits to the first demands of civilization

becomes the source, however, of the noblest cultural achievements
which are brought into being by ever more extensive sublimation
of its instinctual components.

(Freud 1953–74, 11: 190)

Edmund and Fanny are left, in the last sentences of *Mansfield Park*, to
build the civilization that Freud saw as possible if pleasure was abandoned as a dominating force – a new civilization that is more benign
than that of the unbridled patriarchy of Sir Thomas. The father has had
to stand aside for the son, but that standing aside has only been made
possible because another man – in this case Henry Crawford – was
insufficiently integrated into the demands and constraints of patriarchal
civilization. The absence of Henry Crawford's father – both in reality
and as a metaphor for civilization and social constraint – combines with
the excessive presence of Maria Bertram's father to create two characters
for whom an escape to infantile, presocial, pleasure is the one possible
psychic route. Only in the last ironical pages of the novel does it become
clear that in this unrestrained desire for pleasure lies the possibility of the
emancipation of others – particularly Edmund and Fanny – from the
almost certain *absence* of pleasure. In the marriage of Fanny and Edmund
Jane Austen proposes a unity of respect and desire, but it is a unity
tempered by the recognition, later to be documented by Freud, that
neither state is absolute. Absolute desire returns the individual to
infancy, empty respect creates deceit and evasion. The world we leave in
the last chapter of *Mansfield Park* is one which has come to terms with
the irreconcilable differences between egoistic and sexual instincts and
has made, as both Jane Austen and Freud hoped, a civilization capable of
high achievement. The nature of the social order which the marriage of
Fanny and Edmund represents, is, of course, intensely problematic, in
that there is a strong case for arguing (as do Gilbert and Gubar) that
Fanny's role is to reinforce women's subordination in patriarchal culture
(Gilbert and Gubar 1979: 154–5). But the argument advanced here is
that although Fanny, on the level of day-to-day reality, maintains the
patriarchal order, on quite another she fiercely resists her inclusion in
both male fantasy (in the case of Henry Crawford) and male power (the
case of Sir Thomas). What she can be said to represent, therefore, is an
assertion of the part that women can play – through deconstructing
forms of the male debasement of women – in constructing the emotional
conditions in which love and desire unite.

It would be misleading, however, to conclude this essay on a note
which suggests that the only compromise which has been reached at the

end of Mansfield Park is an emotional one. While the explicit sexual desire of Edmund Bertram has been thwarted and tempered, so has the acquisitive capitalist desire to possess of his father. As Jane Austen writes of Sir Thomas: 'Sick of ambitions and mercenary connections, prizing more and more the sterling good of principle and temper, and chiefly anxious to bind by the strongest securities all that remained to him of domestic felicity . . .' (MP, 455). The comment shows a brilliant fusion of the language of commerce and domestic life; 'sterling good' and 'strongest securities', terms appropriate to a commercial market, now become the descriptions of a valuable domestic life. Economic interest has been domesticated.

The person who is largely responsible for the taming of sexual and financial desire in men is the slight figure of Fanny Price. Jane Austen, like Charlotte Brontë, made her most morally forceful heroine small and insignificant in stature. 'Big' women like Maria Bertram and Bertha Rochester come to unhappy ends, both more or less literally confined to attics and both demonstrating to generations of readers women's, just as men's, fears about the unbridled possibilities of women's sexuality. Fanny, like Jane, does not conform to any traditional expectations of femininity: quiet she may be, but she does not seek male sexual approval in the same way as Maria or Julia Bertram. In an entirely radical way, she offers to us a woman who is complete in herself – she does not need to be 'completed' or made whole by a man. The way in which she stands alone in the novel is a vivid portrayal of a woman reconciled, in the sense that Freud understood it, to the condition of femininity. Edmund has begun to see Fanny's social and moral strengths at the novel's end; we might conjecture that in marriage to her he will also learn the limits of conventional masculinity as they had hitherto been constructed at Mansfield Park. In this novel, in many ways the richest, emotionally of Jane Austen's work, we see the working out of universal and ageless patterns of desire. Elsewhere in her fiction other, equally, universal themes are explored – about relations between siblings and parents and children. To all of these themes Austen brings, as Freud was to, the ability to name, and explain, what can appear to be the random events and choices of emotional life.

Acknowledgements

I would like to thank Janet Sayers and David Morgan for reading an earlier draft of this paper. I am especially grateful to Nigel Wood for his careful and thoughtful editorial work on the paper.

SUPPLEMENT

NIGEL WOOD: In your study of *Jane Austen and the State* you portray Jane
Austen's faith in individualism as of paramount importance, that is, society
would crumble if we were subsumed by social conventions. This belief is
created, however, out of a dialectic between two types of conservatism:
that is, acquisitive capitalism, on the one hand, and its opposite: a 'romantic
indifference' to material concerns (Evans 1987: 79). In this piece it seems to
me that you have come to a similar conclusion by a quite different route,
namely that Fanny and Edmund's marriage is representative of a compromise between 'absolute desire' and 'empty respect'. Do you believe that
the psychological and sociological factors behind JA's intentions coexist as
equal partners, or do you see one of them as a more powerful or comprehensive form of explanation?

MARY EVANS: Austen's individualism has always been one of the aspects of her
work which I find particularly interesting, since she both assumes (and
expects) individuals to be responsible for their own fate, while maintaining
an extraordinarily strong sense of the importance of what we now call
'community' or 'society'. So on the one hand she is – as you suggest – conservative, and yet on the other she is quite radical in suggesting that there
are ties between individuals which are of great importance in the maintenance of social cohesion. The word that might now be used to describe
these ties is 'mutuality' – the sense of how people depend on each other
for a viable existence. The marriage of Edmund and Fanny seems to me to
be a vivid embodiment of this ethos. Initially, desire in the relationship lies
with Fanny, but her attraction to Edmund is partly constructed out of her
sense of his commitment to a social ethic. Edmund has to learn to desire
Fanny, partly perhaps because she embodies conscience in such a determined way. (Of which more in answer to the second question.) So in the
relationship between Fanny and Edmund psychological and sociological
factors (or, as I would describe them, social and emotional factors) play
equal, but closely related, parts.

NW: With Gilbert and Gubar's *The Madwoman in the Attic* (1979) in mind, the
strong and silent Fanny Price comes over as a rather patriarchal figure, or, at
least, one that collaborates with the prevailing system, where the 'necessity for silence and submission reinforces women's subordinate position in
patriarchal culture' (Gilbert and Gubar 1979: 154). Is her centrality in the
novel the unacceptable face of a rather banal form of conformity, or is
there more to be said for her than that?

ME: I find Fanny Price an exceptional figure in fiction, in that she seems to me
to represent the possibility of women having that developed conscience
which Freud (and later others including Kohlberg) assumed that they did
not – and could not – have. This position is anything but conformist, in
that Fanny actually rejects empty convention and asserts principles, which
she is prepared to maintain. Fanny Price obviously co-operates with the

form of conventional society, but she also has a uniquely clear sense of values that are not expressed in everyday life. The struggle in the novel between Fanny and Sir Thomas (which in retrospect I would give greater emphasis to) is for control of the moral space at Mansfield Park. In that, Fanny does not do as her cousins (which is to try and sidestep Sir Thomas) but she confronts him in the best David and Goliath tradition.

NW: Does the syndrome of prohibition increasing desire experienced by Henry Crawford and described by Freud in *The Universal Tendency* assume the force of some transhistorical law, equally applicable to every epoch or class?

ME: This question is difficult, if not impossible, to answer emphatically. I would argue that the syndrome of prohibition increasing desire is *probably* universal, but most visible in societies, and communities, which have highly structured patterns of sexual and class relationships. Distinctions about children, about women being 'in' or 'out', about chaperonage and the limits of male–female conversation all create a situation in which the extent of the unknown, and the unknowable, are increased. One of Mary Crawford's first questions about Fanny Price is to ask whether or not she is 'out', and we can read this not only in the terms of the social conventions of the early nineteenth century but also in the more general terms of inclusion/ exclusion of individuals in the adult world of sexuality. Jane Austen makes much of Fanny's simplicity of dress and appearance; Fanny's virginal appearance and its appeal to Edmund and Henry is made clear to the reader. And, of course, there is no other category which is so prohibited as that of the virgin daughter of the house.

NW: You seem to regard the conclusion of the novel as possessing an under-tow that is rather pessimistic, in that the higher achievements that Freud foresaw would accrue if pleasure were bridled are almost poor substitutes for infantile rewards. Edmund and Fanny are, alas, mature. What egoistic instincts remain with them (at all) to meet the demands of the unity you describe of 'respect and desire'?

ME: I do not wish to *be* pessimistic in my conclusions. I suppose it is less a pessimism and more a sense of the limits of Fanny and Edmund as social characters. They will live 'civilized' lives, but without, as far as anyone can judge, any hints of creative neurosis.

NW: Could you apply Freud's ideas to any other JA novels?

ME: Writing this essay on *Mansfield Park* has convinced me that all JA's fiction could be illuminated by, and illuminate, Freud's ideas. The very con-tainment of the context of her fiction provides the first argument in favour of this idea: she writes about the family, and family dramas, with an unrivalled force and intensity. Moreover, she makes connections between the family and society which have long eluded both novelists and sociologists. When she tells the tale of the feckless Wickham and Lydia Bennet in *Pride and Prejudice*, she tells us about every other relationship constructed through romance and maintained through family collusion.

The clarity of her analysis, particularly over issues such as romance, make her a natural ally of Freud, who was equally concerned to strip away ideology and sentiment from marriage and sexuality. The family secrets identified by Laing and Cooper in the late 1960s are known and recorded by Austen in the early nineteenth century. She knew, as exactly as Freud did, that the family was the place of both isolation and intimacy.

CHAPTER 2

The Political Unconscious
in *Mansfield Park*

BREAN S. HAMMOND

[Brean S. Hammond's reading of *Mansfield Park* draws on the Hegelian Marxist positions offered by Fredric Jameson's *The Political Unconscious*. Marxist theories of literature are varied in detail, but stem more or less directly from the view that, while art may seem to be produced just by individuals, we might learn much more about their work if we identify, first, the artist's 'ideology', that is, not a set of codified beliefs, but rather an unphilosophical reflection of how individuals see their roles in class society and the values, symbols and ideas that help explain that role to such individuals and which therefore ties them all the more securely to their inherited context; and second, the basic conditions under which such art can be produced (for instance, conditions of patronage, growth of the mass market, availability of new technologies of production) which establish inexorable limits to the apparent freedoms of artistic activity.

Marx's (and Engels's) terms still provide the original inspiration for Marxist interpretation. In Marx and Engels's *The German Ideology* (1845–6) the 'production of ideas, of conceptions, of consciousness is at first directly interwoven with the material activity and the material intercourse of men'. Thus, thought is the 'direct efflux' of this 'material behaviour', and individuals must be brought to realize that they, in fact, have a hand in the production of their own conceptions, 'real, active men, as they are conditioned by a definite development of their productive forces'. The conclusion is inescapable that 'life is not determined by consciousness, but consciousness by life' (Feuer 1959: 287–8). This is given more specific focus in the Preface to *A Contribution to the Critique of Political Economy* (1859), where it is held as a condition of the 'social production' of one's own life that one enters 'into definite relations that are indispensable and independent of [one's] will, *relations of production* which correspond to a definite stage of development of [one's] material productive *forces'*. This forms 'the economic structure of society, the real foundation, on which rises a legal and political superstructure and to which correspond definite forms of social consciousness' (Feuer 1959: 84). This model seems particularly deterministic, and most recent Marxist analysis regards this 'base–superstructure' divide as a preliminary move, one which if carried through without extra sophistication, reduces all art to its modes of production, a position that makes it particularly difficult to account for individual variations.

The 'definite forms of social consciousness' group themselves in analysis as *ideology*. In order to render such awareness as narrow and partisan (that is, stemming from a class identity, not 'nature' or 'common sense'), there is a need to compare it with some greater entity or notion that proceeds from a more 'scientific' grasp of the total system of social relationships. 'Ideology' was often, then, equated with 'false consciousness'. More recently, 'ideology' has come to be associated with *all* forms of social perception, without which we could not function as members of society. In the work of Louis Althusser the role assigned to art is a major one, for he claims that it is only through the depiction of a process of thought in literary form that the work of ideology can be inspected with sufficient detachment. In his essay 'Ideology and Ideological State Apparatuses' (1969), Althusser finds ideology integral to *all* thought processes. It supplies a focus for definitions, even if actually based on biassed premises. The state apparatuses (among them the Church, the political party, the university and the legal system) 'interpellate' us (encourage us to believe) that we are free individuals, and therein lies their attraction and power (see Althusser 1977: 123–73).

This tendency to differentiate literary from non-literary expression is obviously fraught with the difficulty of defining just what the 'literary' might be, but it also creates a system of evaluation as well as of analysis. For Pierre Macherey, in *A Theory of Literary Production*, literary form was capable of showing up the internal incoherences and multiple contradictions of ideology. The apparent coherence of ideology can only be maintained by a process of repression and economies with the truth. By dwelling on the 'silences' that come to be implied by the work of art Macherey reveals the way that ideology operates and, implicitly, how we can question its hold over us (see especially Macherey 1978: 61–101, and Eagleton 1991: 136–51).

Jameson's great popularity stems from his ability to accommodate the private with the public sphere of analysis. History is not merely 'context' or 'background', but rather something far less unitary; it is perceived in 'ideologies' and several alternative points of access for the researcher. Hegel argued in his *Philosophy of Fine Art* (1835) that there was a very gradual unfolding in particular events of a history which was seen as stages in the development of a 'world-spirit' or an 'idea' or 'absolute', an idealist concept which pointed towards a time (post-capitalist) when form and content might eventually form a harmonious unity. In the work of Georg Lukács and Lucien Goldmann there is an attempt to breathe new life into this perspective, by regarding art as the production of a whole social group whose 'trans-individual mental structures' (Goldmann's term, indicating the group's aspirations and how it makes sense of them) are transposed by the most valuable artists into eventually unified and recurrent structures. For Goldmann, in studies such as *The Hidden God* (1964), structural relations are sought between the literary text, the 'world-view' of the artist's social grouping and its particular historical situation. The tendency is towards an achieved totality of view that can take in something wider than history is more traditionally taken to be. In *The Political Unconscious* Jameson emphasizes this concept of the 'totality' as a standard of judgement, not as a predicted future state (Jameson 1981: 50–7). Ideology confirms a constricted horizon by 'strategies of containment' where limits to reference created by mimetic means (for example, Austen's '3 or 4 Families in a Country Village') enforce an unnecessary frontier to discourse in the interests of 'coherence' or just simply intelligibility. Reading texts as 'symbolic acts' entails 'the will ... [to] grasp them as resolutions of determinate contradictions'. Interpretation becomes a rewriting of the rhetorical text 'in such a way that the latter may itself be seen as the rewriting or restructuration of a prior historical or ideological *subtext*' which is only ever available by self-conscious analytical (re)construction (Jameson 1986: 80–1).

In short, texts never 'tell' us their history; they must be made to do this, and this involves breaking out of what Jameson in 1972 called the 'prison-house of language' (see Jameson 1972: 195–216) and re-engaging with a history which contains several coexistent 'histories' and competing ideologies (see his 'Marxism and Historicism' (1979) in Jameson 1988, II: 148–77). To place the text within the 'totality' is thus also to express what it cannot. Austen does not need to refer to frame-breaking or trade embargoes to be historical.]

NIGEL WOOD

I

Jane Austen is among the elite corps of English authors whose writing has a broad cultural currency. Her novels are not confined to the 'classics' section of the better bookshops, but can be found in the more general category of 'fiction'. In her bicentenary year (1975), she joined Dickens and Shakespeare as one of only three authors to have a set of UK commemorative postage stamps devoted to her work, depicting scenes from *Emma* (8½p), *Northanger Abbey* (10p), *Pride and Prejudice*

(11p) and *Mansfield Park* (13p). (I am not sure if the value of the stamps embodies any literary judgement on their comparative merits!) Later authors have translated her novels into different media: Constance Cox, for instance, has produced dramatic versions of *Pride and Prejudice*, *Northanger Abbey* and *Mansfield Park*. The current list of BBC videotapes includes dramatizations of *Northanger Abbey*, *Pride and Prejudice*, *Sense and Sensibility* and *Mansfield Park*; and a little research in the radio archives would soon produce many more such dramatizations. Follow-up versions of her novels have been produced, such as Joan Aiken's *Mansfield Revisited* (1984) motivated by 'love and admiration', which begins with the 'sudden and unexpected death of Sir Thomas Bertram' and takes Susan Price as its heroine.[1] Innumerable versions of her novels have been produced for children and to suit the needs of different reading schemes. The Rectory at Steventon, Hampshire, where Jane Austen began her life, is a popular place of pilgrimage, as is the grave in Winchester Cathedral which marks the place where she ended it. Long after her death, her name continues to be current in that congeries of places, practices and discourses that amounts to the 'heritage industry'.

What accounts for the continuing public love affair with 'gentle Jane'? For many readers, the name 'Jane Austen' expresses an idealized conception of authorship according to which there is a seamless continuity between the writer and the writing. She has created in her readers' imagination a very close identification between her life and her writing, such that she and her works appear to capture the 'essence' of a certain kind of Englishness, occupying a position in English letters analogous to that of Burns in Scottish. What Edwin Muir has said of Burns – 'for a Scotsman to see Burns simply as a poet is almost impossible . . . He is a myth evolved by the popular imagination' – goes for the English and Jane Austen: though she is a very different kind of myth![2] She converted her life's experience into the raw material of fiction with what appears to be exceptional accuracy, creating a circumscribed pre-industrial landscape which, the reader is convinced, *was* England once. Her novels liberate in the reader a nostalgia that can conceal the extent of the circumscription. The following quotation from Lord David Cecil's *A Portrait of Jane Austen* serves to exemplify the standpoint of very many publications of the 'Jane Austen and her world' stamp:

> She was at ease in the world she was born into. Several things account for this. In the first place the countryside of southern

England, where she spent most of her life, was a pleasing and reassuring region with its green smiling landscape of field and woodland and leafy hedgerows, of spacious skies and soft horizons; and with something at once homely and immemorial in the atmosphere emanating from its thatched villages each centring around a grey old church, its interior enriched with sculptured monuments of successive generations of local land-owners and set in a grassy churchyard populated by gravestones inscribed with the names of successive generations of their tenants; and the two combining to suggest an extraordinary feeling of social and family solidarity and continuity.

(Cecil 1978: 10–12)

Bath, Edinburgh New Town, Chippendale, Sheraton, Wedgwood and Worcester are all mentioned by Cecil in the familiar litany of names that stand as metonymies for 'Georgian England'.

If it is true, as Wordsworth said, that every great writer must create the taste by which he is to be relished,[3] then Jane Austen is a great writer. Her work has been remarkably successful in dictating the terms in which it has later been discussed. These terms are largely ethical. Until recently, much professional criticism of Jane Austen's writing, and the classroom discussion led by its example, has concentrated on the issues of morality and principle that are raised in the novels them-selves. My experience of student essays and examination questions on her work is that they typically replicate and extend the debates that the principal characters themselves conduct or omit to conduct on the pre-dicaments with which they are faced. England at the turn of the nine-teenth century, it might seem to the reader who is not obliged to delve very deeply into *Mansfield Park*, was a country in which the problems of interpersonal relations and the ethical codes that support them were the most pressing. If we were to read the novels as affording direct sociological evidence, we would infer that since most men had an inde-pendent income (albeit varying in adequacy) or a secure profession, their main business was to look for a mate worthy of sharing their social position; while women had to cultivate their natural and acquired attractions in order to edge out their rivals. *Mansfield Park*'s audacity, we would then assume, lies in dramatizing the career of a protagonist who, though devoid of many of these attractions and lack-ing any secure social position from which to market herself, neverthe-less proves successful owing to what the narrator calls 'heroism of principle' – an inner worth that acts as the cuticle on which alone the healthy outer skin of 'manners' can grow (MP, 271).[4] This is the distinction (a key distinction for understanding Jane Austen's work) made by Edmund Bertram in discussing the clergyman's true vocation with Mary Crawford while they are exploring the symbolically designated 'wilderness' at Sotherton:

> The manners I speak of, might rather be called conduct, perhaps, the result of good principles; the effect, in short, of those doctrines which it is their duty [the clergy's] to teach and recommend; and it will, I believe, be every where found, that as the clergy are, or are not what they ought to be, so are the rest of the nation.
>
> (MP, 121)

Thus Edmund attempts to make moral pathways in the 'wilderness'. Within an overview like this, local moral issues can be debated. Ought Edmund Bertram to have seen through Mary Crawford earlier in the novel? Should Fanny Price have refused Henry? What measure of blame can we attach to Sir Thomas for the subsequent loose behaviour of his children?[5]

Discussion couched in these terms is inadequate not only on the pedagogical grounds that in the classroom it can degenerate into mere gossip, further embarrassed by being gossip about unreal people, but it also exposes the inadequacy of a certain kind of literary critical discourse. It fails to transform the language of the original text. It fails to be what the Marxist critic Fredric Jameson would call a 'metacommentary'. A common tendency in much recent literary critical theory has been to expose the inadequacy of interpretation as a critical strategy. Michel Foucault puts the objection wittily when he points out that interpretation, mere commentary, 'must say for the first time what had . . . already been said [in the text], and must tirelessly repeat what had . . . never been said' (Young 1981: 58, from 'The Order of Discourse' (1970)). For Jameson, interpretation of literary works is the rewriting of them in terms of some master code or 'master-narrative' which, far from explaining the text, really only tells us about the ideology the critic wants to perpetuate. By contrast, in what Jameson refers to as 'metacommentary':

> every individual interpretation must include an interpretation of its own existence, must show its own credentials and justify itself: every commentary must be at the same time a metacommentary as well.
>
> (Jameson 1988, I: 5, from 'Metacommentary' (1971))[6]

Elsewhere, Jameson has forcefully exposed the shortcomings of an ethical criticism that can only pose its questions in the form of moral debate:

> we would do better to limit the notion of ethical choices and ethical acts to those situations alone in which individuals face each other as conscious and responsible moral or rational agents, or in which such an autonomous individual or subject confronts his or her own self or personal development. To put it this way is to realize that in the modern world . . . there are many experiences and situations that are far more complex than this, where an individual or a character is faced not with an interpersonal relationship, with an ethical choice, but rather with a relationship to some determining force vaster than the self or any individual, that is, with society itself, or with politics and the movement of history.
>
> (Jameson 1988, I: 124, from 'Criticism in History' (1976))

Ethical criticism, that is to say, discussion of the moral choices confronting rational, autonomous characters in novels, is the aesthetic agenda of what is sometimes called 'liberal humanism'. In a post-Nietzschean world, one 'beyond good and evil' which has witnessed degrees of atrocity unparalleled in human annals, and in a post-Freudian world wherein conceptions of human subjectivity and agency are no longer stable, such a programme has ceased to convince. What conviction it carries is only the result of our categories of literary characterization remaining so stubbornly anthropomorphic. Traditional Anglo-American studies of fiction, as Jameson says, 'remain stubbornly committed to the principle that all elements of a masterwork – style, images, episodes, etc. – cohere in some harmonious ethical or thematic statement, which it is the business of the critic to recover' (Jameson 1988, I: 25, from 'The Ideology of the Text' (1975–6; 1986)). It is the result of certain beliefs about the nature of literary production itself which have until recently organized the discipline of literary criticism in university English Departments and still do organize it in secondary education. Authors – great writers – are the central epistemological category of the study of literature. Literature is produced by the free play of a creative individual's imagination over aspects of experience. The author is the source of the meaning of the work: and we distinguish authors worthy of study from those who are not in so far as the former can impose significant form on their material and use language with special virtuosity. The 'syllabus' author shapes inherited generic conventions into a uniquely intelligent ethical or intellectual outlook, which it is the business of the critic to restate.

Another tendency common to several forms of recent critical theory is the desire to attack this account of authorship. 'Post-structuralist' theories downgrade the status of authorship as part of a wider project – the displacement of all concepts that guarantee meaning from outside language. Conventionally, the idea of authorial intention underpins this confidence in pre-linguistic thought that post-structuralists like Derrida wish to question. 'Psychoanalytic' theories are sceptical of the extent to which any author can be said to control her/his own meanings. Jacques Lacan, the immensely influential French psychoanalyst, called attention in his work to the view that 'language and its structure exist prior to the moment at which each individual at a certain point in his mental development makes his entry into it', thereby denying to individuals any extra-linguistic autonomy (Lodge 1988: 82, from 'The Insistence of the Letter in the Unconscious' (1957)). Roland Barthes, in a famous essay called 'The Death of the Author' (1968), gives a communications-based inflection to the post-structuralist argument by denying to 'great' authors the degree of linguistic innovation and creativity usually credited to them. Language is a system that dwarfs the individuals who use it: writing is 'a multi-dimensional space in which a multitude of writings, none of them original, blend and clash', so that in a sense, writing writes writers. Renaming writers 'scriptors', Barthes characterizes the scriptor's task as 'to mix writings, to counter the ones with the others'. While the *author* is said to 'nourish' her/his book, to exist before it, think, suffer and live for it, to be parent to it as child, the *scriptor* is 'born simultaneously with the text, is in no way equipped with a being preceding or exceeding the writing, is not the subject with the book as predicate' (Barthes 1977: 145). Even more ambitious as a challenge to the centrality of authorship and the ethical criticism that derives from it is the work of Michel Foucault and Fredric Jameson, on whom I shall concentrate before moving to the text.

Michel Foucault's views on authorship are part of a much wider project that amounts to an attack on the current organization of the discipline of intellectual history, or history of ideas. This discipline has been dominated by the notion that there is a continuing, coherent and unbroken intellectual tradition that is forwarded by the achievements of conscious human subjects – 'great thinkers', the records of whose thought partly comprise the documentary evidence on which history itself is built. This approach to history is clearly related to the form of author-based ethical criticism under discussion. Here, the author's *oeuvre* is of importance in tracing the recessive continuities that form our notions of intellectual history. Displacing this cluster of principles in his *The Archaeology of Knowledge* (*L'Archéologie du savoir*, 1969, first published in English in 1972), Foucault lays the foundation for a new study, the study of 'discourse formation'. Asserting the existence of *discontinuities* in intellectual history, denying that the history of human thought is an unbroken tradition, but seeing it rather as characterized by gaps, by sudden eruptions of new 'discursive formations' onto the intellectual scene, Foucault contends that our object of study should be the impersonal way in which, at certain historical junctures, statements are made by a number of writers in many different places, issuing from different institutional sites, within a range of different 'enunciative modalities', which nevertheless can be seen to comprise a coherent discourse of 'natural history' or 'political economy' or 'general grammar'. I quote here one of many passages in which Foucault distinguishes what he calls 'archaeology' from the history of ideas, on the grounds that individual authors and their *oeuvres* are of no significance to archaeology:

> [Archaeology] defines types of rules for discursive practices that run through individual *oeuvres*, sometimes govern them entirely, and dominate them to such an extent that nothing eludes them; but which sometimes, too, govern only part of it. The authority of the creative subject, as the *raison d'être* of an *oeuvre* and the principle of its unity, is quite alien to it.
>
> (Foucault 1972: 139)

On the subject of interpretation, Foucault's opinion is typically as follows:

> The analysis of statements . . . is a historical analysis, but one that avoids all interpretation: it does not question things said as to what they were 'really' saying, in spite of themselves, the unspoken element they contain, the proliferation of thoughts, images, or fantasies that inhabit them . . .
>
> (Foucault 1972: 109)

In an important essay first published in 1969, 'What is an Author?', Foucault argues that the concept of an author performs a particular *function* in discourse. Contrary to the belief that books have had authors' names attached to them since time immemorial, Foucault argues that authors' names first came to be attached to works when it became important to the state to prosecute individuals under blasphemy or libel laws. Authored discourse is *owned* discourse; so that the author function is primarily a legal category. Authors' names are demanded to guarantee literary discourse whereas other discourses (science, mathematics) may not have similar rules of authorization (Lodge 1988: 197–210). Foucault's most valuable insights concern the perceived relationship between knowledge and power. In his account, knowledge is not made by a series of geniuses who make successive breakthroughs and contribute to an uninterrupted progress. Knowledge exists as a bundle of overlapping discursive practices achieving unity by seizing power. Knowledge is powerful discourse. Diane McDonnell gives a simple example to illustrate this: a hospital patient says different things about her body from the hospital doctor, but only some of the statements she makes will be regarded as carrying weight. Her discourse will be less powerful than the doctor's and only his will be regarded as part of 'knowledge' (McDonnell 1986: 2). In seeking out the rules of formation of discourses that have constituted knowledge at different historical junctures, Foucault has been most influential on the Marxist critic and theorist Fredric Jameson, whose work will offer a way into *Mansfield Park*.

For Jameson, the purpose behind literary analysis is to restore works of literature to the social totalities of which they are a part. Although Foucault's work does outline a relationship between knowledge and power, it never satisfactorily considers the specific historical and institutional forms that power has taken in actual human societies. Jameson sees the task of relating specific, historically determined social formations to their imaginative and artistic activities as the fundamental objective of analysis. In many places, he argues the priority of contextual analysis over other forms of interpretation; the case he makes against psychoanalytic approaches, for example, is that if they are stretched far enough, they encounter history when it becomes obvious that they are working with definitions of the *family* that are historically constituted. Any autonomy apparently possessed by structuralist criticism or myth criticism or whatever, is simply the result of arbitrary limitation placed on the interpretative process. He recognizes, however, that traditional historicist criticism as well as Marxist analysis can be appallingly naive about the relationship that exists between historical context and literary work.[7] In particular, the 'vulgar Marxist' view that literary texts directly reflect the ways in which a society produces its wealth (the crude aesthetic conclusion drawn from the Marxist model of base and superstructure) is one that Jameson has set out to combat. His important work is a search after ever more complex ways of representing the relationship between the literary work and the modes of production of the society in which it is written: and Jameson's understanding of what history actually *is* takes him close to post-structuralists:

> History is not in any sense itself a text or master text or master narrative, but . . . it is inaccessible to us except in textual or narrative form, or, in other words . . . we approach it only by way of some prior textualization or narrative (re)construction.
> (Jameson 1988, II: 150, from 'Marxism and Historicism' (1979))

And:

> we need to take into account the possibility that our contact with the past will always pass through the imaginary and through its ideologies, will always in one way or another be mediated by the codes and motifs of some deeper historical classification system or *pensée sauvage* of the historical imagination, some properly political unconscious.
>
> (Jameson 1988, II: 152)

Jameson's thought is complex and it is far from easy to select the key concepts from his most important book, *The Political Unconscious*, but I will make some attempt to do so in what follows.

The central question for Jameson is the question of ideology. How do the beliefs, attitudes and wants of a society, its 'forms of consciousness', relate to the literary works that it produces and how are those forms of consciousness actually replicated in the works? For traditional Marxism, ideology was a pejorative word meaning *false* consciousness, a delusion suffered by the exploited proletariat under capitalism which was necessary to the supporting, stabilizing and legitimation of power. Jameson develops further the thinking of the philosopher Louis Althusser, whose contribution was to show that ideology need not be thought of as *caused* by underlying economic reality, or even as the direct *expression* of it. Rather, our beliefs, attitudes and ideas as they are expressed in the political and legal systems we devise and in the aesthetic objects we produce, are related to each other as elements of an overall structure which is not conditioned by the economy, but rather includes it. Althusser's notable definition of ideology as 'a representation of the imaginary relationship of individuals to their real conditions of existence' (Althusser 1977: 152–9, from 'Ideology and

Ideological State Apparatuses' (1969)) gives the imagination relative autonomy from the material reality that conditions it only in the last instance. Works of art, that is, can be counter-cultural, or not apparently concerned with material reality at all, but history is still their 'absent cause'. To Jameson, ideologies are 'strategies of containment'. Our systems of belief are a way of shutting out, of repressing, underlying contradictions in history, a way of making a coherent system out of elements that do not necessarily cohere. Literary works embody this process more individually: but they are also peculiarly potent in revealing the crisis points of such contradiction. The literary work:

> obeys a double impulse. On the one hand, it preserves the subject's fitful contact with genuine life and serves as the repository for that mutilated fragment of Experience which is her treasure, or his. Meanwhile, its mechanisms function as a censorship, which secures the subject against awareness of resulting impoverishment, while preventing him/her from identifying connections between that impoverishment and mutilation and the social system itself.
>
> (Jameson 1988, I: 15, from 'Metacommentary')

Narrative, for Jameson, is a mechanism through which both the individual and the collective consciousness represses historical contradictions; but it is also, like dreams in psychoanalysis, a site upon which those repressed realities can be retrieved. Critical activity is directed at such a retrieval, but for Jameson this is a gradual ascent up three levels or 'horizons': historical contextualization which locates aesthetic contradiction, leading to the horizon of the social order, where the literary work is reconfigured as a dialogue between antagonistic class discourses; and finally, to the horizon of epochal history, that is to say, to an examination of a work's location in the development of modes of production which is, to Jameson, the determining mechanism of historical change. William C. Dowling, in a helpful introduction to Jameson's thought, expresses the final objective of Jamesonian analysis as recovering 'the ultimate context of reading', which is the production of coherent meaning (Dowling 1984: 184). It remains now to be seen how far we can apply such ideas to Jane Austen's *Mansfield Park*, how far we can open the text to the 'absent cause' of history that the novel seems so wholly to conceal in presenting itself as the accurate mimesis of English upper middle-class life at the turn of the nineteenth century. Our objective is not so much to lay a slavish Jamesonian template over the text, as to show how the critic informed by Jamesonian ideas might ask *questions* that elicit answers different to those found by traditional critics, answers that illuminate occluded aspects of the text.

II

In my opening remarks, I drew attention to a certain cultivated segregation maintained by the discourse of *Mansfield Park*, an impression it creates of being removed from the flux of contemporary events, participating instead in moral debates of seemingly timeless relevance. The parallel with a novel like Charlotte Smith's *The Old Manor House* (1793), a novel that may have influenced the plot contours of *Mansfield Park*, is instructive. Here is a brief summary:

> Orlando Somerive is the second son of an independent farmer, whose maternal aunt, Mrs Rayland, the wealthy owner of a large estate called Rayland Hall, despises her sister for marrying beneath her. Orlando's genial and virtuous character gradually triumphs over her snobbish aristocratic postures and he becomes her favourite. Mrs Rayland's housekeeper-companion, Mrs Lennard, protects an orphan called Monimia, Orlando's female counterpart in virtue, and the young people fall in love. Their liaison prevented by all other parties, they are reduced to clandestine meetings until an army commission is procured for Orlando by his father's corrupt friend General Tracy, who wants Orlando absent so that he can seduce Orlando's sister, Isabella. Orlando is sent to North America to fight the 'rebels' in the American War of Independence. Enduring appalling privations, including capture by 'savages', Orlando returns to find his father dead, Rayland Hall willed out of the family, the paternal home broken up by his dissipated brother, Philip, and Monimia disappeared. Orlando commits his energies to discovering the final version of Mrs Rayland's will that he is assured names him as heir and to finding and marrying Monimia. The story ends happily.[8]

Coming to Smith's novel from Jane Austen, readers must be struck by its angry 'voice', entirely lacking in Austen's detached, ironic poise, and by its overt topicality. Mrs Rayland's uncritical ancestor-worship, her hatred of new wealth gained through trade or merchandising, as well as her contempt for independent yeomen-farmers, and her support for high-church principles, quickly establishes her as a Tory royalist – General Tracy, in conversation with Orlando's father, reports Mrs Rayland to be in favour of Orlando's going to America to fight in the following terms:

> as the British nation is now engaged in a quarrel with people whom she considers as the descendants of the Regicides, against whom her ancestors drew their swords, it is not, I think, very unlikely that she might approve of her young favourite's making his first essay in arms against those whom she terms the Rebels of America.
>
> (Smith 1969, 2, III: 136)

Rayland Hall under her tenure comes to emblematize an Elizabethan England no longer in touch with contemporary reality. All the novel's villains share this set of attitudes and their tyranny over the two lovers symbolizes the wider political tyranny of unlimited exercise of power. Set against them is Orlando's suspicion of rank divorced from merit and his growing respect for the 'rebel' cause when he is in America. By Volume III, the hardships of Orlando's Atlantic crossing which cause him to think about slavery and its attendant miseries, the injustice of the war that exposes notions of military glory as a hollow charade, and his friendship with a Mohawk Indian which belies the common wisdom about 'savages' all combine to construct Orlando as a representative of the new liberalism. The novel's central problematic, anticipating Dickens's *Great Expectations* (1861) and George Eliot's *Middlemarch* (1871-2), is that of vocation: what worthy employment can be found for the second son of a farmer of modest means whose elder son is bent on frittering away the family estate? Ultimately, the issue is ducked as Orlando is permitted to linger on in pursuit of his 'expectations' and to satisfy them through legal chicanery, but the novel succeeds in exposing the hidebound politics of a society that, adhering to traditional hierarchies, has nothing to offer its enterprising youth. Considering the dates of composition and publication of *The Old Manor House*, the period during which supreme power in the French Revolutionary Convention was being fought over by the Girondin and the more radical Jacobin factions, and in which war was finally declared by France on England, it is clear that, like Eliot's *Middlemarch*, the novel has a double focus. Very recent history, the setting of one revolutionary war, serves to define an attitude to another that is currently too dangerous to discuss overtly. Charlotte Smith's novel declares its 'Jacobin' sympathies in its concern for liberty and qualified egalitarianism.

Jane Austen was herself writing in the 1790s and her literary sensibility was formed, as Marilyn Butler has argued, in relation to the events and the fiction of that period,[9] but for the reader fresh to *Mansfield Park* it is difficult to locate any evidence of comparable interest in current political events. Romantic entanglements and the moral worth of those entangled seem paramount. Although, as her recent biographer Park Honan points out, the limits of Austen's parochiality are regularly exaggerated and the claim that she never mentions the burning issues of her time is something of a canard, it is the case that she lived through extremely troubled times without translating a consciousness of this directly into the stuff of fiction (Honan 1987: 223). After 1780, England witnessed a sharp increase in industrial and commercial development based on technological advance, which could not be accommodated without social strain.[10] Production of textiles, iron and coal required forms of social organization very different from those generated by traditional rural economies; and in these new communities, traditional Anglican forms of worship were very much less successful than evangelical nonconformisms like Methodism. The Church of England, whose ministry Austen's father professed, was gradually losing authority in this period. In the metropolis, fashionable Anglican clergymen like Hugh Blair (whose name is mentioned in *Mansfield Park* (*MP*, 120)) would always draw an audience even if the basis of that attraction was theatricality rather than piety. In rural areas, however, the temptation might be to opt for an unstretching life and leave the business of salvation to the charismatics, as Dr Grant is apparently doing in the novel. The question, therefore, of how a parish clergyman could best exercise his ministry, is one of considerable importance. Prior, at least, to the turning sour of the Revolution in 1793–4, when Robespierre's Committee of Public Safety perpetrated the atrocities of the Terror, the watchwords of liberty and equality had some impact on British society. Although the movement for the abolition of slavery had roots going back well before the Revolution, it derived additional momentum from revolutionary ideals. Reforming zeal that motivated individuals like Robert Owen was also generated in part by the Revolution, as is evident in the writings of Tom Paine, whose *Rights of Man* (1791–2) expressed the revolutionary doctrines of political rights and universal brotherhood. England's continuous state of war with France, providing illustrious naval careers for some like Jane Austen's brothers Frank and Charles, but attended by the evils of inflation, manpower shortages and grain famines, spanned virtually the entirety of her writing career. Little enough of this is manifest in her novels. Yet the very eschewing of 'relevance' is itself a political stance, and the imperatives of Austen's famous irony are themselves ideological, as a reading of the opening paragraph of *Mansfield Park* might show.

Usually, this opening is analysed for its use of irony, which is seen to depend on the deployment of 'free indirect speech', a technique if not pioneered by Jane Austen, then certainly taken to a high level of development by her. That technique depends on the ventriloquial merging of the narrator's voice with those of the characters, so that in certain phrases ('allowed her to be at least three thousand pounds short of any equitable claim to it') we hear the lawyer character himself voicing the sentiment, but at a sufficient remove to ironize it. Readers fresh to the novel will find initial difficulty in judging how deeply the narrator's irony cuts. If, as is sometimes said, the intention behind it is to ridicule a society in which the money motive operates in the marriage market, the narrator would be in danger of sawing off the very branch on which she will later perch. The reader coming to the novel from, say, *Pride and Prejudice*, will be well aware that Jane Austen is no unqualified supporter of the 'love-match': her female characters are usually asked to make very considerable compromises with their feelings when it comes to marriage partners. When Elizabeth Bennet expresses astonishment that her friend Charlotte Lucas is prepared to marry the awful Mr Collins, the reply contains a clear reproach to Elizabeth's arrogance and insensitivity:

> 'Why should you be surprised, my dear Eliza? – Do you think it incredible that Mr Collins should be able to procure any woman's good opinion, because he was not so happy as to succeed with you? . . . I am not romantic you know . . . I ask only a comfortable home; and considering Mr. Collins's character, connections, and situation in life, I am convinced that my chance of happiness with him is as fair, as most people can boast on entering the marriage state.'
>
> (*PP*, 165–6)

This is not a viewpoint that gets the pulse racing, but it does receive authorial endorsement in context; and in the opening of *Mansfield Park*, too, it soon appears that the intention is not simply to *replace* dynastic motives for marriage with romantic ones, but rather to ridicule the precision of the tariff system that the small-minded inhabitants of Huntingdon apply. The narrator implies that there is an equation between mercenary and affective motives to be balanced properly. Jane Austen may well be poking fun at the cluster of well-to-do families that constitute 'all Huntingdon', at that time England's second smallest county, but her irony is in the last analysis a pledge of solidarity with that social group.

To see this, we need only consider the time-scale covered in the opening paragraphs, which will indicate how much the narrator is occluding from the reader. If we assume that the 'narrating instant' is shortly before the date of publication in 1814, it is clear that the first paragraph spans a period of some six years from 1784 to the early 1790s, while the second moves us through another decade into the early 1800s. It was the period of the French Revolution and the revolutionary wars in which England was a combatant. Clive Emsley's study of British society during the wars will tell us what 'all Huntingdon' was *actually* exclaiming on when the novel was being written: the Mayor of Huntingdon, he tells us:

> reported that his neighbourhood was infested with vagrants of all ages and both sexes, but admitted that his compassion was aroused by the large numbers of soldiers' wives travelling with their children either to their parishes, or to visit their husbands. Many of these families were distressed, and though it put an additional burden on the already heavy poor rate, he felt he had to assist them.
>
> (Emsley 1979: 164)

English rural society was in desperate straits, due to the war's undiminishing appetite for manpower and for taxation revenue. Poor harvests in 1811 and 1812 exacerbated the problems of a divided and war-torn nation. (Here, at once, is a context for the astounding insensitivity to agrarian needs displayed by Mary Crawford in Chapter 6 when, at harvest time, she requests a horse and cart to transport her harp. Troops were actually being sent into the fields to gather the harvest during the later stages of the war, so urgent was this priority.) So that if, as the narrator says in an intrusion which can seem to be merely a witty quasi-philosophical generalization, 'there certainly are not so many men of large fortune in the world, as there are pretty women to deserve them' (*MP*, 41) that may be because there are not so many men in the world of any kind as there used to be. Around the time of composition of this sentence, some 750,000 Englishmen were under arms. One of them, presumably, was the Lieutenant of Marines 'without education, fortune or connections' who married Frances Price and who is 'disabled for active service' in the next paragraph. Against the background of the war, the narrator's treatment of Lieutenant Price as an invalided wastrel can come to seem unsympathetic. When the proposal is made to Mrs Price that her daughter Fanny should come to Mansfield, at the close of Chapter 1, the narrator's comment ('Poor woman! she probably thought change of air might agree with many of her children' (*MP*, 48)) is very ambivalent. On one level, it betrays her inability to conceive any prospect of *happiness* for a large, socially disadvantaged family in a busy naval port. On a different level, it problematizes the whole conception of the novel's heroine as an *individual* who has stepped out of her class. How does the novel negotiate such exceptional status for Fanny Price, and what happens to those who do not escape to the bosky security of Mansfield Park?

Once we introduce the war as the novel's 'absent cause', history operating on the margins of the text but being repressed by its strategies of containment (of which its pervasive irony is one), we begin to read it differently. A simple exercise might help the reader to gauge the extent of the novel's closure from history. Choose a point in the novel – say, Henry Crawford's elopement with Maria Bertram – and at that point, make a vertically arranged list of the characters in order of social rank; then make another list of the characters in order of moral worth. Obviously, this is very artificial and difficult. The modern reader has to juggle the variables of family background, estate, inheritance and amount and means of income, and it is very doubtful whether married and young women, having no legal status or entitlement to own property, should be on the first list at all.[11] There is clearly no absolutely correct answer, but my lists are as follows:

Social rank	*Moral worth*
Sir Thomas Bertram	Fanny Price
Lady Bertram	Edmund Bertram
Mr Rushworth	William Price
Tom Bertram	Sir Thomas Bertram
Henry Crawford	Mr Rushworth
Hon. John Yates	The Grants
Edmund Bertram	Tom Bertram
Maria Bertram	Lady Bertram
Mary Crawford	Mary Crawford
Julia Bertram	Yates

The Grants	Mrs Norris
Mrs Norris	Julia Bertram
William Price	Maria Bertram
Fanny Price	Henry Crawford

Some spectacular misalignments are immediately clear, whatever version of the list your own judgement produces. The positions of Fanny and William Price and of the Bertram girls are inversely related on the two tables. Sir Thomas Bertram is not firmly on top in both tables; will his absence at the top turn out to be a form of absenteeism, that pervasive malaise of eighteenth-century estate management? Lady Bertram is surprisingly low in moral worth, reflecting the extent to which she vacates the mothering role, and perhaps you found, as I did, that the Crawfords were very difficult to locate on the first table, and extremely mobile on the second, depending on the point in the novel at which you decide to construct the table. They are metropolitan characters, outsiders to the community of Mansfield, whose lack of clear lineage and personal traits of hedonism, flippancy and materialism make them difficult to place.[12] (In the earlier discussion of the narrator's ironic voice I might have made the point that there is something contradictory about Mary Crawford's being condemned for her conversational ironies by an ironic narrator! While the *narrator* is permitted to be ironic, in Mary Crawford it is an index of unseemliness, part of the construction of Mary as too 'forward', as unfeminine.) All this, of course, is part of the novel's ideological significance, clear evidence that the concern is not exclusively with moral conduct, but with that as it relates to social position.[13]

Understanding the Jamesonian conception of history playing on the margin of the text might help us to penetrate more deeply into this narrative economy. Explanations for Henry Crawford's peculiar fluidity might suggest themselves. His outsider status, the result of his metropolitan manners and uncertain birth, has also a specifically historical dimension. Throughout the novel he is implicitly compared with William Price, as a 'disembodied' soldier, a non-combatant in the first era of European total war. When, in Chapter 24, the family is listening to William's tales of derring-do, Henry is emasculated by his own inability to compete:

> To Henry Crawford they [William's experiences] gave a different feeling. He longed to have been at sea, and seen and done and suffered as much. His heart was warmed, his fancy fired, and he felt the highest respect for a lad who, before he was

twenty, had gone through such bodily hardships, and given such proofs of mind. The glory of heroism, of usefulness, of exertion, of endurance, made his own habits of selfish indulgence appear in shameful contrast; and he wished he had been a William Price, distinguishing himself and working his way to fortune and consequence with so much self-respect and happy ardour, instead of what he was!

(*MP*, 245)

What he is, is an effeminate civilian, irrelevant to the war. His presence in Portsmouth, where he goes to visit Fanny, is almost an embarrassment:

They talked of William, a subject on which Mrs Price could never tire; and Mr Crawford was as warm in his commendation, as even her heart could wish. She felt that she had never seen so agreeable a man in her life; and was only astonished to find, that so great and so agreeable as he was, he should be come down to Portsmouth neither on a visit to the port-admiral, nor the commissioner, nor yet with the intention of going over to the island, nor of seeing the Dock-yard.

(*MP*, 393)

William Price and Henry Crawford are contrasting species of masculinity, the one serving his country, the other serving the womenfolk back home. It is no surprise, therefore, that manifest in Crawford's interest in improvement is his desire to sever country houses from their connection with all forms of agriculture and productivity, converting them to the uses of leisure. His advice to Edmund in Chapter 25 on what to do with Thornton Lacey amounts to this:

You talk of giving it the air of a gentleman's residence. *That* will be done, by the removal of the farm-yard, for independent of that terrible nuisance, I never saw a house of the kind which had in itself so much the air of a gentleman's residence, so much the look of a something above a mere Parsonage House, above the expenditure of a few hundreds a year.

(*MP*, 251)

The fact that this advice is being offered in the symbolic context of a card game called 'Speculation' situates Henry's outlook in terms of whiggish financial practices that had long been anathema to conservative landowners.

In similar ways the novel's treatment of Edmund and of Sir Thomas can be, in Jameson's terms, opened to the social totalities of which they form a part. Deeply occluded or repressed as it is, their significance can be stated in terms of pressing contemporary issues. In Chapter 11, Mary Crawford is in her usual way ribbing Edmund about his chosen vocation, trying to tarnish with her cynicism the entire conception of 'vocation':

> 'It is fortunate that your inclination and your father's con-
> venience should accord so well. There is a very good living kept
> for you, I understand, hereabouts.'
> 'Which you suppose has biassed me.'
> 'But *that* I am sure it has not,' cried Fanny.
> 'Thank you for your good word, Fanny, but it is more than I
> would affirm myself. On the contrary, the knowing that there
> was such a provision for me, probably did bias me. Nor can I
> think it wrong that it should. There was no natural disinclina-
> tion to be overcome, and I see no reason why a man should make
> a worse clergyman for knowing that he will have a competence
> early in life.'
>
> (*MP*, 135–6)

Edmund's religious vocation is distinguished here from that of renun-
ciatory extremists, the Methodist and other Nonconformist sects that
were making such headway in this period. When, in the vital Chapter 9, Edmund has distinguished his sense of active ministry from that
of the fashionable metropolitan pulpit idol (another species of actor),
he makes clear that the traditional Anglican understanding of a long-
established parish, central to its community, is his own (*MP*, 120–1).
Implicitly, this is defined against the practice of venal clergymen like
Dr Grant whose preference for grub over God is partly responsible for
a loss of faith in the established Church; but latently, it is also counter-
posed to those evangelical zealots whose swiftly built urban conventicles
were intended to *create* the congregations that they later served. Ironically, Mary's final repudiation of Edmund, as reported by him in
Chapter 47, takes the form of expecting to hear of him as 'a celebrated
preacher in some great society of Methodists, or as a missionary into
foreign parts' (*MP*, 444). Evangelical imagery abounds in the novel,
and that Fanny herself is attracted to the self-reliant Puritanism of the
reformed religion is suggested in the wonderful moment at the close of
Chapter 42 when Henry is asking Fanny's advice on whether or not to
return to his Norfolk estate:

'Shall I go? – Do you advise it?'

'I advise! – you know very well what is right.'

'Yes. When you give me your opinion, I always know what is right. Your judgment is my rule of right.'

'Oh, no! – do not say so. We all have a better guide in ourselves, if we would attend to it, than any other person can be.'

$$(MP, 404)^{14}$$

Edmund is asking Fanny's advice partly by way of staking a claim to her, positioning her as one sufficiently intimate with him to advise him. Fanny's reply, hinting at the operation of individual conscience, testifies to a deep piety that puts his designs to shame.

The 'unspoken' haunting Sir Thomas's character is not that of Methodism, but the equally powerful bogey of slavery. Just as Methodism breaches the silence at one curious moment in the novel, so does slavery, in Chapter 21 when Edmund is exhorting Fanny to communicate more with Sir Thomas, and she replies, 'but I do talk to him more than I used. I am sure I do. Did not you hear me ask him about the slave trade last night?' The novel does not record Sir Thomas's answer, but it does record the 'dead silence' occasioned by the question! (MP, 213). We are never told what exactly is the nature of Sir Thomas's business in Antigua, but it is difficult to imagine that he is anything other than a plantation owner whose estates are worked by slave labour.[15] In Chapter 3, we hear of 'some recent losses' on his West India estate, and shortly afterwards, Mrs Norris speaks of Sir Thomas's means being 'rather straitened, if the Antigua estate is to make such poor returns' (MP, 59; 64), a point she makes while actually refusing to contribute her widow's mite by boarding Fanny. The immediate result of Lord Grenville's Bill to abolish the slave trade, enacting that no vessel should carry slaves from any port in the British dominions after 1 May 1807 and that no slave should be landed in the colonies after 1 March 1808, which received the Royal Assent in March 1807, was, paradoxically, a worsening of conditions for negroes in the colonies. Fresh supplies of slaves being denied, those already working were simply worked much harder and the mortality rate increased. Jane Austen's reader might have imputed Sir Thomas's difficulties to the results of the Bill. In the novel's terms, Sir Thomas's absence in Antigua creates a power vacuum, given that Lady Bertram has abrogated all parental responsibility, which is filled by the theatricals, a projection of Tom's unseriousness and dissipation.[16] It is while Sir

Thomas is absent that the Crawfords insinuate themselves into Mansfield circles. No 'position' on slavery is articulated in the novel but there is enough to make clear that West Indian interests are intimately bound up in the Park's economy, and that they have to be protected.

But the most conspicuous misalignment of social position and moral worth is embodied in Fanny Price, and the fact that the character least 'qualified' to uphold the values of Mansfield Park ends up doing so, is part of the novel's political unconscious. To those who would stress the bedrock Christianity that supports Austen's writing, Fanny's progress is an example of the meek inheriting the earth. In terms, however, of the wider issues associated with class mobility, her gradual upward ascent is less easily assimilable. What kind of statement is Fanny's spectacular social progress making? We might compare her ascent to that of Pamela Andrews, the servant-girl heroine of Samuel Richardson's earlier *Pamela; or Virtue Rewarded* (1740). In this novel, Pamela's almost supernatural virtue converts her master, Mr B., from a designing rake into an attentive husband; but Pamela's character is such that where she led, very few were likely to follow. Her elevation avoids the question of how far England's aristocracy is an open elite, able to be penetrated by exceptional individuals from the lower-status groups, because her mystified 'virtue' claims for her such exceptional status. Although Fanny Price also seems, sometimes, to be too 'goody-goody' for modern tastes, I think that her case really does pose this question, and in a very pressing form. The question is not merely one of how far social assimilation is possible; there is a perceived *need* for such an assimilation to occur. Let us see how far the novel's incidents bear this out.

On the visit to Sotherton, unexpected facets of Fanny's personality are revealed to the reader. She is configured in opposition to Crawford over 'improvement', the fashionable cult of rendering landscape picturesque. Her desire to 'see Sotherton before it is cut down, to see the place as it is now, in its old state', supported by an allusion to Cowper's melancholy traditionalism as expressed in *The Task* (*MP*, 87), indicates her sensitivity in a chapter (Chapter 6) in which Mary Crawford manages to insult everyone, to show an astonishing indifference to the importance of the harvest in a country economy and to make indecent remarks about homosexuality in the Navy.[17] Fanny's sensibility develops as a potent blend of the traditional and the romantic: in Chapter 9, she has been responding imaginatively to Sotherton as an unimproved manor house with 'its rights of Court-

Leet and Court-Baron' and oak avenue, an emblem of former English glory, but is disappointed that the chapel contains nothing of the medieval awe conjured up in Scott's *The Lay of the Last Minstrel*.[18] Edmund has occasion to correct the warmth of her imagination here, but Fanny has now been associated with a strand of romanticism that in the early nineteenth century sang the swansong of European aristocracy, expressing nostalgia for the bygone days of fixed feudal hierarchies. Conversing with Mary Crawford later on in the novel, Fanny rhapsodizes over the 'nobleness in the name of Edmund. It is a name of heroism and renown – of kings, princes, and knights; and seems to breathe the spirit of chivalry and warm affections' (*MP*, 224). Meanwhile back in Chapter 9, Mary Crawford is manifesting a secular irreligiousness that would do justice to Voltaire and the later French Jacobins: 'if the good people who used to kneel and gape in that gallery could have foreseen that the time would ever come when men and women might lie another ten minutes in bed, when they woke with a headach, without danger of reprobation, because chapel was missed, they would have jumped with joy and envy' (*MP*, 115). Henry, by this time, the vulgarian 'improver', is improving the shining hour by desecrating the chapel, using it as a place of adulterous assignation.

Gradually, Fanny's romantic traditionalism, which, however much it is presented as the natural and correct way to feel, is actually an ideological position among others available in the novel, is equated with another strand of romanticism, the Burkean–Wordsworthian nature-worship – a strand that finds nature capable of inspiring awe and impressing the observer with a sense of relative insignificance that can lead to self-discovery. In Chapter 11, Fanny is discovered by Edmund in her usual slightly isolated position, gazing out of the window:

> 'Here's harmony!' said she. 'Here's repose! Here's what may leave all painting and all music behind, and what poetry can only attempt to describe. Here's what may tranquillize every care, and lift the heart to rapture! When I look out on such a night as this, I feel as if there could be neither wickedness nor sorrow in the world; and there certainly would be less of both if the sublimity of Nature were more attended to, and people were carried more out of themselves by contemplating such a scene.'
>
> (*MP*, 139)

Although this is actually something of a literary confection, combining the Burkean sublime and Shakespearean cadences ('on such a night as this' with its allusion to Jessica and Lorenzo's lovers' dialogue in *The Merchant of Venice*, V.i) it associates Fanny with the power of nature in opposition to merely human art. As the novel progresses, Fanny's 'naturalization' will embrace the architecture and environs of Mansfield Park itself. A beautiful passage in Chapter 16 (*MP*, 173–4) depicts the East room as a projection of Fanny's personality, its specularity in playing back to Fanny an image of herself completed by her copy of Crabbe's *Tales*, in which there is a character called Fanny Price![19] A correspondence is established between nature, Mansfield Park and Fanny's instinctive sensibility. It is important that the positions she takes in the novel are endowed with this power. She is instinctively distrustful of theatricals and of acting, embodying neo-Puritan prejudices to the effect that acting is a betrayal of authentic selfhood associated with deception, shape-changing – ultimately loss of individuality. That Henry Crawford is a good *actor* is not a point in his favour. After Crawford's proposal, the full power of the patriarchy is ranged against her. Crawford condescendingly assumes that his hand will be grasped with overwhelming gratitude by a woman without social position or individual will. Sir Thomas and even Edmund attempt to crush her with social forms: the external strength of the case for accepting Crawford can only be resisted by the power of her instinct, which the reader has come to trust.

If my own reading experience of the novel is in any way typical, however, the trip to Portsmouth problematizes Fanny's 'naturalization', that process of imbuing identifiably ideological positions with the power of natural instinct. Portsmouth exposes some of this as 'ideological' in the classic Marxist sense, as a form of false consciousness. For the modern reader, familiar with socialist perspectives only embryonic in the period covered by Austen's novel, Fanny's return home is inevitably a disappointment. It would be naive to think that, brought up in the peace and tranquillity of the Park, Fanny would adjust easily to the lower middle-class commotion of her home life, yet I confess to desiring some celebration of the warmth and energy of Portsmouth, some excitement generated by a busy naval port in wartime, some admission that blood is thicker than water in Fanny's return to the parental fold. Such desires are wholly unsatisfied. Fanny is struck by its smallness, inconvenience, disrepair, absence of ceremony and hospitality. She is offended by her father's boorishness, her mother's sluttishness, her brothers' noisiness:

Fanny was almost stunned. The smallness of the house, and thinness of the walls, brought every thing so close to her, that, added to the fatigue of her journey, and all her recent agitation, she hardly knew how to bear it. *Within* the room all was tranquil enough, for Susan having disappeared with the others, there were soon only her father and herself remaining; and he taking out a newspaper – the accustomary loan of a neighbour – applied himself to studying it, without seeming to recollect her existence.

(MP, 375)

As Fanny surveys the lower middle-class struggle of the overpopulated Price household (almost an illustration of Malthusian demographic theories) she is led only to contrast it with Mansfield:

At Mansfield, no sounds of contention, no raised voice, no abrupt bursts, no tread of violence was ever heard; all proceeded in a regular course of cheerful orderliness; every body had their due importance; every body's feelings were consulted.

(MP, 384)[20]

She is entirely divorced from the mode of production of all that seclusion. How does Fanny think that such leisure is supported, paid for? Her family, with their two servants, are far from rock-bottom by contemporary standards, but her residence in Portsmouth is presented as a state of virtual imprisonment: 'could [Crawford] have suspected how many privations, besides that of exercise, she endured in her father's house, he would have wondered that her looks were not much more affected than he found them' (*MP*, 404). The biblical cadence of 'in her father's house' shocks the reader because the narrator's sentiment is actually so *unchristian* here. Fanny is already close to breaching the first Commandment when she finds that she 'could not respect her parents, as she had hoped' (*MP*, 381). St John's Gospel 14:2 reports Christ as saying to the Disciples: 'In my Father's house are many mansions'. In Fanny's father's house there clearly are not: and being lower middle-class is bad for the complexion. To Fanny it is as if the calm spaciousness of Mansfield is itself given in nature. The reader knows, however, that Mansfield's fortunes are bound up in those of the West Indian estate. Perhaps it is overingenious to detect, in the comparison between the family home at Portsmouth and the adopted home at Mansfield, some projection of Fanny's hatred for post-Revolutionary France? Is her family's noisy brabble a reminder of the *sans-culottes*, the unruly Parisian revolutionary mob so important to the propagation of Revolutionary ideals before they were overtaken by the Terror and in the end by the Napoleonic empire? As Alistair Duckworth has argued, *Mansfield Park* is at the end of a long tradition of country-house literature in which a reciprocal relationship is established between the nation at large and an aristocratic estate that becomes a metonymic representation of the polity (Duckworth 1971: 36–80).

If that is an overreading, Fanny's experience in Portsmouth never-theless permits us to catch sight of the novel's ideological contra-dictions. What is the significance, to return to our earlier question, of Fanny's spectacular migration up the social scale? Such migrations occur in earlier novels – witness Fielding's *Tom Jones* – but in Fielding this is usually expressed through a romance motif in which the protagonist discovers his true gentility prior to getting the girl and the estate. *Mansfield Park*, by contrast, renders social mobility in the mystified notion of 'natural aristocracy'. The irresistible rise of Fanny Price does not configure the possibility of any general class mobility – the Price family as a whole is not Mansfield material – but Fanny's sister Susan is, in a similarly mystified way, marked out as suitable stock for transplanting to the more nourishing soil of Mansfield. (Susan, we are told, 'had an innate taste for the genteel and well-appointed' (*MP*, 409) and it distresses Fanny that she should be left in the parental home.) Yet Austen's protagonists are consciously constructed *against the grain* of novelistic treatments of female heroism ('No one who had ever seen Catherine Morland in her infancy would have supposed her born to be an heroine', is the opening sentence of *Northanger Abbey*) and it is clear that by comparison to earlier characters like Elizabeth Bennet and Emma Woodhouse, Fanny Price represents a new narrative challenge: a woman who is not spirited or precocious and who is rendered passive by her social inferiority and introversion, who nevertheless becomes a magnetic centre of attrac-tion. In the end, however, no adequate explanation is brought to bear on Fanny's exceptional status and she remains a 'heroine'. We *might* read, there is a *danger* of us reading, this plot as an illustration of the aristocracy's need for patrilineal and matrilineal repair: a transfusion of bourgeois blood is needed to put the aristocracy back on its feet. I suggest, however, that the text resists this reading, offering us instead a Fanny Price who is 'naturally' an aristocrat. Her marriage to Edmund comes to seem virtually endogamous. They are more like brother and sister than husband and wife, and Fanny can be taken into the family without creating the impression of any accommodation. The novel apparently dramatizes a process of the English landed aristocracy's putting its own house in order and thereby resisting external challenges; but it represses an alternative reading of its significance, which would endow the scions of the Price family with the more dynamic social energies. In other words, the logic of the plot, which enacts the social advancement of lower middle-class individuals, undermines the aristocratic-conservative interests that the fable is invented to defend; and the only way to avoid the reader drawing this conclusion is to prevaricate between a construction of the Prices as 'typical' and a construction of them as 'exceptional'. Natural aristocracy, as applied to Fanny and Susan (less so to William because he, after all, has a social structure for advancement, a career ladder), is the ideally obfuscatory, perfectly ideological tool for accomplishing this work.

III

It remains to indicate how my approach to the text marries with the theoretical positions outlined in the opening section. I began by diagnosing a pedagogical problem, that discussions of Jane Austen too often fail to transform the text, limiting themselves to unfolding the wisdom that the text already contains. What Catherine Belsey refers to as the 'expressive realist', assumption, that 'literature reflects the *reality* of experience as it is perceived by one (especially gifted) individual, who *expresses* it in a discourse which enables other individuals to recognize it as true' (Belsey 1980: 7), prevails because Jane Austen offers us a vision of English country life that we very much want to have been true. Lionel Trilling's very last lecture (which, sadly, he did not live to deliver) was to be given on the subject 'Why we read Jane Austen'. An incomplete version of it was published in the *Times Literary Supplement*, which, though it does not get round to telling us why *he* read her, offers this account of why his students did: they

> believed that . . . they could transcend our sad contemporary existence, that, from the world of our present weariness and desiccation, they might reach back to a world which, as it appears to the mind's eye, is so much more abundantly provided with trees than with people, a world in whose green shade life for a moment might be a green thought.

Trilling then offers another reason that is quite the reverse of this escapist motive, based as it is on the *similarity* between the world of Austen's characters and that of his students' own experience:

> these fictive persons [Austen's characters] would be experienced as if they had actual existence, as if their 'values' were available to assessment, as if their destinies bore upon one's own, and as if their styles of behaviour and feeling must inevitably have a consequence in one's own behaviour and feeling.[21]

What this adds up to saying is that *Mansfield Park* is an ideological work in the sense defined by Althusserian Marxists – that is, it is a representation of an imaginary but compelling sense of reality, resolving crucial contradictions in conceptions of the self and the social order. As my opening section explains, much recent literary theory attempts to reveal the literary text as a construction that does ideological *work* of this kind; and in my approach I have foregrounded strands in literary theory that seek to show how a text expresses certain ideological positions as a matter of conscious authorial intention, but is also itself *placed* in ideology in ways that the author might not perceive or, according to Jameson, might repress and banish to the 'political unconscious' of the text. The materialist critic James Kavanagh is actually discussing Shakespeare when he calls the author 'a principal – but not the only – agent of a productive ideological practice, most of whose conditions remain out of his control: the patronage system, the market/audience, the technical possibilities of the theatre, the political constraints and social ideologies in place, even the exigencies of his own personal formation', but much of it applies, *mutatis mutandis*, to Jane Austen ('Shakespeare in Ideology', in Drakakis 1985: 148). This imposes limits on 'individual genius' and on the superior wisdom of the great writer, limits that our culture finds difficult to accept, such is the power of the 'creativity' mythos.

In my view, Marxist-materialist thinkers have been particularly suggestive, Fredric Jameson pre-eminently so, in modelling the relationship between a literary text and the historical conditions of its cultural production. This relationship is one of only *apparent* continuity. Actually, the literary text is not organically related to its cultural matrix. It is often riven by contradiction, characterized by gaps, silences, loose ends and blind alleys. These characteristics provide clues to the fault lines in the culture itself. Audaciously, Jameson has combined materialist and psychoanalytical perspectives to postulate that a literary text can repress traumatic aspects of history: war, class conflict and what he sees as the scandal of exploited labour. Doubtless, Jameson's three 'horizons' of meaning are too schematic. In practice, they can be difficult to distinguish and it is doubtful whether a three-level analysis can be applied to individual texts. His own examples in *The Political Unconscious* go beyond the text to examine entire *oeuvres* and entire literary formations which are exemplified in many individual works. Bearing such difficulties in mind, my Jamesonian approach to *Mansfield Park* will not be complete. It has attempted, however, to reveal how the work is shaped by extratextual historical forces (and in particular the French Revolution) so systematically excluded from conscious mention that Jamesonian repression becomes a feasible hypothesis. A more explicitly ideological novel, Charlotte Smith's *The Old Manor House*, was used as a control text to show the extent of Austen's editing out of the topical. Fanny Price's status in the novel is the site for the second stage in Jamesonian analysis – the reconfiguration of the work as dialogue between antagonistic class discourses. Do we read Fanny as in any way exemplary, typical? Does she represent the possibility of bourgeois mobility, her penetration of the elite signalling the openness of English aristocracy to permeation by the lower classes? Or does she remain a 'heroine', not typical but exceptional, marked out by her own particular gifts and talents, blazing no trails for others to follow? In my reading, the novel toggles uneasily between these possibilities, betraying anxiety that is unconsciously rooted in the social instability of the period. While the war lasted, communal effort held it in check, but only a short time after Austen's death, it was to erupt in its ugliest form in the massacre at St Peter's Fields in Manchester, mordantly called Peterloo.

The third stage of Jamesonian analysis is beyond the scope of this essay, and perhaps of this writer, but allow me to offer a few hints towards it. Here, we are asked to consider a text in relation to the simultaneous presence of dominant, residual and emergent ideological strands in the cultural formations of any particular historical epoch. Following Raymond Williams's thinking in *Marxism and Literature* (1977), Jameson is here offering a flexible cultural analysis that recognizes the inadequacy of isolating any single set of features and claiming that these are representative of thinking in the era' (Williams 1977: 121–7). 'Residual' and 'emergent' elements refer to experiences, meanings and values which may be carried over from the past, or may be pointing towards further development in the future, and which are not fully assimilated into the dominant. We might show that for all their surface differences, Austen's novel and Smith's (and, we might add, other radical novels like Robert Bage's *Hermsprong* (1796) in which the privileges of inherited rank are challenged) share the same difficulty in envisaging systematic class mobility. Edmund Bertram's inherited parish allows him to circumvent the problem of making a living; indeed, he is allowed to settle into comfortable incumbency of two livings, a practice that is explicitly considered immoral in the early part of the novel. Orlando Somerive (in *The Old Manor House*) is allowed to *have* the problem, but he solves it in the same way, by inheriting an estate. Following Jameson, we might try to show that all the fiction of the period shares this structural difficulty in devising an outcome. As Jameson argues in 'Metacommentary', the nature of literary plots is, in the last analysis, traceable back to the nature of the society that furnishes the raw material:

> Thus the appearance of a melodramatic strain in classical plots (particularly towards the middle of the nineteenth century) is a sign that events no longer cohere, that the author has had to appeal to Evil, to villains and conspiracies, to restore some of the unity he felt it beyond his power to convey in the events themselves.
>
> (Jameson 1988, I: 8–9)

What the reader experiences as a failure of nerve, or as the compromising of narrative realism – the magical happy ending – can be related to economic and social changes attendant upon industrialization. Once the effects of industrialization have been assimilated, and England's rural economy has been thoroughly urbanized, the destinies of novelistic characters like Pip in *Great Expectations* or Frank Vincy in *Middlemarch* also change, as opportunities other than legacy hunting come their way. So much for the men. As the work of the Marxist-Feminist Literature Collective has indicated, however, in its work on mid-Victorian women's writing (*Jane Eyre*, *Shirley*, *Villette* and *Aurora Leigh* are the texts they discuss), the fates of *female* characters in novels continued to evade the determinations of actual women's fates, in respect of class position, kinship structures and upbringing (Barker *et al.* 1977: 185–206). Like Fanny Price, these later heroines are orphans or quasi-orphans whose class position is uncertain and who have no father-figure to exchange them in marriage. Residual 'romance' elements are employed to invent a destiny for them that the reader might experience as implausible. What this might suggest is that gender is an operator in the identification of 'residual' and 'emergent' strands in an ideological formation, a possibility not canvassed by Williams. This might spark off a Jamesonian reinvestigation of the nature of literary realism, or, as it has been termed, 'classic realism' which established a dominant position as a literary mode in the mid- to later nineteenth century. But that is another story.

SUPPLEMENT

NIGEL WOOD: Jameson's Marxism concentrates on a definition of ideology in terms of 'strategies of containment', a limitation of subject-matter or treatment that provides a reassuring unity. An analysis of the political unconscious would therefore confront this partial view with a 'totality' of social practices and ideologies that compose the whole social formation. You mention this on pp. 65–6. Does Austen evade the more complicated view of social working? Or rather, does the conscious intention of the author count in this analysis?

BREAN S. HAMMOND: Jameson's view, and ultimately, I suppose, the tendency of all materialist criticism, reduces the extent to which an author's conscious intentions can be said to determine the overall significance of a literary work. The Marxist 'bottom line', I guess, is that being determines consciousness, even if we do have to add qualifying phrases like 'in the last analysis'. So if the part played by conscious will and intention in creating the literary work is permitted to grow too large, the author will be perceived as the shaper of experience rather than as significantly shaped by it. Recent materialist criticism therefore speaks of intentions that the author does consciously hold and that are expressed more or less successfully in the work (or may be expressed in extratextual sources like letters, television interviews or whatever) – and in so far as a reader knows about these, they constitute another source of knowledge about the work, but not a source that has any special *privileges* – and a wider notion of 'intention' that the author may not be aware of at all. We might speak of this as the 'intention' manifest in the 'totality of social practices and ideologies' (to use your phrase) that operates as a matrix for the work.

An example: I might write a novel in which I have various pungent things to say about the present state of gender relations in our time. The incidents in my novel might suggest that men have had a very bad deal as a result of feminism, that every man is now suspected of being a rapist, that the view that women have suffered under patriarchy, however historically accurate, is now being employed to blot out the real suffering endured by men. This might be my conscious intention, the kind of thing that I tell Melvyn Bragg (presenter of Independent television's *South Bank*

Show). A critic who appears on the show with me might demonstrate however, that my book is part of a far larger anti-feminist or pro-masculinist backlash that has resulted from, among other things, changed economic circumstances in which women have tended to oust men from their jobs, have usurped the traditional male position as breadwinner, have made men feel emasculated by lesbian experimentation, and so on. *I* didn't see myself as any part of a wider movement. I don't think of *myself* as a sociological statistic. I am in conscious control as the shaper of my artistic vision. Yet the validity of the critic's view might be undeniable, and I might end up agreeing that the critic knows what I wanted to say better than I do myself.

NW: In your penultimate sentence you whet the appetite for a wider-ranging analysis, one that places certain forms of realism in a social context. What does formal realism's dominance in the nineteenth century lead one to suppose?

BSH: I have to confess that I become a little esoteric in my closing sentences, partly because the fish I am trying to fry get too big for the pan. The issue that I gesture towards here is the issue of 'realism'. The Victorian period is often spoken of as the era of 'realism' and sometimes of 'classic realism' (see MacCabe 1979: 13–32). What this might mean is that Victorian novels develop a set of procedures that secure the ends of 'plausibility'; procedures that manage to disguise their status *as* procedures so effectively that they convey the impression of transparency. The reader looks *through* the text directly onto the world represented by the text, the text itself offering minimal resistance to the act of reading. This helps to 'naturalize' the fates of the characters and to render them convincing. Credible individuals are firmly rooted in a 'realistic' milieu, securely anchored in their vividly rendered environment. This is perhaps why certain kinds of Marxist critic, notably Georg Lukács, are so enthusiastic about realism. It is a form in which it is easiest to teach the lessons of ideology, with relatively little interference from 'style' or difficulty or obliquity.

The quotation I give from Jameson on p. 86, however, suggests that he does not accept this account of 'realism'. Even those Victorian novels most celebrated for their realism, like George Eliot's *Middlemarch*, for example, can be shown to employ melodrama, coincidence, 'romance' elements – elements that evidence the degree of structure and artifice that goes into even the most realistic of fiction and that may tell us something about the 'hidden agenda' of the author. To take another example, Elizabeth Gaskell's *Mary Barton* is for some of its length an unflinchingly 'realistic' account of poverty in working-class Manchester in the 1840s, but the take-over of a melodramatic plot in its later stages seems to be a shying-away from the revolutionary consequences of the earlier analysis, and the novel's ultimate desire is the avoidance of confrontational class violence. What the Marxist-Feminist Literature

Collective has to add to this, however, is that Victorian works only have even their *supposed* plausibility for the fates of *male* characters. Anyone reading Victorian novels with gender issues in mind would not even have been *tempted* to locate 'classic realism' there because the novelistic fates of female characters seem to be inconsistent with the destinies of actual women as evidenced by historical and sociological documents.

NW: Can we find a consistent ideology in Jane Austen's work?

BSH: This question really puts me on the spot, and I can only answer it by giving a 'bare-bones' summary of my entire piece. The ideological implication of *Mansfield Park* appears to me to be that the aristocracy, traditional guardians of the nation's moral and political values, are not doing their job, for one reason or another. (The Park itself does, I think, function as a symbol of nationhood, at least of the essential, desirable part of the nation.) This lays them open to very radical penetration by the lower classes (which, in France in the 1790s, had taken the form of revolution) and, to avoid that, they have to be called back to a sense of their proper responsibilities. That Fanny Price should be the instrument for achieving this is the main source of ideological indeterminacy, and therefore of complexity, in the novel. Notions of 'natural aristocracy', which fudge the nature/nurture issue and offer a hybrid between genetic notions of social position and socioeconomic (class) notions, are employed to avoid confronting the question squarely. If I am asked whether this is a deliberate, conscious avoidance of the issue on Jane Austen's part, I would probably say that it is not: that the terms of a class-based analysis of this question are barely available to the writers of her generation and would anyway have proved uncongenial to her. It was the hallmark of conservatism in her era to present social hierarchies as absolutely given in 'nature', as Edmund Burke argues in the early part of *Reflections on the Revolution in France*. In defence of hereditary monarchy, for example, Burke says:

> This policy [of hereditary monarchy and peerage] appears to me to be the result of profound reflection; or rather the happy effect of following nature, which is wisdom without reflection, and above it. A spirit of innovation is generally the result of a selfish temper and confined views. People will not look forward to posterity, who never look backward to their ancestors. Besides, the people of England well know, that the idea of inheritance furnishes a sure principle of conservation, and a sure principle of transmission; without at all excluding a principle of improvement. It leaves acquisition free; but it secures what it acquires. Whatever advantages are obtained by a state proceeding on these maxims, are locked fast as in a sort of family settlement; grasped as in a kind of mortmain for ever. By a constitutional policy, working after the

pattern of nature, we receive, we hold, we transmit our government and our privileges, in the same manner in which we transmit
our property and our lives. The institutions of policy, the goods of
fortune, the gifts of Providence, are handed down, to us and from
us, in the same course and order.

(Burke 1968: 119–20)

One can imagine Fanny Price and Jane Austen cheering that to the echo,
although neither would actually be considered part of the political nation
on the grounds of Burke's argument.

NW: Jameson combines psychoanalytic theory with more materialist
readings in *The Political Unconscious*. Are there special factors that lead
you to prescribe this line to students – or to apply it yourself?

BSH: I would like students to develop more self-consciousness about the
ways in which they read texts. I would like them to, so to speak, look over
their own shoulders while they are reading and ask: 'Why am I
approaching the text in this way? Why am I asking *these* questions of the
text, and not other questions, such as . . .'. Although materialist readings
are most satisfying to me, I appreciate that we study texts in a pluralistic
culture. Students will be exposed to other colleagues who take
psychoanalytic or deconstructive or feminist approaches, examples of
which can be found in this volume. Perhaps I can persuade you of my
openness when I say that the reasons *why* materialist readings satisfy me
are doubtless to be found in the psychoanalytic domain! So it is not that I
want all students to turn themselves into materialists. I do want them,
however, to turn themselves into *something*, to theorize about and to
interrogate their readings. Personally, I want to open texts to history, and
to do so in a way that does not use history as an 'objective' standpoint
from which to survey the text, but rather acknowledges that history itself
is given to us in textual form and will also present problems in reading. It
is less important to me, however, that students should learn to do just
this, than that they should discover a way of approaching texts that makes
sense to them and imparts value to the enterprise of approaching texts at
all.

CHAPTER 3

Gender, Theory and Jane Austen Culture

CLAUDIA L. JOHNSON

[In choosing Carol Kay's essay on 'Canon, Ideology, and Gender', Claudia L. Johnson is not preparing the ground for the application of a new set of theoretical premises. As Kay points out about the theoretical tendency to reduce every genre of writing to 'language', theory has been fixated with epistemological questions, that is, to do with how we come to 'know' anything. It has not often addressed political questions, content to find politics in every sphere but politics. Challenging the canon does not just imply the promotion of certain works at the expense of others, as the real challenge would be to the structures of thought that organize the whole academic study of the subject, that indeed constitute it as an object for study in the first place. Turning to Mary Poovey's study of the woman writer, *The Proper Lady and Woman Writer*, Kay is impressed by the way that she reintroduces matters of individual agency into 'the enterprise of social description' (Kay 1986: 65). As examined in the Headnote to Brean Hammond's essay, there have been Marxist redefinitions of 'ideology', and it now often comes to signify the very means by which anything is intelligible in a given society. The language we use to differentiate between 'philosophy', 'politics' and 'literature' is a form of ideological divide-and-rule. In the eighteenth century, for example, much more writing was literature, and vice versa, art did not often strive for inclusion in the realm of aesthetics alone.

Our judgements about past texts depend on careful historical discrimination. One of the most immediate would be that most records of the past were written by men for men. Significant writers such as Mary Wollstonecraft are marginalized in order that safe traditions can be perpetuated. This raises the questions as to *whose* history we are to study and *why*? Inevitably, the enquiry is framed by prior considerations of contemporary relevance. Just as 'Janeite' culture answered some past social need, we need to reassess our *present* cultural context, not so as to doctor the evidence so that we come up with a 'Jane Austen' that fits our society, but rather to discover how she challenges her ideological constraints while living within them – and so, how she can confront our own.

The task of a feminist historian of literature is thus to emphasize the enforced silences or self-censorship that allow women to slip out of history. In Jane Austen's case, it is necessary to reinvent the 'domestic' and its sphere of influence. Judith Lowder Newton's identification of women's alternative power-bases has implications for how we regard Austen's fiction: when a woman's power as an individual is signed away in marriage, how can she accommodate herself to such pressures? Newton stresses 'the peculiar dominance in these novels of tension, disguise, and ultimately disjunctions of form' (Newton 1985: 9), where marriage, *in and outside* the pages of literature, is a deeply ambivalent event. Is women's writing just a site of 'compensating fantasies' or a 'site of protest' (Newton 1985: 11)? Johnson is, therefore, acutely aware of how power has the capacity to inhabit many superficially innocent forms of influence and how it is this domain of 'common sense' or 'nature' (so eminently transportable from age to age) that deserves urgent redefinition.]

NIGEL WOOD

At the 1989 convention of the Modern Language Association in Washington, DC, a panel entitled 'Jane Austen's Politics' drew the kind of crowd generally associated with racier topics. The discussion of politics very soon developed into a debate about feminism, for the feminist premise that gender is the work of ideology and not of nature has fundamentally transformed what we recognize as political in Austen's work. After the panel was over, a reporter from the *New York Times* approached me, having been curious about the crush of people spilling from the aisles into the hallways, which he had evidently been scouting for material to use for that publication's annual MLA-bashing article. 'Tell me, professor,' he asked, his pencil poised in readiness at a tiny memo-pad, '*was* Jane Austen a feminist?' Something told me I was being set up. When I began to explain that this was perhaps not the most productive way of thinking about Austen's treatment of gender, his face clouded and he wandered off in search of someone who would give him the news-byte he craved.

I will return to the reporter's question at the end of this essay. For the beginning of it, I would like to explain why he considered the panel not merely a hot topic but also a ludicrous one. As the very existence of the *Theory in Practice* series attests, recent developments in literary theory – feminism, deconstructionism, Marxism, psychoanalysis, and new historicism, to name only a few – have changed both how we study literature and how we think about what we are doing when we study literature. But even though Austenian studies, as this particular volume proves, have surely benefited from the theory revolution, the work of Austenian critics interested in theory has, I think it is fair to say, encountered resistance of a distinctively vehement sort. This, of course, is not because Austen's fiction itself is inimical to such analyses, but rather because the culture that has grown up around Austen and her novels repels the methods, objectives and discourses of critical modes that are so aggressively abstract, irreverent, and complicating.

By 'Jane Austen culture' I refer in part to the largely amateur Jane Austen societies which thrive across England and North America. Their members are enthusiastically, indeed idolatrously, committed readers whose command of Austenian minutiae can put established scholars to shame, and whose activities (teas, costume balls, games, readings, quizzes on the novels, and the like) are animated by an antiquarianism that seems dotty to academics for whom literary study is a far more sober business. Academics take for granted the justness of their dominance over the study of literature, but such non-professional societies, whose energy and ubiquity have no parallel with any other author I know – the Browning and Trollope societies seem tame by comparison – certainly challenge this presumed hegemony. The Austen Janeites celebrate – not with campy abandon but rather with brisk self-control – epitomizes normative clarity, good manners, good taste, common sense, and an arch sort of knowingness. In doing so, they of course partake of a long tradition of Austenian commentary. Scott praised Austen for her 'exquisite touch which renders ordinary commonplace things and characters interesting' (Southam 1968, 1: 106); Whateley had commended her novels because their 'moral lessons' were put forward 'clearly and impressively' rather than 'offensively' (Southam 1968, 1: 95); and a whole line of critics from Henry James (his impatience with 'everyone's dear Jane' notwithstanding) to Chesterton and beyond singled out her common sense as a product of her decorous and unpretentious submission to limitation (Southam 1985, 2: 179, 340).[1] Modern-day Janeites compound such admiration with a powerful sense of nostalgia and (in the United States especially) a vigorous anglophilia.[2] Small wonder, then, that critical theory was slow to come to Austenian studies, for it routinely problematizes the very same qualities – clarity, decorum, common sense, stability – that Austen's novels were thought to honour.

But Janeism is no merely amateur affair: *mutatis mutandis*, it has characterized much Austenian criticism within the academy even through the 1960s and 1970s, and has lingered with such remarkable tenacity that vestigial traces are discernible even in the works of critics influenced by the theory boom of the 1970s.[3] In his *Jane Austen: A Critical Bibliography* (1953), R.W. Chapman brushes away Samuel Kliger's study of Austen's 'neo-classicism' on the grounds that it is 'polysyllabic, and open to the familiar objection that its subject would not have understood it', opining further that Austen would 'turn over in her grave' if she heard critics employ big words to explain her work (Chapman 1953: 53). I wish to set aside Chapman's low estimate of Austen's understanding for abstraction, and to turn instead to the decorum he defends. If the dean of Austenian studies judged offensive words as innocuous as 'antithesis' and 'premeditated', the more demanding lexicon of post-structuralist discourse would surely have struck him as radically hostile to and even desecratory of the modesty and delicacy of Austen's *oeuvre*.

It would be nice to suppose that the mannerliness Chapman urged has had its day, but his *Oxford Illustrated Jane Austen* (1932–54), replete with appendices detailing Regency fashions in dress, carriages, and modes of address, remains authoritative for advanced students and scholars alike, and validates the antiquarianism of Janeites.[4] Chapman, of course, distinguished himself in several areas of English literary scholarship, and my aim here is neither to detract from his erudition nor, certainly, to place everything that is reactionary about Jane Austen culture, inside the academy and out, at his door. Rather I seek to identify and ponder a certain anti-intellectualism that is part of the decorum of Jane Austen culture as he partook of it. By now, of course, Austenian studies are far from a backwater, but critics and scholars interested in critical theory still comment on the recalcitrance of this decorum and the social agendas it underwrites.[5] To judge from the many incredulous, aggrieved and/or indignant reviews that have greeted recent feminist, Marxist, and Foucauldian studies of Austen, there are still many critics – critics who presumably are professors as well, teaching advanced courses and directing advanced research – who appear to regard the procedures and interrogations of their own profession as pretentious claptrap that always goes too far whenever it addresses Austen, who persist in maintaining that Austen is and ought to remain among the few cherished places in the canon where one may turn for respite, where high art can be enjoyed in all its prestige without requiring the rigours and risks of criticism. For many academics, too, the world projected by Austen's fiction has seemed so exquisitely integrated, so sufficient to its own forms and rituals, so exempt from gaps or excesses that analysis itself is a sort of violation – invasive, irrelevant, unnecessarily complicating.[6]

Jane Austen culture discloses powerful fantasies about history, gender, class, and national identity, and although these are interrelated, this essay will foreground the issue of gender. In doing so, I wish to call attention to the assumption that Austenian consumption and criticism ought to reproduce the decorums thought to be observed in the fiction, that it ought, in short, to conduct itself like a social call. Austen is supposed ignorant of high-falutin words, of course, because she is a woman, and the largely male business of criticizing this female author has accordingly had the character of 'polite society', as Carol Kay has explained it with respect to eighteenth-century drawing rooms. The word 'polite' here signifies the mixed company of men and women alike; where men, if they are gentlemen, not only refrain from swearing and smoking, but also put aside the uncouth pedantry of their formal learning, and submit instead to the tastefulness and polish that the company of ladies alone is thought to impart (Kay 1986: 63–76).[7]

Even when Austenian studies opened out, underlying and unacknowledged assumptions about the civilized and civilizing complementarity of the sexes, and the decorum respecting it, remained. In so far as Lionel Trilling's several essays on Austen, for example, elevated her work to the highest levels of moral and intellectual import, they are emphatically not Janeite, and as such they licensed the appearance of later analyses which did not hesitate to use concepts with which Austen could not have been familiar without appearing to worry overmuch about disturbing her repose. But though Trilling certainly recognized and lamented the reactionary impulse behind Janeism, his own work exemplifies it in muted forms, especially where the question of gender is concerned. When, in the widely influential introduction to the Riverside Edition of *Emma*, Trilling meditates on the names 'Jane' and 'Austen' – 'the homely quaintness of the Christian name, the cool elegance of the surname' – I am struck by his complacency towards a figure whose sex had already deprived her of the dignity of weightier signifiers. True, Trilling is explicitly addressing the aura in which authors and their works live, but it is impossible to imagine him thinking in comparable ways about

Matthew Arnold's names or Georg Wilhelm Friedrich Hegel's (although he does mention Charlotte Brontë's), let alone supposing such musings significant enough to print in a text designed to teach a generation of students how to think about the authors under study. Trilling dutifully chides extraliterary preoccupations with Austen's 'sex, her celibacy, and her social class', but these are his preoccupations as well.[8] His essay on *Mansfield Park* is ahead of its time in the brilliance and economy of its analysis of the sexual hostility to Austen expressed by such readers as Emerson, Twain, Lawrence, Garrod and Brontë. But Trilling distances himself from their rage against feminized domesticity only to vindicate the accuracy of their sense that Austen elevates a distinctively feminine complacency to an ideal. Trilling finds in *Mansfield Park* a profoundly anti-modern yearning for stasis over assertion, artifice over process, inertia over activity which turns out to be grotesquely embodied – and hence, obviously, engendered – in Lady Bertram, about whose person Trilling expresses ambivalent, not to say contemptuous, views which perhaps say a good deal more about himself than Austen, to whom he smoothly attributes them: 'Middle-aged, stupid, maternal persons are favorite butts for Jane Austen', he maintains, implying that the disgusting but regressively blissful state of being 'a vegetable' ('solid, simple, and sincere') which Austen maddeningly valorizes in this novel were inescapably attached to the female body itself ('*Mansfield Park*' in Trilling 1955: 227, 230).[9]

How do such phenomena strike a feminist critic, and in what manner will she/he interrogate them? It is crucial, first, not to genericize a critical mode whose explanatory power has been so supple, complex and extensive. Feminisms – and I stress the plural – have generally not proceeded from single, privileged, authoritative texts, and have remained distinctly *critical* in refusing totalizing paradigms. As a feminist, I am committed to thinking about how individuals are constituted as men and women, how sexual difference itself is constructed; about what is at stake in this differentiation; about what social apparatuses are deployed to enforce differentiation and to make it as well as its enforcement seem natural. As these questions and my subsequent discussion of them in *Mansfield Park* make explicit, although gender as an instance of ideology bears on men and women both, the subject of ideology is so reflexively assumed to be male that for the most part only feminists and men working in the now emerging fields of gender studies and/or gay and lesbian studies have had a stake in thinking about how sexual difference is constructed and what this entails. As a historicist who came of critical age with literary theory, I address these questions to literature as well as to the discourse about it, and I attempt to answer them through a project of historical contextualization sensitive to intersections of feminism, political theory, and fiction itself. Precisely because gender relations are not natural, they must be rooted out and unmasked for all their variable specificity; and precisely because narrative is ideologically charged, we must read closely, attending as carefully to what a novel does not and cannot say as to what it does, in order to trace how and in what moods it moves towards the conclusions it endorses and how it shuts down the counter-readings it nevertheless cannot entirely occlude.

For these reasons, I have chosen Carol Kay's essay 'Canon, Ideology, and Gender: Mary Wollstonecraft's Critique of Adam Smith' as a loose sort of model for my enterprise here. I have done so not because it is 'abstract' theory which can then, in a crude or mechanical way, be 'applied' to literature, but because it presumes the integration of the two modes. What I consider most suggestive about Kay's discussion is its critique of the ahistorical ways in which our knowledge and our theory have been institutionalized. Wollstonecraft, for example, is rarely even mentioned in histories of political philosophy even by feminist scholars because the discipline of philosophy as currently understood generally assumes and thus reproduces exclusion of women from the outset; discussions of Wollstonecraft emanating from English Literature departments similarly charge her with assuming the masculine discursive role of a philosopher in order (futilely) to evade her femininity. But observing how the boundaries which differentiate and often also gender our current academic disciplines actually ensure some of the very exclusions we protest against, Kay argues persuasively on historical grounds that, given the far broader territory covered by the term 'philosophy' and the far looser and more permeable distinctions that generally obtained among philosophy, literature, history, politics, education, psychology, and so on, Wollstonecraft could indeed stake some claim to a philosopher's authority. Literary history, in teaching us about the interpenetration of literary, political and philosophical discourses, can restore marks of the cultural system we are studying and can help us understand writing as a variably gendered social practice.

As an author who has so often been deemed apolitical precisely because she is a certain kind of woman writing domestic novels at a certain time, Austen, too, has suffered at the hands of academicians for whom the domestic itself means private, feminine and apolitical. Taking cues from Kay, I will challenge each of these codings, and contend that the 'domestic' novel itself was, as Kay says specifically of writings on education, never inherently non-political, and least of all during Austen's time, when it was conspicuously polemical.[10] Kay calls for a 'new literary history' committed to 'the enterprise of social description' (Kay 1986: 65), and the ensuing discussion proceeds by paying close attention to the diverse practices – economic, educational, affective – through which English gentry ruled at the outset of the nineteenth century.

Having put some critical cards about feminism and literary history on the table, I would like to return to the theory-resistant character of Jane Austen culture. To the extent that I and others like myself feel obliged to preface our discussion of theory, or feminism, or politics and Jane Austen with little apologies, we testify to the power of Janeism, and we betray our anxiety that maybe she really is fluff, really is *a*feminist, really is *extra*political after all, that our efforts really are rather silly, or at the very least that they require special pleading. But Janeism itself has a history, and one which is gendered and politicized in ways we may no longer recognize. Just before World War I, Frederic Harrison described Austen as 'a rather heartless little cynic . . . penning satires against her neighbors whilst the Dynasts were tearing the world to pieces and consigning millions to their graves'. Harrison continued, in words that have since become famous: 'Not a breath from the whirlwind around her ever touched her Chippendale chiffonier or escritoire.'[11] To be sure, Harrison's letter is contemptuous. But it would be a great mistake to conclude that contempt is all that it expresses. His letter sketches out two arenas of history which, as it turns out, bear greatly on the way we conceptualize Austen's fiction and its relation to her time. First, there is the history we chart in terms of political and military change, change effected by Dynasts who carve up the world as they succeed one another. Since the 1970s, of course, scholars arguing towards widely divergent conclusions – such as Marilyn Butler, Warren Roberts, Gene Ruoff, Mary Evans and myself – have contested the claim of Austen's isolation from politics so understood. Second, there is the history we chart by marking changes in the ways domestic life is conducted, including the styles of furnishings: Chippendale tables in the dining room or parlour. Now, Marxist and Marxist-inspired criticism over the past twenty years has done nothing if not demonstrate to us how these kinds of history are mutually constituted. For Harrison, however, this is clearly not the case. He discusses Austen's writing table as though it could be bracketed from social and political events. In his hands, Austen herself becomes a sort of Chippendale, since she and her furniture both occupy the world of antiques: enjoyable objects produced in the past, yet somehow basically detachable from the history that made them the way they are.

Austen would be loved for this presumed extra-historicity once the Dynasts of our own century went at it, and her unmomentousness would be cherished for the same reasons that listeners burdened with complexity would adore Mozart for his supposed cheerfulness and simplicity. The tradition of regarding Austen as outside politics takes shape with the men of the trenches, forming a foundation on which the New Critics would mount their close readings. Among the first Janeites explicitly so named was not a little lady scribbling at her escritoire, as blithely oblivious as Austen is imagined to have been to the world blowing up around her, but Kipling's artilleryman from the front line, Humberstall, who read Austen's novels to escape the horrors of the Great War: 'Jane', he averred, was the '*non pareil*' for a 'tight place' (quoted in Southam 1985, 2: 103). Kipling's story 'The Janeites' (1924) did not stretch the truth. As Christopher Kent has shown, soldiers suffering from post-traumatic stress were indeed advised to read Austen's novels. H.F. Brett Smith, an Oxford tutor, served in World War I as an adviser in British hospitals, and his special responsibility was the prescription of salubrious reading for the wounded. For 'severely shell-shocked' soldiers, his treatment was always Jane Austen.[12]

The taste for Austen evinced by shell-shocked men – men whom war has rendered helpless, hysterically sensitive, and in short, feminine – is promising material indeed for gender-based analysis. By considering the provenance of Janeism, we can begin to challenge and to uproot the late twentieth-century Western European and American assumption that fiction written by women is also written and marketed *for* women and that the constructions of the 'feminine' are somehow for women only. Early 'Janeism' is a distinctively and professedly male mode of Austenian appreciation. Shell-shocked Janeites value Austen for her presumed remoteness from the Dynasts and their carnage. Historically, women readers and (especially) women writers – think, for example, of George Eliot and Charlotte Brontë – have been chillier about Austen generally, more inclined to regard the pared-down scale of her fiction as oppressive and confining rather than safe and cosy. But for soldiers whose minds were shattered by Dynastic history, the circumscribed, anti-global dimensions of Austen's fictional world feel manageable and therapeutic; her placid feminine interiors furnished in Chippendale feel civilized, and her presumed triviality feels redemptive.[13]

The Austen we conjure when we apologize for discussing the politics, ideology, or gender in her novels is, one need hardly stress, a profoundly wishful one, and it is absurd to persist in privileging it unquestioningly when it itself emerges from such specific historical conditions and carries such transparent agendas. The public–private boundary upon which it is premised is drawn not primarily or merely in order to exclude women from the big world, but rather to create a feminine space to which men may retreat for sanctuary, thus enabling them to partake of the 'feminine' without courting the opprobrium that is attached to 'effeminacy'. And though the world to which this Austen belongs is in the past, it is not strictly speaking a historical or historicized one so much as it is a pre-historical one, that is to say, a nostalgic one. What made her novels so appealing to the men of the trenches is the fact that they are imagined to take place in a world *before* our own, *before* history blew up, *before* rules and codes stopped making sense, and *before* those codes lost their efficacy in defining masculinity in relation to other men in terms of warlike valour, heroism and honour, and only secondarily in relation to women. Janeism has been so durable because the notions of feminine propriety it implicitly circulates – such as transparency, intellectual as well as affective restraint, tidy domesticity, orderliness, and poise – are understood both to have helped ensure masculine lucidity and self-definition at a time when it was under duress, and, as Kipling's story suggests, to have sustained the attractiveness of English national identity itself when the empire was creaking.[14]

It is hardly surprising, then, that Austenian studies should be so hostile to theory when 'Jane' was deployed precisely to shore up what theory exposes as ideologically freighted. Feminist analyses in particular have upset this nostalgia even more radically, because their critiques are so intimate, insisting as they do that the premises and practices of paternal, spousal, sexual privilege are no less ideological than the affairs of Dynasts. Like Kay, I take my cue here from Mary Poovey, who explains why she does not use the term 'ideology' simply to refer to 'false consciousness':

> Ideology, as I use the term, governs not just political and economic relations but social relations and even psychological stresses as well. Ideology, in other words, is virtually inescapable; for simply by living together, men and women establish

priorities among their needs and desires and generate explanations that ratify these priorities by making them seem 'natural.' In this respect, despite its inevitable kinship with power, ideology *enables* ideas and actions; it *delimits* responses, not just in the sense of establishing boundaries but in terms of defining territories.

(Poovey 1984: xiii–xiv)[15]

Wielding historical details confidently over a broader array of disciplines, Kay demonstrates the truth of Poovey's last sentence more persuasively than Poovey herself sometimes does, particularly when it comes to considering writing itself as a social practice, and the counter-strategies ideology itself makes possible for 'authors' and their 'careers', categories she and I are not willing to forgo in the wake of post-structuralist critiques of the subject. As feminist scholars, Poovey and Kay alike address the ideological content of the natural-seeming 'priorities' that account for as well as make possible the relations of 'men and women' – relations experienced as natural, secure, private, non-contestable.

As if introducing the possibility – indeed, the inevitability – of domination or conflict in domestic relations between the sexes were not unsettling enough, feminist critiques also subvert the tenets of liberal humanism, of which Janeism is a part, when insisting that all reading and writing are executed from a position. Naming and conceding their own interests, agendas and emphases, feminist critics challenge colleagues who, assuming their universality rather than their difference, speak and read as though they did not occupy subject positions conditioned by sex, class, education, nation, ethnicity, or religion. Naming women as readers as well as subjects of literature – a move which some post-structuralists have found problematic in that it presupposes the availability and coherence of 'women' itself as a category – has proved an enormously productive critical strategy capable of transforming completely how we entertain Austen's novels, from their broadest outlines down to their subtlest details.[16] Opting not to privilege the love story and the economies it underwrites by positing it as at once the meaning and the mastercode of Austen's novels, feminist critics paid attention to aspects of the novels which had been insignificant or altogether invisible to 'humanist' readers, and to observe the agendas served from such inattention and unknowing.[17] Those of us who read from feminist positions have not been inclined to consider Austen's fictional world as safe and well-ordered as Janeites have had it. We will probably note that the plot of *Emma* begins because Emma finds that the half-mile between Hartfield and Randalls – a distance Emma herself calls 'such a little way' (*E*, 40) – is 'not pleasant' (*E*, 56) for a solitary female such as herself to undertake alone, even if she *is* handsome, clever and rich; that Colonel Brandon supports the woman and child Willoughby has abandoned in *Sense and Sensibility*, and to remember that this fate could plausibly have befallen the portionless and unprotected Marianne; that Fanny Price's father, who had made lewd jokes to Fanny every time he noticed her, declares that he would give an adulterous daughter 'the rope's end as long as I could stand over her' (*MP*, 428). I could multiply such examples. My point is simply that Austen's fiction is not placid. If we are sensitive to the ideological content of what Poovey calls 'psychological stresses', it will become clear that Austen depicts the anxiety and vulnerability that comes along with being a woman in a male-dominated society with some detail – though the heroines who bear such stress rarely contest the priorities that cause them as carefully as we might – and that this specificity discredits the contention that Austen was an elegant chronicler of a wise and gracious time when men were gentlemen, women were ladies, and everyone liked it this way and got along just fine.

Feminist critique, then, not only confounds the fantasy of heterosexual intelligibility – that is, for a sense that sexual difference is clear, just, and mutually fulfilling – but also challenges and delimits our authority as scholars, and insists that our world, to say nothing of Austen's, is as conflicted and splintered as that of Kipling's artilleryman. But although I can testify personally to the indignation feminist Austenian criticism has aroused in conservative readers of both sexes deeply committed to institutions that feminism and literary theory in general challenge, it would be exceedingly misleading to imply that resistance to such criticism has proceeded only from the right. Far from it. Some Austenian scholars who identify with the left lament even as they insist upon Austen's reactionary social and political affiliations,[18] and for them feminist criticism is refused not as an intrinsic outrage but rather as subjective and insufficiently historical. Although Marilyn Butler, for example, now acknowledges that the eighteenth-century tradition of 'Tory feminism' is worth thinking about, she finds that 'American "literary-historical" feminist criticism' reads literature from the past too selectively and too 'harshly through the spectacles of the twentieth-century feminist movement' (Butler 1975: xxxiii, xlv).[19]

As a historically-minded feminist – one, moreover, who has been fundamentally enabled by Butler's pathbreaking *Jane Austen and the War of Ideas* (1975) even though I dissent from much of it – I heed this warning about anachronism. But if we take seriously the notions of ideology Kay and Poovey recommend, regarding it not merely as a set of tenets and codes that can be articulated by an author in his or her letters, or by characters in novels, but rather as a set of often contradictory assumptions and priorities that are *lived*, and which are most telling when the author is not aware of them, then the force of this objection is diminished, for any author's or character's texts will reveal ideologically charged contradictions and resistances she/he did not contrive, and we call attention to them precisely because our angle of vision is different. Nor is it nearly as simple as Butler implies to put the 'spectacles' of our own historical situation aside. When so rigorous a historian as Butler herself codes sentimentality and psychology in and of themselves as individualist, subjectivist, and (hence) radical, without meaning to she is saying more about the political codes of the late 1960s and 1970s – when her book was written – than about the status of sentimentality and psychologizing in Austen's own time. Elinor and Marianne Dashwood's struggles in *Sense and Sensibility* with wishing, hoping, expecting and believing, to say nothing of Fanny Price's moral ideas about memory, show that Austen was deeply taken with the psychology of the individual's experience with desire in time which Johnson – one of her favourite authors, and hardly a proto-Jacobin – develops throughout *The Rambler*, *The Idler* and *Rasselas*.[20] And the most extravagantly sentimental document of Austen's time was Burke's *Reflections on the Revolution in France*, a book which, notwithstanding its centrality to Butler's argument, utterly reverses her crucial terms, coding rationality as radical and bad, and feeling as conservative and good.

Historicist assertions can thus be as anachronistic as those of any partisan, and perhaps more dangerously so precisely because of their air of objectivity. Certainly one very conspicuous feature of the dominant ideology of *our* period is that 'feminism' is singular and very recent, and that, up until today, gender was serenely accepted as natural. A wily feature this is, too, for by relegating its legitimate sphere to the new, it ensures the permanent ephemerality of feminism. But as I have argued elsewhere, issues pertaining to women's nature, women's manners, and women's rights were debated very hotly in the 1790s and after, as during all times of deep ideological rupture.[21] A literary history animated by feminism can help us to shed our deeply anachronistic liberal assumption that canonical texts – in literature, and, Kay reminds us, philosophy and politics as well – are gender-neutral. Virtually all of the ideological tensions represented in *Mansfield Park* are played out over the issues of femininity itself, the proper deployment of which was understood by reactionaries in particular to be essential to the continuance of authority and the preservation of order in the household, in the neighbourhood, and in the nation. As I will argue in the following section, far from endorsing conservative practices concerning the formation of women's minds through education and the disposal of women's hands in marriage, *Mansfield Park* opens up gaps and contradictions within reactionary ideology about gender in order to resist them.

Feminine Lawlessness, Feminine Loathings: *Mansfield Park* and the General Nature of Women

What sets *Mansfield Park* apart from Austen's other novels is the astonishing obtuseness of all its principal characters. None of the figures in whom we conventionally place confidence – earnest clergymen, dignified fathers, good little girls, vivacious young ladies – are reliable. Like many eighteenth-century writers, Austen is fascinated by stupidity. But the failures of mind persistently dramatized here are generally not served up for the reader's enjoyment as they are, say, in *Sense and Sensibility* and *Pride and Prejudice*. I am thrilled and amused when Elizabeth Bennet drops the civility required of public conversation and calls Mr Collins 'a conceited, pompous, narrow-minded, silly man'; and I am relieved that her father agrees and refuses to force her to marry him anyway, as Mrs Bennet urges (*PP*, 174; 152). But in *Mansfield Park*, everybody's understanding is so clouded that important and fairly obvious things about each other, let alone about themselves, go unnoticed. Let us consider Mrs Norris, that great grotesque, for example. Far from taking her for a nasty fool, Sir Thomas licenses her interventions; far from spotting her preternatural viciousness to Fanny, Edmund believes that it would be wonderful for Fanny to go and live with her at the parsonage; and far from finding something wrong with her command that Fanny always regard herself as the lowest and the last, Fanny entirely concurs. Although Austen's irony is systemic, we are not encouraged to laugh at such blindness. The dangers which obtuseness produces cannot be contained if they cannot be recognized, and if that obtuseness, moreover, is somehow a matter of interest rather than capacity, then it will appear too culpable for laughter.

Discernment is one of the few qualities Austen invariably treats with affection and respect, and if no one in *Mansfield Park*, Fanny not excepted, possesses it, I suspect it is because the novel in part undertakes to represent something not unlike the workings of ideology itself, particularly with respect to female manners. All of Austen's novels are richly well suited to the study of the ideology of gender because they do nothing if not dramatize the systems of priorities that regulate her characters' lives as they experience desires and make and rationalize their choices. As a matter of course, the characters in *Mansfield Park*, for example, think about primogeniture, sexual mores, paternal authority, filial duty, education, and domestic affections (such as gratitude, veneration, shame). But, as is not the case in the other novels, *Mansfield Park* always shows us how the characters' priorities and assumptions are 'false consciousness' rather than knowledge. Time and time again, the narrator invites us to see all of the mystification, doubletalk, and contradiction they engage in but do not themselves perceive even when they believe themselves to be most rational. Having been granted access to the 'truth' outside their unknowing, we are obliged to see and to ponder how their interests and assumptions enable their lives as well as occlude alternatives, blocking recognition of subjects which (as Sir Thomas says of Fanny's refusal of marriage) their 'comprehension does not reach' (*MP*, 316).

Given the obfuscation that (literally) reigns at Mansfield Park, it is surprising that *Mansfield Park* is often considered the most strenuously and programmatically conservative of Austen's novels, the most committed to vindicating the values, practices, and authority of the ruling classes, despite the few, ostensibly in-house criticisms it is sometimes acknowledged to make of it here and there.[22] Jane Austen's previous novels were planned during the 1790s, when Austen was in her early twenties and when the social and political issues raised by the revolution in France and the prospects of social change and/or disruption at home were debated with immense energy, stridency and freshness by Austen's (in some cases only slightly) older contemporaries. *Mansfield Park*, on the other hand, was the first novel drafted and completed entirely in Austen's adulthood, during an atmosphere of massive political reaction and reconsolidation, and it is tempting to speculate that the scathing but decidedly unexuberant and unhopeful irony that marks this novel owes something to the immovability of the problems it is taking on. Readers who idealize Mansfield Park implicitly or explicitly take it on the say-so of its most obsequious and most disastrously indoctrinated inmate, Fanny, for amidst the squalor of Portsmouth it is she who rhapsodizes:

At Mansfield, no sounds of contention, no raised voice, no abrupt bursts, no tread of violence was ever heard; all proceeded in a regular course of cheerful orderliness; every body had their due importance; every body's feelings were consulted. If tenderness could be ever supposed wanting, good sense and good breeding supplied its place.

(*MP*, 384)

Fanny envisions the stately country manor at its most attractive – where hierarchical differences subsist unconflictually, where persons are affiliated by the affective bonds of solicitude from above and gratitude from below, and wisely harmonized into a thoughtfully, not a despotically, regulated whole, conducing to the happiness and fulfilment of all. Fanny's vision of domestic order is an intrinsically (not merely analogically) political vision as well. If the way twentieth-century academicians divide the disciplines is such that 'women who study women usually feel excluded from philosophic discourse', as Carol Kay has observed, the same is true of women who study politics (Kay 1986: 66). In both cases, good history helps us shake off this restriction. The adjective 'domestic', after all, refers as much to affairs within the state as it does to those within a household, and in *Mansfield Park* these two sites interpenetrated in ways that were perhaps far more conspicuous in Austen's time than our own. Twentieth-century readers typically assume that men and women functioned in 'separate spheres', the public and political falling to men, the private and 'domestic' falling to women. But this boundary, firmly in place when shell-shocked soldiers sought asylum on 'Jane's' side, was still very much under construction in the early nineteenth century, and such a model clearly does not obtain at Mansfield Park. A man like Sir Thomas is not simply the father of a family, but also a member of parliament, and the space inside his doors is still very much a public site, visited by stewards and bailiffs (*MP*, 206); and it goes without saying that *within* the houses of men like Sir Thomas – as in the halls of any justice of the peace – neighbourhood disputes are resolved and judgements meted out.

But Fanny's vision is emphatically not the Mansfield we have seen and she has experienced. Austen had just finished *Pride and Prejudice* before turning to *Mansfield Park*, after all, and she knew how to make the country estate such as Fanny imagines it look good. This is manifestly not what she had in mind. Far from being governed – as Pemberley is – by wisdom, moral imagination, and benignly vigilant authority, Mansfield nourishes delusions that are always described as pathological – note the frequency with which characters pronounce *other* people's minds 'diseased' (*MP*, 363), 'vitiated' or 'tainted' (*MP*, 442), and plot 'cures' (*MP*, 79; 98; 394; and *passim*) and 'medicinal projects' (*MP*, 363) for their sakes. Indeed, granting the dire importance of all the material differences between Mansfield and Portsmouth, the moral differences are not nearly so great as Fanny imagines. Her own memory is deceiving her, as she has told us memories are wont to do. So at least Austen's rather painstakingly contrived details would seem to suggest. At Portsmouth, Fanny is disgusted to see her sisters quarrel over a silver knife, but the Bertram sisters have warred as passionately, albeit a lot less openly, over the attention of their favourite, Henry Crawford; at Portsmouth, Fanny laments the rowdiness of spoiled sons, but Mansfield is being drained by Tom Bertram's massive debts; at Portsmouth, Fanny is pained to find that her father 'scarcely ever noticed her, but to make her the object of a coarse joke' (*MP*, 382), but at Mansfield, Sir Thomas also (much to Fanny's acute embarrassment) marks with surprise her sexual maturation – indeed he discusses her 'person' at great length with Edmund – and, like her real father, he notes that the time is coming to marry her off. Fanny's praise is thus an unwitting indictment: contention and indelicacy are indeed never 'heard' at Mansfield, and that is part of the problem. As could be expected in a novel where *acting* is so important, Mansfield may excel at the manner and gestures of graciousness and probity, but does not possess the substance of it, to borrow a distinction to which her characters so frequently recur, however pathetically Fanny herself – so suspicious of acting in general – is 'taken in'.

Anarchy is as rife at Mansfield as at Portsmouth, however more modulated, and Sir Thomas is to blame. He, the narrator declares, 'was master at Mansfield Park' (*MP*, 365), and his mastery is nowhere more misguided and misconceived than with respect to the women under his care. Brean Hammond observes that Austen's prose lacks the political details that mark that of her more engaged contemporaries (see p. 70), and his point is surely well taken, but we should not equate the topical or polemical with the political. Most of the basic preoccupations, situations, structures, and even character types that make up Austen's fiction were already coded as political and politicized without anyone having to make any announcements about it. Moreover, as I have suggested earlier, feminism itself has changed what we recognize as political, and has made us more sensitive to the highly gendered character of political debate at the end of the eighteenth century.[23] By figuring Sir Thomas's failures of authority as failures to control or protect women, Mansfield Park unmistakably situates itself in a political context, for this was one of the most conspicuous features of conservative discourse. As Kay remarks, in Burke's reactionary senti- mental vision, woman becomes 'a sheltered symbol of the fragility of the whole social order' (Kay 1986: 69).[24] This vision is reproduced in *Pride and Prejudice*, where Darcy's guileless sister is prey to the machinations of the scheming Wickham. But reactionary discourse does not always figure women as this helpless. Whereas Burke evokes a queen's vulnerability to the lust of marauders in order to arouse the chivalry of men,[25] later reactionary writers would dwell on such vul- nerability in order to underscore the necessity for the strict discipline of women. In *Mansfield Park*, women are agents not victims of disorder: Mary Crawford refuses the authority of clocks and miles, and Maria and Julia refuse the authority of husbands or fathers. The novel, it is true, does give some space to the ungovernability of males. Tom Bertram runs through his family's wealth with the careless extravagance typical of pampered heirs. But even though his depredations cause some crisis *in* the novel, they are too normal to cause the crisis *of* the novel, and thus remain curiously outside the plot. He can impoverish his brother without as much as a second thought – this, after all, is his prerogative – but 'affliction' (*MP*, 439) in the form of a knock on the head, and more importantly, a sister's loss of reputation can reach him: only that can bring *him* shame; in reflecting on him, it makes him reflect.

Watching out for the honour of the womenfolk, however, is of course not a purely affective imperative. In Austen's time great households and the neighbourhoods of which they formed a central part were still the basic political units, and their survival depended on the 'name of the father', in the economic rather than the Lacanian sense,[26] although the two eventually converge. The first and most fate- ful act of paternal solicitude Sir Thomas commits is on behalf of his name. Anxious that the poor girl he plans to bring into his home might marry one of his sons and thus take on his name and everything attached to it, Sir Thomas accepts Mrs Norris's argument that raising Fanny as a sister to his own children would forfend against marriage by making it seem like incest. But this solution only aggravates the problem. If Fanny is raised like a daughter, how can he preserve the distinctness of his own daughters' names: 'how to preserve in the minds of my *daughters* the consciousness of what they are, without making them think too lowly of their cousin; and how, without depressing her spirits too far, to make her remember that she is not a *Miss Bertram*' (*MP*, 47). Sir Thomas wants his daughters always to know 'what they are', bearers of his name, for the transmission of wealth and the enlargement of alliances through marriage depends on such identifications. But the patrilineal succession of property through male heirs also depends on female propriety, for only in this way can men be assured that they know their names. After Maria commits adultery, Sir Thomas sequesters her on some remote estate not, it would appear, to shield her from shame, but rather because, bearing his name still, she may endanger other men's names: 'he would never have offered so great an insult to the neighbourhood, as to expect it to notice her' or 'be anywise accessary to introducing such misery in another man's family, as he had known himself' (*MP*, 449–50).

It is not for nothing, then, that strictures on female manners and education figured so prominently in counterrevolutionary fiction and conduct literature, for female modesty itself was a matter of national security during a profoundly reactionary time.[27] Sir Thomas, Edmund, Tom and even, as the narrator observes (excoriating the double standard in sublunary justice), Henry Crawford himself are rendered powerless by the phenomenon of female immodesty. Observing Crawford's attentions to Fanny at the ball, Sir Thomas 'advises' Fanny in his presence to go to bed in order 'to recommend her as a wife by shewing her persuadableness' (*MP*, 286). Persuadableness ensures governability without risking the possibility of defiance or the exposure of authority, and Sir Thomas advertises Fanny's because he assumes, rightly, that all men want their wives to trust that their husbands know best and to submit to their wishes without obtruding a will of their own. By Sir Thomas's standards, Lady Bertram, a 'cipher' (*MP*, 182), is also a perfect wife: always mild and trustful, she absorbs whatever opinions he suggests to her. Stunningly impercipient, Sir Thomas sees the same qualities in his daughter Maria. Rather than take alarm at her manifest indifference to her fiancé, he is happy to think that precisely because her 'feelings were not acute', precisely because she is not afflicted with 'the prejudice, the blindness of love', she will submit without discomfort to a marriage that would 'bring him [Sir Thomas] such an addition of respectability and influence', and merely become 'but the more attached to her own family' (*MP*, 215). By rendering women so cheerfully malleable that they co-operate with the plans of husbands and fathers, the system of female manners is supposed to ensure that the hierarchy of sex functions stably and without necessitating any show of force from without.

In *Pride and Prejudice*, we know that Darcy and Elizabeth Bennet are attracted to each other precisely because they disagree, and the happy conclusion to that novel invites us to think that their marriage, though ecstatically fulfilling, will be enlivened rather than compromised by the differences strong people will always have. *Mansfield Park* addresses more squarely and more critically the reactionary linkage of social disorder with female independence and sexuality. Men here evince a lot of worry about domestic stability and women's capacity to disobey and disgrace them. This anxiety produces stunning contradictions in the way femininity itself is conceived. On the one hand, it is constituted by 'gentleness, modesty, and sweetness', qualities 'essential' to 'every woman's worth' (*MP*, 297) which add up to the same sort of ductility Sir Thomas recommends. With these sorts of notions in mind, Edmund counsels Fanny not to decide for herself, but rather to comply with what Henry and Sir Thomas ask, in other words, to accept Crawford's proposal: 'You have proved yourself upright and disinterested, prove yourself grateful and tender-hearted; and then you will be the perfect model of a woman' (*MP*, 344). Gender is being used here, then, to police a woman's behaviour by threatening her with disapproval on the score of unnaturalness. It is not feminine to resist, to make a fuss for one's own sake, to disappoint the desires of others by insisting on the primacy of one's own. It goes without saying, of course, that the docility central to femininity so constructed precludes the possibility of erotic independence. When Mary Crawford shows herself capable of speaking about the Rushworth scandal with 'no feminine – shall I say? no modest loathings' (*MP*, 441), to Edmund's mind she transgresses the nature of woman as heinously as Maria herself did when she, giving rein to desires outside established means of control, broke her marriage vows. The woman who could speak of adultery without loathing could commit it without loathing, and thereby surrender all claim to femininity itself.

At the same time, femininity is always already defined as an essential waywardness, an inborn proclivity to lawlessness which legitimizes the authority rational men should exert over them. Mutually exclusive as these two notions of femininity may appear, however, they conduce to each other. At the end of the novel, Sir Thomas laments that he did not inculcate his daughters with active principles. But, as we shall see, if his daughters had the capacity as well as the prerogative to be independent agents, Sir Thomas would have been the first to excoriate them as unfeminine. Mary Crawford is never more charming to

Edmund as a woman than when she is indulging in 'feminine lawlessness' (MP, 122) in the wilderness at Rushworth's estate. Before the
conclusion, which damns her as a siren, Edmund praises her not only
for her 'good humour' but also implicitly for her feminine sweet
temper when he enthuses that she 'would never give pain! . . . how
readily she falls in with the inclination of others!' (MP, 139). Clearly,
if a woman is approved of as feminine to the degree that she shows a
readiness to please others rather than to satisfy herself, she will also be
inclined towards the sort of volatile and morally uncentred playfulness
of which 'good' men disapprove. Given the fact that female lawlessness, which sometimes appears delightful and sometimes menacing,
is described as an a priori of women's nature, feminine modesty will
always seem secondary, compensatory, and hence subject to doubt as
a ruse. Indeed Henry Crawford calls Fanny an 'angel' (MP, 340)
because he has never seen the modesty she possesses in a woman before.
Henry learned his 'lessons' (MP, 76) about women from the Admiral,
'a man of vicious conduct' (MP, 74) who flouts decorum by bring-
ing his mistress under his roof and who contends on the basis of what
appears to be his own vast experience that no modest women exist.
Such 'lessons' make Henry reluctant to settle down, 'unwilling to risk
[his] happiness' (MP, 76) by making it dependent upon women who
will turn out to be rakes at heart. Fanny is 'the impossibility [the
Admiral] would describe' (MP, 296) because she is both modest and a
woman. When Crawford later declares his 'fullest dependence' on
Fanny's 'decorum', 'faith' and 'integrity' (MP, 298) he is saying that
he knows she will not yield to 'feminine lawlessness' or compromise
his name.

One of the deepest and best-protected ironies of *Mansfield Park* is
that Henry Crawford is, in one very important way, wrong about
Fanny. She is not an exception among her sex, but indeed exemplifies
its intolerable contradictions. When Crawford undertakes to make
Fanny fall in love with him, he fully expects to take possession of a
virgin heart – 'It would be something', he muses to himself, 'to be
loved by such a girl, to excite the first ardours of her young, unsophis-
ticated mind!' (MP, 245), but the narrator stings male vanity where it
lives, and once again invites us to mark the error in which the characters wander: 'All those fine first feelings, of which he had hoped to be
the excitor, were already given' (MP, 242). Fanny is not innocent or
pure of erotic desire; her 'ardours' have been excited by Edmund for
quite some time, and she knows exactly what they are all about. She
recognizes that the lessons Edmund gives Mary in horsemanship

constitute a sort of erotic instruction as well; dumbfounded that good gentlemen could be drawn to women of such high spirits and intrepid pleasures, she struggles not only with 'discontent and envy' (*MP*, 104) but also with thwarted sexual passion that makes her weak, nervous, pale. Fanny, in short, is what no modest woman ought to be: erotically independent. Not conveniently malleable or safely asexual, as Sir Thomas could wish, her 'ardours' smoulder secretly without solicitation or authorization – well under her own control, of course, but self-control has a potentially subversive kick all its own. Henry Crawford had piqued himself on his wariness of romantic or marital 'take ins', but attributing Fanny's glow to fraternal passion alone, he too, is duped by the lawlessness of woman's passion.

The contradictions about femininity thus take a conspicuously heavy toll on Fanny herself. To her, 'no' means 'no'. But according to the notions of femininity circulated in *Mansfield Park*, particularly by Sir Thomas himself, Fanny's 'no' must really mean, 'Not until my uncle says so' or it is not feminine at all. Fanny's internal resistance strikes him as the height of ungovernability, and his bitter harangue makes it clear that he considers the problem radically pernicious:

> '. . . I had thought you peculiarly free from wilfulness of temper, self-conceit, and every tendency to that independence of spirit, which prevails so much in these modern days, even in young women, and which in young women is offensive and disgusting beyond all common offence. But you have now shewn me that you can be wilful and perverse, that you can and will decide for yourself, without any consideration or deference to those who have surely some right to guide you – without even asking their advice . . .'
>
> (*MP*, 318)

Unlike Darcy, Sir Thomas is represented not merely as an exemplary landowner, but also as a consciously reactionary one and as something of an ideologue, animadverting on the alarming disrespect for authority prevalent in these 'modern days', and singling out *female* 'independence of spirit' as it relates to matrimonial choice as 'offensive and disgusting', as 'wilful and perverse', and later as 'a gross violation of duty and respect' (*MP*, 319) due to fathers and guardians. Sir Thomas, it would appear, has attended to lamentable 'tales of the times' about headstrong young ladies – their heads spinning with noxious ideas about equal rights, the indignity of submission, and the duty of independence, platforms attributed to proponents of reform, such as Mary Wollstonecraft.

More striking than the acrimony of Sir Thomas's speech is an erroneousness so glaring as to oblige us to see it as a misrecognition made necessary by the exigencies of reactionary ideology itself. Characters in *Mansfield Park* see Fanny partially – Mrs Norris sees a sneaky 'spirit of secrecy' (*MP*, 323); Tom, a 'creepmouse' (*MP*, 168); Edmund, 'an interesting object' (*MP*, 53); and Henry Crawford, a pure woman worthy first of flirtation and later of courtship. No one but Sir Thomas could suppose hers a 'young, heated fancy' prone to 'wild fit[s] of folly' (*MP*, 318). Fanny's refusal of Crawford is acceptable and proper *before* Crawford consulted with Sir Thomas. But her refusal after he authorizes the match stymies his understanding almost as much as his gravity had earlier overawed her: 'There is something in this which my comprehension does not reach' (*MP*, 316). To comprehend Fanny's decision as lucid rather than crazed would be tantamount to admitting that she does, after all, have the right to differ with him, to desire and decide for herself, and to conceding that his authority can therefore legitimately go no further. Because Sir Thomas can allow none of this, he must discredit her choice by deeming it insane, a matter of perverse 'unaccountableness' (*MP*, 317). Thus the 'choice' she is given is indeed only, as Tom Bertram says in another context, 'the pretence of being asked, of being given a choice' when one in fact is obliged 'to do the very thing – whatever it be!' (*MP*, 146). Sir Thomas speaks here of his 'right' to 'advise' Fanny, but the paternalist discourse of power here and throughout *Mansfield Park* merely conceals the bruter operations of power. The novel is unequivocal on this issue. Sir Thomas uses the word 'advise', the narrator states, but his is the 'advice of absolute power' (*MP*, 285), power which never needs to bruit its strength because it can always expect instant cheerful compliance, and which as a consequence need never recognize itself. Daughterly defiance is so portentous because it can bring power to the brink of such knowledge. Unhampered by any sense that his power ought to be gentle and educative, Mr Price, by contrast, enforces the law corporeally, without the restraint which, in his view, inhibits 'the courtier and fine gentleman' who likes women too much to discipline in the good old way. If the adulterous Maria Rushworth 'belonged' to him, he declares, 'I'd give her the rope's end as long as I could stand over her' (*MP*, 428). A fine gentleman, on the other hand, must equivocate. Thus Sir Thomas scolds Fanny, 'You cannot suppose me capable of trying to persuade you to marry against your inclinations' (*MP*, 329), even though (as we know) he is indeed intent upon such persuasion, because he must palliate the force his coarser brother-in-law exerts without apology.

Unlike Austen's smart heroines who inhabit novels where lucidity is available, Fanny never understands, much less really protests against, a situation we are always invited to see as unjust. It is she who asks about the slave trade in Antigua, and we have no reason to suppose that her interest is critical. Herself a perfectly colonized subject, she, too, is one of Sir Thomas's slaves, every bit as bound to and constituted by the system that oppresses her as the hero of Edgeworth's appalling story *The Grateful Negro* (1802).[28] Convinced of his essential benevolence, she finds his angry objections to her refusal as 'unaccountable' as he finds the refusal itself: 'She had hoped that to a man like her uncle, so discerning, so honourable, so good, the simple acknowledgement of settled *dislike* on her side, would have been sufficient', and although she can conclude '[t]o her infinite grief' (*MP*, 318) that this is not so, she cannot doubt his discernment, much less suspect him of the same meretriciousness towards her that he showed towards Maria when forwarding her marriage to Rushworth. Nor can she justify her refusal, because self-defence is an offence, one which could only lend credence to his charges of wilfulness, the infraction considered particularly revolting in women. At Portsmouth, Fanny is amazed to find herself doing things 'in *propria persona*' (*MP*, 390), and she enjoys this autonomy. But it is certainly not what Sir Thomas would consider a feminine prerogative: Fanny is banished to Portsmouth exactly because she showed an unfeminine proclivity for deciding for herself. Thus Fanny can only repeat the charges – 'Self-willed, obstinate, selfish, and ungrateful' (*MP*, 319) – she has already heard before when she refused to take part in the theatricals. At that time, however, she was unable to withstand the urgings of those to whom she owes so much in the way of gratitude and complaisance. 'Was she *right* in refusing what was so warmly asked, so strongly wished for?' (*MP*, 174), she asked, and as her eventual capitulation shows, her answer then was 'no'.

Because Fanny has abjected herself so dutifully before a figure whose authority she generally associates with the sublime – thus quaking with dread, awe, terror, fear, horror at the thought of opposing him or witnessing his wrath (given Sir Thomas's chariness about baring his paternal anger, Fanny's association here says more about her oversensitivity than it does about his severity) – she cannot resist his urgings in such a manner as might force her to think about him and herself in a new manner. At Portsmouth, Fanny is 'startled' by the 'fearless, self-defending tone' (*MP*, 373) Susan takes when denying one of her mother's patently unfair accusations. But if Fanny is shocked it is not only because fearless self-defence is an act of assertion from which good girls shrink, but also because it is a not-so-implicit challenge to the justice of parental government, which no good girl can mount while remaining within the boundaries of propriety as delineated in the novel. Drawing on an idealized reading of gentry graciousness which enables her to believe that even though she 'knows' her place (rating 'her own claims to comfort as low even as Mrs Norris could' (*MP*, 233)), Fanny cannot believe that she is merely instrumental but trusts that even she has 'due importance' (*MP*, 384). Obliged, then, to oppose Sir Thomas without forcing any rupture, Fanny does not have much room to manoeuvre:

> she trusted, in the first place, that she had done right, that her judgment had not misled her; for the purity of her intentions she could answer; and she was willing to hope, secondly, that her uncle's displeasure was abating, and would abate farther as he considered the matter with more impartiality, and felt, as a good man must feel, how wretched, and how unpardonable, how hopeless and how wicked it was, to marry without affection.
>
> (*MP*, 323)

Fanny's 'trust' in Sir Thomas veers without intention into an arraignment of him. Carried by a youthful enthusiasm for the holiness of true love towards judgements which Austenian narrators never endorse (in *Pride and Prejudice*, for example, Charlotte Lucas's desperately expedient marriage to Mr Collins is not deemed wicked, however far from ideal), Fanny damns the course of action Sir Thomas authorizes in severely moral terms. She stops well short, however, of the conclusion to which her own logic leads her. If a good man – a man of feeling – would see that the action he is promoting is wicked, unpardonable, hopeless, wretched, then Sir Thomas must not be the good man she has taken him for.

Mansfield Park brings Fanny and Sir Thomas to an impasse over the limits of paternal authority and the propriety of female choice, and the denouement that eventually takes them out of it shuts down the conflict that brought them there without resolving it. Fanny is brought neither to submission nor to an unladylike persistence in refusal; Sir Thomas is compelled neither to recognize the nakedness of the authority he exerts nor to apologize to Fanny for its illegitimacy. I take the narrator at her word when she writes 'Let other pens dwell on guilt and misery. I quit such odious subjects as soon as I can' (*MP*, 446). The conclusion of *Mansfield Park* averts the guilt and misery towards which the rest of the novel has been heading. But just because *Mansfield Park* ends with a marriage does not mean that the ending is 'happy' or that the novel fundamentally affirms the conservative interests of patriarchal domination that marriage serves, for the novel in fact disturbs the foundations on which such happiness and such domination rest.[29] The unwonted authorial intrusiveness here invites us to regard this escape as purely conventional – the way you end a novel – rather than as a 'realistic' or organically appropriate solution to the ideological problems uncovered throughout its course. True, designed to wrap up the novel tidily, the conclusion appears to recuperate female modesty and the values it upholds. The disclosure that, *if* Henry Crawford had persevered, 'Fanny must have been his reward – and a reward very voluntarily bestowed – within a reasonable period from Edmund's marrying Mary' (*MP*, 451) seems to vindicate Sir Thomas's refusal to let Fanny's 'no' stand.[30] But this admission is one small part of so dense a sequence of conditional clauses that the entire novel would have to be radically different for it to obtain. As for Fanny's marriage to Edmund, her ensconcement at Mansfield, and the moral and social regeneration all this is supposed to portend, it seems fantastically wishful to take so much consolation from a union undertaken in such enervation and as a matter of default at the last minute. Considering how everything in Mansfield's previous policy had been calculated to prevent Fanny from entering into this very union, and that the 'instant annihilation' (*MP*, 430) of Maria and the demonization of Mary Crawford are necessary before Mansfield lets her in, the prize seems tarnished for me, if not for Fanny. And finally, the mythic abruptness with which the evil characters are cast out and the good huddle together suggests to me an author not so much committed to reconstituting the gentry household as self-conscious about how she appears to defend it; one, who bent on quitting guilt and misery, has contrived to avoid delivering a *coup de grâce* to the ethos represented throughout the novel with such withering irony.

As over-determinedly tidy as the conclusion is, however, in some respects it breaks rather than completes the circle. The introduction of Susan into the household seems particularly disturbing, suggesting as it does that the Bertram family, stung by its striking unsuccess at extending itself outward, can only regenerate itself through the absorption of its underclass. Where else, I wonder only half-jokingly, could the Bertrams ever find a wife for Tom? And yet, Susan Price is not another Fanny. Not coming from a propertied family, she has not been disciplined into a version of female propriety calculated to help fathers consolidate and extend their property by disposing of their daughters in marriage. Fearless and self-defending rather than cringing and long-suffering, moreover, Susan is a stranger to the sentiments which constitute the affective front of gentry ideology. Unfazed by the scandal that has shaken Mansfield Park at its foundation, Susan takes her seat in the carriage wearing 'the broadest smiles' which are 'screened by her bonnet' and 'unseen' by companions (Fanny and Edmund) who would regard them as impertinent (*MP*, 433). These smiles take us, once again, outside the ideology within which Edmund and Fanny function. Upon her arrival at Mansfield, Fanny had been 'mortified', 'overcome', 'abashed' and 'awed' by a place whose power depends in part on its capacity to impress persons inside as well as outside its doors with just these sentiments. But Mansfield does not awe Susan with the dignity of its power, or melt her with a sense of its graciousness. Susan's visions are material: 'silver forks, napkins, and finger glasses' (*MP*, 434). For her, it is a place full of the trappings of class and little of the moral mystique that has benighted her sister even as it has also enriched her. Installed there at the novel's end, she may fare better for her greater clear-sightedness.

Conclusion

Challenges to the legitimacy of feminist approaches to Austen almost invariably proceed from the premise of her Tory conservatism, which in turn depends on identifying Austen's class affiliations, and on supposing that she was so smoothly integrated within it that she perforce reproduced all its values in her fiction. Once we take seriously the value of interrogating gender, the business of denominating political allegiances becomes more complicated and less illuminating, especially once we surrender our own ideologically loaded assumption that feminism is germane only to political radicals from the 1970s. 'Woman' was a politically sensitive issue during the decades Austen wrote, and to place Austen's fiction within this context is by no means to suggest that she was a 'radical'. Indeed, radical ideology of the 1790s – inspired as it was by a tradition of commonwealth republican-ism which idealized masculinity – was in some respects more hostile to women than the culture of the old regime, which at least granted women of the upper classes place and influence publicly in salons and at court. The female duties of domesticity and maternity were advocated by Jacobins and bourgeois conservatives alike.[31] Feminist inquiry sensitive to historical specificity thus helps us disclose how a commonwealth 'radical' like Mary Wollstonecraft may ultimately be more entangled in oppressive romantic and/or masculinist values than a 'reactionary' writer like Hannah More, whose appeals to divine authority at times formed an unshakeable basis on which to construct her own.[32]

If we want to consider how female manners and education figured in national agendas during a profoundly reactionary time, then questions such as 'Was Jane Austen a Tory?' or 'Was she for or against the French Revolution?' are not likely to be the most incisive or productive. Feminist historical scholarship is disruptive as well as exciting precisely because it so often cuts across these more conventional ways of denominating political and social affiliations. Obviously, the question 'Was Jane Austen a feminist?' is loaded and in some respects irrelevant: one that implies goals, alliances, and possibilities – about employment, wages, law, language, sexuality, and so on – which she could not have been aware of when what we now call 'feminism' was developing in conjunction with modern democratic movements. Austen never rallied for women's rights to political representation or reproductive freedom. But assuming the moral equality of the sexes, her fiction represents the construction and enforcement of sexual difference as politically motivated elements of gentry life, and it protests against the costs these exact from women.

SUPPLEMENT

NIGEL WOOD: You suggest in your conclusion that feminist history is especially liberating because it cuts across class-based and sociological analyses of context. Does it offer just an alternative, or do you find areas where it actually falsifies the impressions of such non-gender-specific work?

CLAUDIA L. JOHNSON: First, a clarification. I wrote that feminist historical analysis was 'disruptive as well as exciting', not that it was 'liberating'.

I am struck by the ways in which this question itself may be counter-productive. In so far as it could be taken to imply that Austen's novels are some integral truth which critics, wielding their 'isms' – in this case, feminism and Marxism, say – fight over, it runs the risk of reproducing the problem I tried to address at the outset of my essay: the tendency to view Austen as a contained interior, set apart from clamour and conflict. Of course, literary critics of no matter which author commonly put all positions but their own beyond the possibility of contestation. But what I have called 'Jane Austen culture' has been particularly prone to isolate Austen from the discursive gunfire of competing claims. This ought to be examined.

This reservation aside, your question addresses the long-standing tension between gender-based and class-based analysis. For the sake of those who are coming to this debate for the first time, I will simply state that I do not accept that either class or gender is primary and determinative. This is less of an issue now than formerly. Only the most doctrinaire Marxists – and there are not many left – would deny the legitimacy of genders as political and social categories, and although more recent theorists (Jameson is an eminent example) may not be particularly interested in feminist analysis, their work certainly complements it. Not that the bad old days are over. The ease with which so sympathetic and helpful a critic as Terry Eagleton can assume Austen's perfect coextensiveness with the ideology of her class (see, for example, the scattered comments in Eagleton 1976: 71) indicates an almost reflexive tendency to erase sex in the interests of class. Feminist theorists (Teresa de Lauretis being among the most formidable) search out and critique these – and other – blind spots on the level of critical theory. By the same token, feminist literary criticism from the 1970s – Gilbert and Gubar's *Madwoman in the Attic* (1979) for example – tended to elide class in a drive to underscore the oppression of women by men, thus overlooking (among other things) differences *within* the category of 'woman' – for instance, posed by characters such as Emma, Harriet Smith, and Hannah (the Woodhouses' servant) – which preoccupy feminist critics and scholars of the 1990s.

Because class-based and/or sociological study interests feminists, too, I would say that feminist inquiry, rather than 'falsifying' or standing merely as 'alternative' to them, fundamentally and productively complicates them.

NW: Carol Kay concludes her essay on Wollstonecraft by claiming that a 'new literary history cannot dispense with a new political science' (Kay 1986: 75), one that embraces 'matters of individual agency' and *also* 'the enterprise of social description' (Kay 1986: 65). How far do you feel your approach to Jane Austen has been affected by this?

CLJ: Clearly, my approach has been profoundly affected by this. My essay demonstrates what 'the enterprise of social description' might look like within the context of text-based criticism, examining how the domestic politics of the gentry as represented in the novel relate to larger issues of social and political domination. Readers might well want to continue this enterprise of contextualization by exploring such social practices as education, medicine, reading, writing, theatre, household economy, and fashion, to name but a few.

The part of your question I would really like to address concerns the matter of 'individual agency'. In my essay, I mainly approached this as it related to characters variously enabled and repressed by the ideal of independence which is part of the political philosophy underlying so much fiction of the late eighteenth century. But, like Kay, I also think that, within the context of this same political-philosophical tradition, there is a lot of room for thinking about 'individual agency' as it relates to authors as they intervene in the political struggles of their time. In a way, this gets back to your first question, for Marxists have had a lot at stake in de-emphasizing individual agency and the philosophical tradition that serves it. Just as feminist critics and African Americanists were trying to make women and 'minority' authors visible and powerful in literary history, post-structuralist Marxist critics – along with other post-structural theorists – were demystifying bourgeois individualism, decentring the self, and dismantling authority *per se*. But once we accept elements of this critique, it ought to be possible to consider an author not as a transcendent or transhistorical agent, but precisely as historically constituted. This is in part what I have tried to do by thinking about the role domestic fiction itself played in the post-revolutionary controversies of the 1790s and by situating Austen within this context.

It is worth thinking about how this enterprise has already changed the map of literary history. It was not very long ago, after all, that Ian Watt lamented the chasm of 'mediocrity and worse' that yawned between Richardson's and Fielding's novels in the mid-eighteenth century and the masterpieces Jane Austen published in the early nineteenth, and he dismissed intervening 'fugitive literary tendencies such as sentimentalism or Gothic terror' as digressions from the great realistic tradition with 'little intrinsic merit' (see Watt 1957: 290). Feminist critics played a large role in resuscitating and repositioning the literature of this period (including Gothic, sentimental, domestic, and polemical fiction and non-fiction) and in fact in restoring it to the prominence it enjoyed during its own time, precisely because our critical practices tend to centre on ideological as well as aesthetic rupture, and because we are committed to exploring the role narrative plays in resisting as well as reproducing dominant values.

CHAPTER 4

Discovering 'A New Way of Reading': Shoshana Felman, Psychoanalysis and *Mansfield Park*

BARBARA RASMUSSEN

[Shoshana Felman's Lacanian reading of James's short story, *The Turn of the Screw* (1898) emphasizes the inevitable implication of the reader in narratives. In psychoanalytic terms the process is always one of 'transference', where the reader invests fictional items with positive or negative qualities according to the deep patterns established in response to the first significant experiences with family members. Critics seem authoritative, yet they are condemned (as are all readers) to play out between them the conflicts between the fictional characters or evident themes of the story, always in the service of an illusory pursuit of full meaning.

The Turn of the Screw is an apt narrative to choose to demonstrate this. The story is set in a large country house (Bly), where a new governess takes up her post in charge of two children in the absence of a father. She is employed by the children's uncle, who has given her strict instructions not to bother him with news about their progress. Flora and Miles exhibit a mixture of attractive manners and secretive anxiety. One day, the governess sees two former employees of Bly, the steward Peter Quint and the ex-governess, Miss Jessel, both of whom she later discovers are dead. She cannot establish whether the children can see these ghosts as well, as they are particularly evasive when questioned, and so she fears the worst: that they are both under an evil ghostly power. When challenged directly, Flora is very disturbed and falls ill. On confronting Miles, the governess sees Peter Quint at the window and attempts to protect Miles and so exorcize the ghost's power. She is unsuccessful, as the frightened boy dies in her arms.

As the tale is told just from the governess's point of view, there is a central doubt as to whether she is mad, actually sees the ghosts or just hallucinates. The tale provides us with an especially open terrain, and yet it functions just as a marked instance of all reading experiences, where we attempt to assert mastery over the text and yet find it mastering us: 'In Lacan's model of transference the analyst is 'absent' so that the analysand is forced to analyse for her/himself. The 'subject supposed to know' refuses this position, much like the absent master of Bly and the necessarily absent author' (Wright 1984: 130). Without these authority-figures, there is an uncertainty in interpretation that involves a pursuit without final knowledge: 'the Master's discourse is very like the condition of the unconscious as such: Law itself is but a form of Censorship' (Felman 1977a: 145). This is by way of an introduction to Lacan's work on the 'subject', which is considered very much an effect of the linguistic system rather than a cause. A traditional view of the means by which we attain expression in language derives from the basic assumption that it involves a compromise between our unconscious desires and the public negotiation with an inherited language. Whenever we enter linguistic self-consciousness, we give ourselves up to a pre-existing system of signifiers assigned individual meanings by such a system. Lacan noted that, alternatively, we take up 'subject-positions' within a distribution of relations (for instance, male/female, I/you), and so are not totally in charge of our meaning. Indeed, it is a condition of our use of language that meaning is rendered unstable – never captive, but always in view. For Freud, our unconscious drives cannot be expressed through language. If desire is formless and unknown, language apparently supplies form and intelligibility – a clarity quite foreign to the language of the unconscious which is too instinctive to be fully semantic as traditionally understood. Lacan refuses this division between a pre-existing unconscious and its ensuing expression, as he regards the unconscious as emerging simultaneously with language, which actually *structures* our desires. (This is why Lacanian phraseology and written style is so complex, obliging the reader to 'work through' to the specialized associations of the signifier.) As Colin MacCabe describes it, this 'play' between imagined presence and the inevitable absence of non-linguistic corroboration *produces* the unconscious and its unadmitted desires (see MacCabe 1979: 6–7). Lacan's reading of Freud recovers some of the realization that these desires are not biological instincts but rather 'drives' activated by a sense of lack or prohibition. What is at stake here is a sense of 'character' or 'subject' as traditionally understood. When a child perceives itself reflected in a mirror for the first time, it is led to identify with an image that promises unity and distinctiveness. Lacan regards this as a misrecognition, based on the *desire* to possess such unity yet which is never actually experienced, and is termed by him as the 'imaginary' state. This identification with an image, a 'dyadic' mental structure, is a pleasurable activity and yet one to be invaded by a third and intrusive term. With linguistic maturity, there is an inevitable entry into a system of differences (present/ absent, here/there, as well as male/female), which Lacan calls the 'symbolic', associated with the Father's prohibition of incestuous desire. The easy equivalence of a 'signifier' (the child) with its reflected 'signified' (the image) is thus disturbed and the direct path to reality thwarted. Instead we grow to associate with an endless relay of *linguistic* and so hollow signs. Lacanian literary criticism derives from the realization that, just as the unconscious might be structured *like* a language, it may be an effect *of* language. The metaphors of a literary text figure the unconscious rather than represent it in the signified. The usual formulation (since Saussure's linguistic work) is that the signifier is sustained by what it signifies ($\frac{s}{S}$). The bonding may be arbitrary, as a physical object such as a hairy quadruped that barks can be a 'dog', 'chien' or 'hund', yet once locked into the specific *langue*, the bonding becomes a secure one. For Lacan the algorithm should be better expressed as $\frac{S}{s}$, where the signified 'slides' beneath a signifier which 'floats'; the bar between the two signifying a division rather than a relation, that is, the signifier obeys no 'law' of the signified. For Freud, the unconscious expresses itself through dream images which may be 'condensed' (a combination of several at once) or be 'displaced' (a constant shift of significance from one image to a contiguous one). Lacan calls these rhetorical features the 'metaphorical' and 'metonymic' respectively.

Both of these textual tendencies are symptomatic of a response to the obstruction of desire. The metaphor transforms the apparent 'signified' (for example, 'the ships ploughed the ocean'), whereas metonymy always supplies allied references rather than similar ones to the apparent 'signified' (for example 'the pen is mightier than the sword', 'the decisions made by Downing Street'). This obliquity or evasion is not a route, however indirect, to some signified deeper 'meaning', the unconscious desire. It is the very condition of language that it is never able to speak of what it desires to say. Consequently, when I use the first-person pronoun, 'I' am assigned a subject-position, in a symbolic sense, but not describing the disjointed self at all. There is always an *absence* at the centre of our determination to represent, and we cannot avoid either providing a substitute for or deferring such contact with the realm of desire in and through language. Literary expression, as with all linguistic use, provides a constant stream of signifiers, which only ever attain temporary meaning retrospectively, through the noting of their difference from one another. The desire to express the inexpressible is a mechanism which unsettles the symbolic order's impositions of meaning. In practice, however, no one can define one's matrix of desires so as to control it, that is, in Lacan's terms, to occupy the position of the Other. Despite this, we continue to use language to attempt just that: to become the origin and so guarantor of meaning.

A 'subject' can thus never be an autonomous observing non-participant. Similarly, the text will never be fixed in form and content. On the contrary, it is riddled (quite literally) with discontinuities and inconsistencies to the point where it is always 'decentred', free of governance by a fixed authorial subject. Similarly, readers may feel that they are grasping meaning in their readings, yet it is more the case that the story appropriates its readers through their transferred and projected desires.]

NIGEL WOOD

The knowledge that one errs does not eliminate the error.[1]

The Blindness of Mastery

This is an essay about reading and psychoanalysis: about the lure of meaning – our desire for the definitive interpretation – and the impossibility of finally mastering it. Shoshana Felman's 'Turning the Screw of Interpretation' (1977a) seeks to demonstrate both the force of this desire and the impossibility of its fulfilment. To attempt to explicate her essay – to summarize its meaning and to work through its implications in a reading of *Mansfield Park* (a novel which has, to date, yielded many and various interpretations) would seem, then, to be a thoroughly contradictory endeavour. To grasp meaning is to ignore the complex textual performance which has produced it. Mastery of meaning would seem to depend on blindness – to be its own contradiction and deconstruction. Paradoxically, then, it would seem that I can only hope to elucidate Felman's exposure of error by repeating the error she exposes.

'Turning the Screw of Interpretation' is important because it marks a radical break with the traditional concept of the relations between Freudian psychoanalysis and literature. As Felman herself points out, 'a reading can be called "Freudian" with respect to *what it reads* (the *meaning* or thematic *content* it derives from a text) or with respect to *how it reads* (its interpretative *procedures*, the techniques or *methods* of analysis it uses)' (Felman 1977a: 117–18). Felman is interested in the latter understanding of what constitutes a Freudian reading – an understanding derived from the work of the French psychoanalyst Jacques Lacan. This is because, as Felman notes, 'The gist of Freud's discovery, for Lacan, thus consists not simply of the revelation of a new *meaning* – the unconscious – but of the *discovery of a new way of reading*' (1977a: 118). She goes on to quote from an unpublished talk given by Lacan in which he asserted:

> [Freud's] first interest was in hysteria. . . . He spent a lot of time listening, and, while he was listening, there resulted something paradoxical . . . that is, a *reading*. It was while listening to hysterics that he *read* that there was an unconscious. That is, something

he could only construct, and in which he himself was implicated; he was implicated in it in the sense that, to his great astonishment, he noticed that he could not avoid participating in what the hysteric was telling him, and that he felt affected by it.[2]

What Lacan suggests here is that Freud constructed his theory of the unconscious because he noticed that in the dialogue between analyst and analysand (patient) something happened – the analyst became involved and was affected, in a way which went beyond his conscious understanding or mastery. He thus discovered his own unconscious. (An unconscious reading was taking place 'within' Freud (Felman 1987: 23). He could not master it – only register its effects – the way it involved him in the story.) That is, as Felman notes, 'the unconscious is not only *that which must be read*, but also, and primarily, *that which reads*' (1977a: 118). Psychoanalysis, in this perspective, does not operate through the analyst's mastery of unconscious meaning but through a dialogue in which analyst and analysand both have to learn to listen to their own 'ignorance' (Felman 1987: 82) – to those effects of any discourse which exceed our capacity for conscious mastery.

Freud himself gives perhaps the clearest gloss on this when he writes:

Psychoanalysis sets out to explain . . . uncanny disorders; it engages in careful and laborious investigations . . . until at length it can speak thus to the ego:

'. . . A part of the activity of your own mind has been withdrawn from your knowledge and from the command of your will . . . you are using one part of your force to fight the other part . . . A great deal more must constantly be going on in your mind than can be known to your consciousness. Come, *let yourself be taught* . . . !'[3]

What Lacan points to then is the way Freud let himself be taught by his discovery of his own unconscious. It was important, he realized, for the analyst to avoid succumbing to the effects of the text – becoming involved. Rather the analyst, by guarding against such involvement, yet noticing the effects of the text, could return them to the patient – as precisely that part of her/himself which she/he was overlooking – the unconscious.

This, as Felman argues (1977b: 5–10), has interesting implications for the relationship between literature and psychoanalysis. Traditionally, psychoanalysis has been conceived as offering literature 'a reliably professional "answering service" ' (Felman 1977a: 105) – as an authoritative source of knowledge which could be *applied* to the literary text. But to emphasize that the 'unconscious', including the unconscious of the analyst, 'is a reader' (Felman 1987: 22), suggests rather that literature and psychoanalysis are involved with and in one another. Literature and psychoanalysis both have to do with language and the effects of language. If the unconscious is a reader, undermining the authority of consciousness, then neither the literary critic nor the psychoanalyst can claim a position of mastery. Literature and psychoanalysis can learn from a 'dialogue' (Felman 1977b: 6) with each other. Each may help the other to rethink the very question of reading, of what happens when we read fictional narratives like *Mansfield Park* – the question of the effects of narrative and how we become involved in narratives beyond the grasp of our conscious understanding.

David Lodge, for example, quotes some pertinent comments on *Mansfield Park* that relate precisely to the paradoxical effect of its narrative performance (Lodge 1988: 94–5). Lionel Trilling declares that it 'is a great novel, its greatness being commensurate with its power to offend' (Trilling 1955: 211), and Miss G.B. Stern speaks of being 'contentedly spell-bound', though she confesses her inability to understand why some of the events of the novel assume such importance for the reader (Quoted in Lodge 1988: 19–20). Clearly, *Mansfield Park* involves its readers and affects them in a paradoxical way – a way that goes beyond the reader's conscious grasp – a way thus not dissimilar to the effect that Freud's patients' stories had on him.

Felman is interested in such reading effects and thus she focuses her article on *The Turn of the Screw* since the intensity of the critical debate which it has evoked would seem to make it 'one of the . . . most *effective* . . . texts of all time' (1977a: 96). An examination of Felman's essay should then allow us to return to *Mansfield Park* with new insight into its 'reading-effects' (1977a: 102). What Felman notices is that, examined closely, the critical debate uncannily repeats the drama of the story, with the critics trying to rescue the text from the misreadings of their critical opponents, just as the governess in the story tries to rescue the children from the ghosts. Most notably, Edmund Wilson's psychoanalytic reading of *The Turn of the Screw*[4], which sees the ghosts as merely imagined by a neurotic, sexually repressed governess, has incensed other critics who trusted her account. Yet in contesting each other's readings, critics, far from finally mastering this ambiguous story, actually echo it. Where, for example, the governess sees the children as possessed by the ghosts, one critic, cited by Felman, accuses his Freudian opponents of themselves being '*strongly prepossessed*' (1977a: 101). Felman thus concludes that:

The critical interpretation . . . not only elucidates the text but also reproduces it dramatically, unwittingly *participates in it*. Through its very reading, the text . . . acts itself out. As a reading effect, this inadvertent 'acting out' is indeed uncanny: whichever way the reader turns, he can but be turned by the text, he can but *perform* it by *repeating* it.

(Felman 1977a: 101)

In her choice of words here, Felman clearly alludes to Freud's concepts of the repetition compulsion and of transference and to their reformulation in linguistic terms in Lacan's work. A brief consideration of these concepts, then, should help us in following Felman's argument further.

In *The Interpretation of Dreams* (1900) Freud argued that 'an unconscious idea' transferred 'its intensity' onto the 'day's residues' and, under the cover thus provided, it could achieve representation in a dream in displaced guise (Freud 1953–74, 5: 562–4).[5] In *Beyond the Pleasure Principle* (1920), where Freud focuses particularly on the compulsion to repeat traumatic experiences, he recounts his experience of the way patients could not always simply remember what they had repressed. Where they could not remember, they acted out (repeated) repressed fantasies and wishes in relation to the figure of the analyst, wishes often going back to thwarted love relations and conflicts with parental figures (Freud 1953–74, 18: 7–64). The patient thus transfers and re-enacts an earlier experience in the current relationship with the analyst. The traumatic conflict has been repressed; and *precisely because* the castrating division between conscious and permitted behaviour and unconscious wishes that the trauma and its repression entailed has not been dealt with consciously, it returns unrecognized, to haunt the patient.

In relation to the compulsion to repeat Freud wrote in his 'Analysis of a Phobia in a Five-Year-Old Boy' (1909): 'a thing which has not been understood inevitably reappears; like an unlaid ghost, it cannot rest until the mystery has been solved and the spell broken' (Freud 1953–74, 10: 122). Unconscious wishes persist and are unwittingly acted out, as opposed to being consciously apprehended. When this happens in analysis the analyst may make use of the situation to bring the patient to a conscious awareness of the repressed wishes, to give them symbolic, substitutive form in language and thus to lift the repression or lay the ghost. This will involve an acceptance of contradictory or ambivalent feelings by the patient and thus a loss of her/his sense of self-unity. Far from being in a position of self-mastery, the patient has been repeating or acting out an unconscious reading quite inappropriate to the current situation with the analyst.

Here, then, we can see the connection Felman makes with the fierce hostilities and passions evoked in the critical debate over *The Turn of the Screw*. The critics as readers and interpreters, Felman suggests, are 'turned by the text . . . can but *perform* it by *repeating* it' (1977a: 101). What they do not understand *performs* them. They unwittingly repeat, in their conflict with each other, the conflict of meaning in the text which they have repressed or excluded by insisting on a univocal reading. The unconscious, reading rhetorically – reading the language of the text as figuring desire – has the critics acting out a conflict which they have repressed from consciousness. A meaning other than conscious meaning or 'literal' meaning (a 'trope' or figurative *turn* of language) is in play, without the critics recognizing it. It is this uncanny reading-effect – the return of something familiar but repressed (not understood) – that Felman notices and which opens up a number of more general questions concerning the nature of reading, of reading-effects and the relations between literature and psychoanalysis which are explored in the remainder of her essay. Since her concern is with literature, with *letters*, it is not surprising that she draws on Lacan's rereading of Freud, a reading which draws heavily on Saussurean linguistics.

In Saussurean linguistic theory, language is a system of differentially related signs; the sign being composed of a signifier (verbal or acoustic image) and a signified (concept), the two initially quite arbitrarily related but fixed by convention. It is through language as a system of differences that we make sense of the world. Language does not reflect meanings already present in the world, though its familiarity may seduce us into assuming that it does. Lacan reversed the priority of signified over signifier implied by Saussure, privileging instead signifier over signified: $\frac{s}{s}$. To understand why he did this we need to consider how meaning is always the product of a whole system of differences and does not inhere in any one differential element. For example, when we read a book, the meaning of any word, sentence, episode will be dependent on what precedes and what follows it. Thus meaning shifts as we read on. Lacan suggests that meaning constantly slides under the chain of signifiers and is not tied to any one of them. But even to say this is reductive in relation to Lacan's argument, for he also notes that Saussure identified two axes in the relational structure of language: the syntagmatic or horizontal axis along which meaning unfurls as we utter a chain of words (as in this sentence); and the paradigmatic or associative, vertical axis – all the other words associated with an individual word in the syntagmatic chain which are not present but which might be used instead of it.

This is, then, a way of understanding Lacan's assertion that the unconscious is structured like a language. The *presence* of meaning along the syntagmatic axis depends paradoxically on a whole system of *absent* differences. A position or meaning is produced for the subject to identify with in the syntagmatic chain, but this position depends on the absence of the differences which constitute that position. Lacan refers to these excluded differences as the Other. Subjectivity is thus produced by these differences rather than being in a position of mastery over them. Moreover, the subject of the utterance, of the speech *act*, is disjoined/divided from the subject spoken about or from *what* is said. This is the distinction Lacan makes between the subject of the enunciation (*énonciation*) – the process of utterance – and the subject of the enounced (*énoncé*) – of what is stated. We are constituted in language as *split* subjects. As MacCabe writes:

> The unconscious is that effect of language which escapes the conscious subject in the distance between the act of enunciation (in which the subject passes from signifier to signifier) and what is enounced (in which the subject finds him or herself in place as, for example, the pronoun 'I').
>
> (MacCabe 1979: 9)

Lacan illustrates this with the example of a person saying 'I am lying'. The 'I' who utters this, the 'I' of the enunciation, is divided from the 'I' of the enounced or statement. Identification with the 'I' of the enounced involves a misrecognition since it excludes the subject of the process of the enunciation, the process which produces the enounced.[6] Consciousness of meaning requires repression of the differences that produce it. The bar between signifier and signified really is a bar. Thus, Colin MacCabe argues: 'The unconscious is the result of the fact that, as we speak, what we say always escapes us – that as I (the ego) say one thing, it (the id) says something else' (MacCabe 1979: 7). What we consciously think we say is in a figurative relation to another speech. As Felman suggests, the unconscious reads 'not literally but rhetorically' (1977a: 137). The unconscious as a reader turns 'literal' meanings to its own purposes which are beyond conscious knowledge. It is the excess in the patient's utterance beyond what she/he consciously registers that the listening psychoanalyst returns to the patient. Just so, it is the gap between the univocal meaning which the critics seek and identify with in *The Turn of the Screw*, and the differences on which such meaning depends which return in the divisions of the critical debate, that Felman as textual analyst points to.

For Lacan, a baby first achieves a sense of unity by misidentifying its disunified being with an alien mirror image. Lacan calls this the imaginary. In the imaginary the child does not separate itself from what surrounds it but rather, fuses with it. This imaginary sense of incestuous unity with the world (the [m]other) is punctured by the child's accession to conventional language. In Lacan's linguistic version of the Oedipus complex the castrating presence of a third term – the paternal metaphor, the Name-of-the-Father (the *Nom-du-Père*) – divides mother from child, repressing incestuous desire, creating the unconscious, which can now only find substitutive figurative expression in the Father's terms. Language (the Symbolic order – the system of conventional differences) is the third term. In French 'nom' sounds like 'non' or 'no' and the Father's Name does indeed negate desire, allowing it an outlet only in the arbitrary signifier or word which forever defers satisfaction. The child must submit its desire for incestuous oneness to the cultural law of linguistic substitution.[7] Unconscious desire can only manifest itself through its own contra-diction – the conventional signifiers of conscious discourse which are in an arbitrary relation to the signified. What we consciously think we ask for is never what we (unconsciously) mean. The satisfaction of a specific need will never satisfy our hunger for this imaginary lost oneness. The articulation of need in terms of a demand always leaves a residue of desire.

Unconscious desire informs our interpretation of signifiers, making us transfer authority onto them as full of meaning – as capable of satisfying desire – but, forever disappointed, moves on down the chain of signifiers. As MacCabe writes: 'While at one level the conscious subject rests in the world of the signified, at a different level there is an *other* and dominant subject which races along the differential paths of the signifier and constantly disrupts the imaginary unity of the first' (MacCabe 1979: 73). We are ineradicably split subjects: the meaning we think we grasp in the enounced, like the child misrecognizing itself in a mere alien mirror image, is but differentially and negatively related to the signified which the unconscious subject of the enunciation pursues. Unconscious desire moves on down 'the differential paths of the signifier' (MacCabe 1979: 73) in pursuit of a satisfaction which the very negative status of the arbitrary *Nom-du-Père* makes impossible.

The unconscious comes into being with our subjection to this 'no' of the Father yet we constantly try to close the gap which thus opens for us with more words – words with which we try to account for, *narrate*, our desire (see Wright 1984: 111–13). Yet all we do thereby is to repeat the repression – the contra-diction – which produced the unconscious in the first place. Lacan thus understands the repetition compulsion in terms of language and our subjection to it. We compulsively transfer our desire for imaginary oneness onto signifiers – allowing ourselves to be seduced by them, forgetting their merely figurative status – taking conscious meaning as whole and authoritative.[8] 'Transference' says Lacan, 'is love . . . addressed to knowledge', to 'the subject presumed to know'.[9] But the granting of authority to a signifier is always a misreading. Transference for Lacan 'is the acting-out of the reality of the unconscious'.[10] Felman speculates whether it may not then always be 'the acting-out of a *story*' (1977a: 133) – the performance of a story of desire which has been repressed from consciousness. We perform/enunciate what our identification with a position in the enounced simultaneously blinds us to. What we fail to understand governs us. We unwittingly *act out* unconscious desire.

Desire touches upon the Real. The Real for Lacan is what language always 'misses'.[11] The 'referent', 'the origin', 'the beginning' (all key terms in Felman's analysis of *The Turn of the Screw*) is that from which our reading of the world through language always divides us. It is always already lost, since birth separates us from the mother's body, plunges us into a world already differentiated by language. The oneness that the small child experiences is always already imaginary – always already lost. This is why Felman understands the critics of *The Turn of the Screw* to be inevitably mastered by the story which they assume they can master. Transferring authority onto its signifiers – treating the text as 'the subject presumed to know' – like the child narcissistically misrecognizing itself in an alien mirror image – the critics identify with a position *in* the story. They identify with a position in what is narrated (in the enounced) ignoring the enunciation, the process of differentiation on which it depends. Interpreting meaning inevitably excludes the process of producing that meaning. Yet since a critical reading, an interpretation, is a further act of enunciation, the story as performance – as the repressed differences upon which any meaning depends – is repeated, in displaced form, in the *act* of reading which exceeds its own interpretative grasp of meaning. The critics unwittingly repeat the story in their interpretations, like a patient acting out, instead of consciously understanding, repressed wishes.

Felman points to Edmund Wilson's psychoanalytic reading of *The Turn of the Screw* as an example of an attempt to master the story which involves a misreading (misrecognition) that excludes the very differences on which meaning depends. Wilson comes up with a univocal reading in line with the traditional conception of psychoanalytic criticism as capable of mastering the literary text. The 'answer' (Felman 1977a: 105) to the ambiguity of the story is that the governess is suffering from repressed sexuality. If the text is rhetorical (figurative), then Wilson penetrates the ambiguous symbols to come up with the answer – sexuality – understood literally and univocally, not rhetorically, as 'positive *act* or *fact*' (Felman 1977a: 111). Felman shows that this is a misreading of Freud's conception of sexuality. The concept of sexuality in Freud involves 'both *more* and *less* than the literal sexual act' (Felman 1977a: 110) and sexuality itself is constituted by 'libido' and 'repression' which are in conflict with one another.[12] In Lacanian terms our sexuality is defined by what it is 'allowed to be'[13] – that is, by the substitutive form that the *Nom-du-Père* (repression) allows libido (desire) to take. As Felman notes, this implies that the '*meaning*' of sexuality '*is its own contradiction*' (1977a: 111). The meanings we consciously grasp are produced through the repression of desire which has to make do with the narrow route provided by the arbitrary signifier. Thus unconscious desire, unconscious meaning – lack of satisfaction – is produced and reproduced precisely through that repression.

Felman therefore argues that 'sexuality *is* rhetoric, since it essentially consists of ambiguity . . . Sexuality is the *division and divisiveness of meaning* . . . meaning *as* conflict' (1977a: 112). Unconscious desire is paradoxically produced by what divides it from direct knowledge of itself. It is this self-division – knowing unconscious meaning only through what contradicts it, the *Nom-du-Père* – that generates more unsatisfied desire and hence more signifiers. Sexuality (desire) is sense (meaning) misrecognizing itself. Ambiguity is inevitable because what we consciously think we mean does not match our unconscious desire – what *it* means.

What is interesting, then, is that Wilson reduces this conflictive, ambiguous meaning of sexuality to a univocal literal meaning. He excludes division. Freud postulated a traumatic primal scene in which the child witnesses an act of sexual intercourse, registers *sexual division*, and hence the possibility of its own division/castration. Unable to master what is seen, the child represses it. The ambiguity of *The Turn of the Screw* confronts the critics once again with a traumatic division of meaning. Felman thus writes of 'the primal scene of the text's meaning as division' (1977a: 113). The critics cannot master it, instead they repress it by offering a univocal interpretation. But the repressed returns: the critics act out the division of meaning even as they struggle against

it. Felman quotes a classic example of a critic saying: '[My] interpretation . . . has the virtue of *extreme inclusiveness* though I fear *there is no
room in it* for . . . Mr. Wilson'.[14] The claim to an inclusive interpretation
of *The Turn of the Screw* is contradicted by the exclusion of Wilson's
interpretation. What the critic thinks he means is different from what
he *act-ually* says. Contradiction, apparently banished from the text,
reappears in displaced form – acts itself out, unnoticed, in the critic's
self-contradictory claim. Just so the critical debate as a whole – the
struggle between the critics – acts out the conflict of meaning which it
seeks to deny.

Felman turns to speech act theory in theorizing this division and its
consequences. Specifically, she invokes the seminal work of J.L. Austin[15]
who tried to divide *performative* utterances such as 'I promise to marry
you' which 'accomplish an *act* through the very process of their enunciation' from *constative* utterances or '*statements* of fact' (Felman 1983: 15) –
statements such as 'The cat is on the mat'. While the latter may be
'logically true or false' the former 'cannot be either logically true or
false, but only successful or unsuccessful' (Felman 1983: 15–16). However, since 'constative utterances' can be seen as 'implicit performatives'
(1983: 17) (for instance, 'I assert that the cat is on the mat') it would
seem that speech is always an *act* – a performance – whose 'force of
utterance' (1983: 18) always exceeds any statement or meaning. Felman
refers to a 'referential residue . . . a performative excess' (1983: 81)
which, like the Real for Lacan, is only negatively evinced in that meaning 'misses' it (1983: 73–85).

The performative effect of enunciation may be to seduce us into thinking we grasp full meaning (a literal statement of fact) but the meaning
we grasp does not take account of its own differential process of production. We grasp the meaning of a speech act from within language – we
never achieve a transcendental position of knowledge 'outside' language
(Felman 1977a: 201). The unconscious 'knows'[16] but it is divided from
its own knowledge by the misrecognition of consciousness. Thus what
we consciously think we say only figures what we *act-ually* say – the act
of saying (the enunciation) involves more – an excess of force – over
what we consciously grasp as the meaning (the enounced) of our utterances. Our speech acts exceed our conscious grasp of them and our
attempts to close the gap – our resort to further signifiers – paradoxically only repeat (re-enact) the division in displaced terms. We do
not decode some final meaning: as speaking beings we are condemned
to use signs whose apparent *decoding* or reading is really only a further
encoding, the replacement of one set of signs by another.[17] So when we

read (interpret) stories, we do not reach a final meaning but instead *re-code them*, turn them 'into their own substitute and their own repetition' (Felman 1977a: 133). Thus Felman argues that in the critical contest over the meaning of *The Turn of the Screw*:

> Criticism, to use Austin's terminology, here consists not of a statement, but of a performance of the story of the text; its function is not *constative* but *performative*. Reading here becomes not the cognitive observation of the text's pluralistic meaning, but its 'acting out.'
>
> (Felman 1977a: 114–15)

Paradoxically, while the critics do not consciously master what the story means, they do act out its meaning: 'the truth of the text as its own contradiction' (1977a: 115). The critical conflict over the text dramatizes the very 'heterogeneity of meaning' (1977a: 113), the impossibility of pinning meaning down in some ultimate literal formulation. Our impulse to master the text attests to the seductive power of signs which, simultaneously, blinds us to their substitutive status as mere figures of unconscious meaning, which they negate. Thus, our so-called definitive interpretations and the debates they generate, act out, repeat, what we repress – 'meaning *as* division, meaning *as* conflict' (1977a: 112).

Thus, instead of undertaking the self-contradictory project of trying (finally) to decode the meaning of the story in terms of what can only be a further encoding, Felman seeks rather to practise the 'new way of reading' which Lacan finds in Freud. She seeks to 'investigate' the story's self-divided, ambiguous 'structure'. What she wants to explore is not *what* the story means but rather *how* that meaning perpetually eludes us, how it takes 'flight' down a chain of signifiers which, as mere substitutive, rhetorical, figures of unconscious desire, have the effect of perpetually both promising and deferring any access to final meaning (1977a: 119).

Examining first the prologue which frames the story of *The Turn of the Screw*, Felman shows how it divides the story from any originary self-presence, since it comes to us always already divided from itself by a performance of a reading. Language, which, as a substitutive mark, signifies the non-presence of what it stands for, must always already have preceded the events themselves for those events to have differentiated themselves for and from the interpreting mind.[18] The story is always already divided from itself then, *by a reading* – an interpretation – through which it is at once constituted and misapprehended. The inside and outside of the story thus become confused, since the inside comes to us on the outside – as a reading which makes the story *ex-centric* to itself. The story thus resembles the unconscious which is paradoxically constituted as *unconscious* by a reading in the substitutive terms of the *Nom-du-Père*. The *Nom-du-Père* produces the unconscious by negating incestuous desire and substituting for it. Further readings of the story thus only repeat the story of the 'constitutive loss' of its 'origin' (1977a: 122).

Since narration is always the *performance* of an interpretation, of a reading, the force of which exceeds its meaning, a story is paradoxically always preceded by its own repetition, by a repetition of its 'loss'. A story, like, indeed, the story of the unconscious, is always the story of its own 'loss' of 'its origin' – of the self-division inherent in the interpretative *act* (1977a: 122). The frame of *The Turn of the Screw* foregrounds this by featuring three narrators each of whom 'to relay the story, must first be a *receiver* of the story, a *reader* who at once records it and *interprets* it, simultaneously trying to make sense of it and *undergoing* it, as a lived experience . . . a *reading-effect*' (1977a: 124). It is the reading-effect, the force of the performance of a reading, in so far as it exceeds the meaning consciously grasped by the reader, which generates a re-performance of the interpretative act. This re-performance is another set of signs, which in their turn re-produce the reading-effect of a split between the mobile reading subject of the process of the enunciation and the fixed subject position with which we consciously identify in grasping meaning. Thus *The Turn of the Screw* is indeed like 'the story of the unconscious' which comes to us always already 'constitutively' divided from itself by a reading – a reading which is not in possession of itself, can never overcome its self-division – and which thus can only generate further readings which repeat the division, re-enact the story of the story's 'constitutive loss' of 'origin' (1977a: 122).

The story of *The Turn of the Screw* which involves an absent master, is aptly, then, never in a situation of mastering itself. Yet the story survives because of the transferential relation between the narrators. Each falls in love with a previous narrator – is seduced by the powerful effect of a reading-performance into the reading error of attributing authoritative self-presence to a mere sign of an absence (for example, Douglas is seduced by the fixed, idealized image of the governess that her reading produces – an image in the enounced that does not correspond to the governess as mobile subject of the enunciation). Douglas *wants* to be seduced because her image of authoritative self-possession mirrors back at him his own wished-for self-mastery. He is caught up in an imaginary, transferential relation to the sign as full of meaning. Seduced, as the governess is seduced by her own performance, Douglas, as a performer of more signs than his conscious interpretation comprehends, repeats the performance, gives a reading, and in his turn seduces the third narrator. Thus the story transfers itself from one performance, one set of signs, to another – always knowing more than it consciously knows – always thus divided from itself.

The story points indeed to its own linguistic status, since the manuscript of the story is copied and sent from narrator to narrator as a letter, asking for a total comprehension which both the writer's and reader's situation *within* language makes impossible. As Felman notes, 'a letter is the materialization of the absence of the beginning of a story' (1977a: 140). So this chain of letters, this story, itself involving the governess's failure to write a letter to the absent master about facts which she is not in possession of, is paradoxically generated by its own impossibility. The letters which constitute the story only materialize 'the absence of the beginning of' the 'story', the story's lack of self-possession, its failure to master, to *know* itself fully. Thus, Felman argues that:

> it is precisely *because* the letters *fail* to narrate, to construct a coherent, transparent story, that there is a story at all: there is a story *because* there is an unreadable, an unconscious. Narrative paradoxically, becomes possible to the precise extent that a story becomes *impossible* – that a story, precisely, 'won't tell.'
>
> (1977a: 143)

The governess, blind to her own transference – to the authority or self-presence she mistakenly grants to mere signs – seeks to master the ghosts which, like meaning, appear only in the form of their own negation, as signifiers of an absent presence (1977a: 150). Not surprisingly she ends up clasping a mere empty signifier, the corpse of a child. Critics, unconsciously seduced by the fictional authority of the signifiers which constitute the tale, have repeated her reading-error, and in seeking to master the story have only succeeded in re-enacting it, being mastered *by* it. They have produced yet more signifiers which only repeat the story's 'constitutive loss' of self-knowledge – its ineradicable ambiguity. The signified perpetually takes '*flight*'.

The *Turn of the Screw* was deliberately written to trap its readers;[19] not so *Mansfield Park*. Yet the latter has nevertheless generated 'heated critical debate' (Southam 1976: 27) and, as with *The Turn of the Screw*, its critics take sides, are divided, over its meaning. Some see Fanny as a true heroine who, guided by Edmund, acquires a fine moral sense and the capacity to judge properly. For these critics Fanny stands for principle, duty, self-knowledge and self-restraint and gets her just reward in marriage to the man she loves. But critics on the opposing side see Fanny as a 'prig-pharisee',[20] dull and self-righteous, and champion the Crawfords as lively, human and unjustly excluded from Mansfield.

Yet when we review the critical debate it does indeed bear an uncanny resemblance to the conflict within the novel – as though the latter, far from being resolved, had merely displaced itself, re-enacted itself, on the critical scene. For example, key ideas in the novel, couched in particular terms and structuring the way one group of characters views another, are repeated in the way one set of critics sees its opponents. Thus Fanny's adverse judgement of those in the novel who follow their instincts and do not recognize the need to govern individual inclination in the interests of general social good is repeated by Lionel Trilling in *his* opposition to *critics* who do not appreciate Austen's advocacy of 'constraint', critics who manifest 'the biological force of the resistance which certain temperaments offer to the idea of society as a limiting condition of the individual spirit' (Trilling 1955: 210).

The related idea in the novel, that a proper unselfishness requires that individual inclinations be subordinated to an authoritative code of principled and therefore scrupulously discriminating judgement, is repeated by David Lodge, when, in spite of his own usual 'instinctive moral preferences' (Lodge 1988: 94) and those of some of the novel's more hostile critics he concludes his analysis of *Mansfield Park* with the argument that Austen 'puts every generation of readers to school . . . in learning her own subtle and exact vocabulary of discrimination and evaluation', and adds authoritatively, thereby excluding critics who disagree, 'we submit to the authority of her vision' (Lodge 1988: 113).

The difficulty of making proper moral interpretations and the rejection of those characters who fail in this respect, are echoed in Margaret Kirkham's dismissal of superficial *readers* of *Mansfield Park*:

> Austen created in her, [Fanny] a heroine whom the unwary might take for something like the Rousseauist ideal of the perfect woman, but she expects her more discerning readers to see through it, and gives them a good many indications that this is not a proper reading.
>
> (Kirkham 1983: 104)

The triumph of moral integrity in the novel over selfish and inconstant worldliness, through principled adherence to a traditional code, is echoed in Tony Tanner's dismissal of hostile critics of the novel:

In a more general way the book does seem, as some critics have noted, to speak for repression and negation, fixity and enclosure, the timidity of caution and routine opposed to the exhilaration of risk and change. But if we are sympathetic to the symbolic implications of the world of the book we can see that, at its most profound, it is a book about the difficulty of preserving true moral consciousness amid the selfish manoeuvring and jostling of society.

(*MP*, 31)

Moreover, it would seem that when critics outlaw as wrong a key positional term or interpretative stance in the novel, it has an uncanny way of returning (like the repressed) in the very terms they adopt to *defeat* their opponents. Thus Reginald Farrer, who sides with Mary Crawford *against* Fanny – 'fiction holds no heroine more repulsive in her cast-iron self-righteousness' (Southam 1985, 2: 264) – nevertheless uses against Fanny and against Jane Austen and her critical supporters, the very argument employed against Mary Crawford in the novel. It is not Mary but Jane Austen who has been led astray by her associates. Edmund argues that Mary does not have 'a cruel nature', rather, in her response to Maria's elopement, she speaks simply 'as she had been used to hear others speak . . . Her's are faults of principle . . . of . . . a corrupted, vitiated mind' (*MP*, 442). Contesting this interpretation of Mary, excluding it as a misreading, Farrer nevertheless uses precisely the argument of a good 'nature', 'vitiated' by bad associates to condemn Austen:

> *Mansfield Park* is *vitiated* throughout by a radical dishonesty, that was certainly not in its author's own nature. One can almost hear the clerical relations urging 'dear Jane' to devote her 'undoubted talent to the cause of righteousness.'
> (Southam 1985, 2: 262–3; emphasis added)

Rejected as a reading *of* Mary, the idea of a tragically 'vitiated' nature returns as a reading of her first readers (Edmund and Austen as his supporting narrator), and is used to reject *them*:

> [Austen's] purpose of edification, being not her own, is always at cross-purposes with her unprompted joy in creation . . . this dualism of motive destroys not only the unity of the book, but its sincerity.
> (Southam 1985, 2: 263)

> Had it not been for its *vitiating* purpose . . . *Mansfield Park* would
> have taken highest rank.
>
> (Southam 1985, 2: 265; emphasis added)

Exactly the same return of the repressed, return of what is rejected from
the novel in an analysis of what is wrong with its readers, marks
Kingsley Amis's interpretation of *Mansfield Park*. Mary is misread; not
she but her misreader – Austen herself – is morally 'corrupted' (Amis
1957: 40).

With *Mansfield Park*, as with *The Turn of the Screw*, it would seem
then to be the case that: 'The scene of the critical debate is thus a *repetition*
of the scene dramatised in the text. The critical interpretation . . . not
only elucidates the text but also reproduces it dramatically, unwittingly
participates in it' (Felman 1977a: 101).

Significantly, what none of these critics can countenance is duality.
Even if it implies rejection of the book, a 'proper' reading must be
found. But, as Felman notes, when critics resist division it has a way of
returning in their own interpretations: 'Contradiction reappears with
ironical tenacity in the very words used to banish it' (1977a: 114). Thus,
when Lionel Trilling seeks to show us that the novel 'undertakes to . . .
affirm literalness' (Trilling 1955: 208), and 'discovers in principle the
path to the wholeness of the self which is peace' (Trilling 1955: 230), he
nevertheless does so by a resort to rhetoric, by paradox:

> That the self may destroy the self by the very energies that define
> its being, that the self may be preserved by the negation of its own
> energies . . . makes a paradox, makes an irony, that catches our
> imagination.
>
> (Trilling 1955: 218)

The very critic who perspicaciously notes that *Mansfield Park* uses
'irony' to defeat 'irony' (Trilling 1955: 224) does not notice the self-
contradictory force of this rhetorical ploy and himself repeats it to affirm
the 'wholeness' of the self when directed by principle. Not surprisingly,
and like the critics of *The Turn of the Screw*, Trilling can but end up
affirming 'contradiction in the very act of denying its existence in the
text' (Felman 1977a: 114). The split self, divided by contesting conscious and unconscious readings, enacts its return in the very sentence
that succeeds his triumphant affirmation of 'wholeness':

> [*Mansfield Park*] discovers in principle the path to the wholeness of
> the self which is peace. When we have exhausted our anger at the
> offense which *Mansfield Park* offers to our conscious pieties, we

find it possible to perceive how intimately it speaks to our secret inexpressible hopes.

(Trilling 1955: 230)

What Felman notes about criticism of *The Turn of the Screw*, equally proves to be the case with *Mansfield Park*:

Criticism . . . here consists not of a statement, but of a performance of the story of the text; its function not *constative* but *performative*. Reading here becomes not the cognitive observation of the text's pluralistic meaning, but its 'acting out.'

(Felman 1977a: 115)

Far from disheartening us however, this unconscious acting out of repressed textual contradiction in the contesting and self-contradictory criticism that *Mansfield Park* has engendered, might prove instructive. It might precisely be viewed as a telling performance, rather than a cognitive grasp, *of the divided structure of meaning itself*. The story's structure is such that the textual performance or enunciation which produces an effect of knowledge or meaning in the enounced will always fail to be grasped by that conscious meaning. We cannot master a chain of signifiers, a *process* of signification (of *making* meaning) with the illusion of fixed meaning, of knowledge, which such a process engenders as one of its effects. As Paul de Man writes: 'any speech act produces an excess of cognition, but it can never hope to know the process of its own production . . . there is never enough knowledge available to account adequately for the delusion of knowing' (de Man 1979: 300).

Thus we cannot grasp the mobile subject of the enunciation, a subject in process down a chain of signifiers, from the fixed subject position produced in the enounced. The critic who finds her/his mastery (unified self) reflected in the illusion of full meaning that the enounced offers, is thereby divided from the critic as re-writer of the text, re-performer of its process of enunciation in the act of interpreting it. The critic as conscious master of meaning cannot but be divided from the unconscious subject of the differential process of signification that produces the pleasing illusion of mastery. As Felman argues: 'The necessity of shutting one's eyes actively partakes, indeed, of the very act of seeing, knowing, reading' (1977a: 167).

However, if we learn Freud's lesson of 'a new way of reading' and instead of attempting to grasp a final transcendental signified, follow instead the endless 'flight' of meaning down the chain of signifiers that constitutes *Mansfield Park*, then, as Felman puts it, we may begin to push 'thought beyond the limit of its self-possession' (1987: 96), learn something about our own self-division as readers, and about 'the necessity and the rhetorical functioning of the textual ambiguity' (1977a: 119).

Starting then, as Felman does, with the story's frame – its framing narrative discourse – it is apparent that this narrative of a search for *proper* meaning itself comes to us not as some final authoritative self-present meaning *but as simply another reading of the story's content* which is thus always already different from itself. The very opening of *Mansfield Park* introduces us to this ongoing process of meaning's 'flight' and self-division:

> About thirty years ago, Miss Maria Ward of Huntingdon, with only seven thousand pounds, had the good luck to captivate Sir Thomas Bertram, of Mansfield Park . . . All Huntingdon exclaimed on the greatness of the match, and her uncle, the lawyer, himself, allowed her to be at least three thousand pounds short of any equitable claim to it.
>
> (*MP*, 41)

If 'good luck' and 'captivate' sound like summary repetitions of conventional (and thus not, perhaps, very subtle) responses to such a marriage, then this impression is confirmed by the second sentence, 'All Huntingdon exclaimed . . .'. The narrative discourse is repeating other readings, echoing other voices. The narrative discourse replaces one set of signs – already a reading of the story – with another. Like *The Turn of the Screw*, the 'story . . . originates in a frame through which it frames itself into losing its own origin' (Felman 1977a: 122). The story comes to us through a reading of previous readings, of previous signifiers, themselves differential substitutes for an always already absent presence. Since, as we have seen Felman argue, a signifier 'is the materialization of the absence of the beginning of a story' (1977a: 140) the beginning of the story of *Mansfield Park* seems to be constituted by its own 'loss' (1977a: 122).

The story, like that of the unconscious, comes to us only exteriorized from, 'ex-centric' to, itself, in a reading which divides it from its own self-presence (Felman 1977a: 123–4). The narrator's voice is an 'alien' one, re-counting '*the other*' (already a reading or readings of the story) '*in the other*' (in language) (1977a: 125). The narrator's voice only divides the story further from itself. As a voice it is divided from what it re-counts, not only by time ('About thirty years ago'), but also by the ongoing process of enunciation, its *own performance* of a reading which fails to master itself. The 'reading-effect' of the enunciation of the opening lines is in excess of any meaning we try to grasp. Is such a marriage a fortunate one or is 'good luck' to be taken ironically as its opposite? Are such fortunate marriages the result of 'luck' rather than desert? Our own re-performance of the narrator's 'act of *reading*' (Felman 1977a: 126) reproduces the split between performance and meaning. Grasping a meaning as authoritative involves the exclusion of other possible meanings. Apparent mastery of meaning is always blind mastery – like Sir Thomas's.

The narrative discourse, in apparently decoding, only further encodes – produces the story 'as its' own 'substitute' and its 'own repetition' (1977a: 133). The effect of a split that we undergo between our ongoing experience of the performance of the story and the interpretations we make has, paradoxically, the further effect of generating more signs, more interpretations in an attempt to 'catch up' (Wright 1984: 113) with, to fix, the story in presence-to-itself. The narrative of *Mansfield Park* takes us once again on the characters' search for proper meaning and, though the end of the novel might seem to mark the success of the search, the fierceness of the subsequent critical debate, the conflicting re-readings (which are also re-writings) of the story, suggests otherwise. This tale of a failure of mastery reproduces itself in repeated failures of mastery – the final meaning of *Mansfield Park* eludes us. While we seek to master the text it masters us – holds us – even down to the 1990s, with the ever elusive promise of proper and final meaning.

If no one masters the story, how, then, has it survived? The answer would seem to be by the power of its rhetoric to seduce us with the promise of proper meaning. Seduced by the apparent authority of the narrative and its authorial narrator, we transfer onto the text as 'the subject presumed to know'. If transference according to Lacan is the enactment of unconscious desire, is 'love . . . addressed to knowledge', then we are, as readers, indeed acting out an old, unconscious story. We are repeating a demand for wholeness of meaning – addressed to a signifier, which, as a signifier, censors or negates that demand. We repeat in our relation to the text an older conflict between our desire for imaginary oneness with the (m)other and our subjection to the enforced substitution of the *Nom-du-Père*. Unwittingly we act out our desire in the reading process as we are 'reading not literally but rhetorically' (Felman 1977a: 137). The conscious meanings we grasp substitute for unconscious meaning, unconscious desire which, unsatisfied, moves on down the chains of signifiers – generating more transference, more writing, more critical re-readings of *Mansfield Park*.

We can see this process of transference prefigured and reflected upon critically (shown to involve a reading-error, a misattribution of authority) in the story itself. The first Fanny Price transfers her affections onto Mr Price. Disappointed, his authority proving 'illusory' (Felman 1977a: 131), she transfers her demands to Sir Thomas – who functions in the story like the *Nom-du-Père*, the very figure of the law: ' "Advise" was his word, but it was the advice of absolute power' (*MP*, 285). Yet rather than offering 'absolute' satisfaction, his word only defers it. Mrs Price receives 'advice', 'money and baby-linen' and 'letters' (*MP*, 43) but she also suffers loss and separation and has to submit to not entirely satisfactory substitution. Not she, but significantly, her namesake – our Fanny Price – (a kind of displaced signifier of her mother's desire) is received into the patriarchal domain of Mansfield Park, parted from her (m)other. Not surprisingly then, the first chapter ends on a note of dissatisfaction: 'Poor woman! she probably thought change of air might agree with many of her children' (*MP*, 48).

Transference continues with the second Fanny Price. After the kind ministrations of her cousin Edmund: 'Fanny, with all her faults of ignorance and timidity, was fixed at Mansfield Park, and learning to *transfer* in its favour much of her attachment to her former home, grew up there not unhappily' (*MP*, 56; emphasis added). Here again, we might note, substitution leaves a residue of desire, 'much' but not all of Fanny's love is transferred. There is a residue of unsatisfied desire, generating more signs – the ongoing narrative.

It is onto Edmund in particular that Fanny transfers as 'subject presumed to know'. Edmund substitutes at Mansfield for her brother William, who at home in Portsmouth had been 'her constant companion and friend; her advocate with her mother' (*MP*, 52). The 'pain . . . of the separation' (*MP*, 364) from her first home and from William, itself repeating the pain of an earlier experienced alienation from her mother (*MP*, 366), is assuaged by transference onto Edmund who now serves in William's place, as her 'advocate' and friend; but significantly this substitution implies division: 'she loved him better than any body in the world except William; her heart was divided between the two' (*MP*, 57). Fanny's love for Edmund is, unwittingly, a mere figure of (a rhetorical substitution for) an earlier, lost love.

Fanny and Edmund enter into a mutual mirroring relationship. At one point Mary Crawford tells Fanny (referring to Edmund): 'You *have* a look of *his* sometimes' (*MP*, 188). Mary wants Fanny at this point to play Anhalt (Edmund's part in *Lovers' Vows*) to her own Amelia. Yet once again the text returns difference: 'Fanny joined in with all the modest feeling which the idea of representing Edmund was so strongly calculated to inspire; but with looks and voice so truly feminine, as to be no very good picture of a man' (*MP*, 189). Edmund at an early stage finds Fanny 'an interesting object' (*MP*, 53) and by the time of the Crawfords' arrival: 'Having formed her mind and gained her affections, he had a good chance of her thinking like him' (*MP*, 95). At the end of the novel she is 'dearer by all his own importance with her than any one else at Mansfield' (*MP*, 454).

Like psychoanalytical transference the relationship between Fanny and Edmund is 'primarily discursive and linguistic' (Felman 1977a: 130), a 'situation of dialogue and of *interlocution*' (1977a: 130). Douglas, the second narrator of *The Turn of the Screw*, 'charmed by the governess . . . becomes narcissistically infatuated' with her 'so that he *adds faith* . . . to the authority of her idealized mirror-image of herself' (1977a: 131) – her image in the enounced. So, too, Fanny and Edmund's relationship is one where each is asked to confirm the other's *integrity*. Hence their frequent dialogues, each seeking the other's confirmation of correct behaviour and proper judgement. Thus when Edmund decides to participate in the play he seeks Fanny's approval: 'Give me your approbation . . . I am not comfortable without it' (*MP*, 176). At the end of the novel Edmund, knowing Fanny's 'mind' has been 'in so great a degree formed by his care' (*MP*, 454), can propose with 'no fears from opposition of taste, no need of drawing new hopes of happiness from dissimilarity of temper' (*MP*, 455). But this state of narcissistic integrity is only achieved by the elision of difference, by the exclusion of those (the Crawfords, Maria, Mrs Norris) who see and act differently.

The authority attributed to the other by transferential love is illusory. Each thinks the other holds the key to authoritative meaning. But this is really the interlocutor's 'own story as unknown' (Felman 1977a: 135). The other 'does not know *what* it knows' (Felman 1987: 92) – can only return division. What the mutual admiration of transference occludes is each subject's *lack* of self-mastery – the castrating *division* which cannot be faced, between conscious meaning and unconscious desire. This is why in psychoanalytical transference the analyst must avoid this mutuality, remain aloof in order to disconfirm it.

In the case of Fanny and Edmund it is clear that unconscious desire interferes in conscious judgement, they see and interpret with eyes suffused with love, they are 'reading not literally but rhetorically' (1977a: 137). Fanny, for example, cannot give her 'approbation' to Edmund's acting but just as Edmund's judgement of propriety here is

coloured by his infatuation with Mary Crawford, so Fanny's inten-
tionally principled opposition is coloured by her jealousy of Mary and her
love for, and faith in, Edmund. Edmund is not blamed: 'Alas! it was all
Miss Crawford's doing' (MP, 177). If transference 'is the acting-out of
the reality of the unconscious', then Edmund and Fanny are each here
acting out what they do not understand but are nevertheless troubled
by – their 'own' unconscious 'story as *unknown*'. Their authority as
readers is shown, like the governess's in *The Turn of the Screw*, to be
'itself a fiction' (1977a: 131).

Thus, again, when Mary sends a message that she hopes to take part in
the play, the narrator tells us that Edmund manages, 'with the ingenuity
of love, to dwell more on the obliging, accommodating purport of the
message than on anything else' (MP, 154). This gap between performance and the meaning attributed to it is again noted in the case of
Fanny. When she tries to reject Crawford's addresses we are told:
'Fanny knew her own meaning, but was no judge of her own manner'
(MP, 326). Indeed the authority of her reading of others is frequently
undercut by the narrator. For example, she disputes Fanny's belief that
Mary's 'darkened' mind would remain unenlightened even after marriage to Edmund (MP, 362). Similarly, Fanny's conviction that she
could never love Crawford is undermined in the last chapter when we are
told: 'Would he have persevered . . . Fanny must have been his reward'
(MP, 451).

The narrative discourse constantly points in this way to the ironic gap
between what the characters perform (do, see, feel) and their conscious
understanding of their own performance, but it, too, is troubled by the
same gap. Paul de Man has argued that 'rhetoric' when viewed 'as a
persuasion . . . is performative, but when considered as a system of
tropes, it deconstructs its own performance' (de Man 1979: 131; quoted
in Felman 1985: 25). The narrative discourse may persuade us at the end
of a mutually satisfying love between Fanny and Edmund, where signifier
and signified seem virtually to mirror one another, and which fully meets
with Sir Thomas's approval. Ironically, however, we are also reminded
that this is the very opposite of Sir Thomas's 'early opinion on the subject'
(MP, 455). This reminder takes us back to the first chapter where Sir
Thomas has allowed himself to be persuaded by Mrs Norris that, 'brought
up . . . like brothers and sisters', any match between the cousins would
be 'morally impossible' (MP, 44). Overtones of incest thus threaten the
lawfulness of the happy ending and indeed to the very last chapter Fanny
and Edmund's 'brotherly' and 'sisterly' relations are repeatedly mentioned.[21] Yet of course we know that they are not brother and sister,

that this ascription is only figurative. The dream which William shares with Fanny on their trip to Portsmouth, of a life together in a 'cottage' (*MP*, 369) is substituted for by Fanny's life in the parsonage with Edmund. The persuasiveness of the happy ending depends on an incestuous oneness which is lawful because it involves its own negation – is only figurative. Apparent oneness depends on difference, on substitution and loss.

Difference is indeed foregrounded by the narrator's conclusion of this paragraph with an ironic reflection on the disparity, the self-difference implicit in the 'contrast . . . between the plans and decisions of mortals' (*MP*, 455). Yet the narrative discourse immediately goes on to overlook the difference in the next paragraph by arguing that intention is matched by reward. Sir Thomas's 'kindness' to Fanny is repaid: 'His liberality had a rich repayment, and the general goodness of his intentions by her, deserved it' (*MP*, 456). Yet again an ironic gap immediately opens up, difference returns in that the 'mutual attachment' between Fanny and Sir Thomas and Fanny's marriage to his son creates a hole in arrangements at Mansfield. Susan has to 'supply' Fanny's 'place' with Lady Bertram. She becomes her '*substitute*' and (through transference) 'perhaps, the most beloved of the two' (*MP*, 456; emphasis added).

The statements of the narrative discourse which seeks to persuade us of oneness are thus constantly troubled by a difference which returns and which foregrounds not fullness but lack, and the need for figurative substitution. Fanny substitutes for Maria as 'the daughter' Sir Thomas 'wanted' (*MP*, 456). In a repetition of this movement of blind substitution, Susan in turn replaces Fanny. What the novel gives with one hand it takes away with the other. Decoding turns out to be only a further encoding, the narrative turns out to be, through a transferential 'love-relation' which overlooks difference, its 'own substitute' and 'its own repetition' (Felman 1977a: 133). Sir Thomas's readiness to exclude 'part of himself' (*MP*, 450) in Mrs Norris is repeated in the narrator's exclusion of 'guilt and misery' (*MP*, 446) to achieve the effect of a happy ending. Satisfaction is achieved only at the price of its own contradiction. Transference onto a substitute and the repression of difference it involves, are constantly held up for attention even as we are seduced by the suasive force of the novel's rhetoric. The novel deconstructs any authoritative finality in its own conclusion – at once concealing and revealing its mere substitutive status.

There is, then, a fantasy of wholeness, of mastery and integrity, consistently in play in *Mansfield Park* which is just as consistently undercut. In fact the whole novel manifests itself as a hole, revealed and occluded by letters. It offers the story in otherness to itself, in the substitutive form of language – linguistic signs – material attestations of the absence of what is alluded to. *Mansfield Park* is a letter or, rather, a chain of letters, addressed to us, its readers, but our very resort to critical accounts of the text reveals the 'unreadable' status of the letter, its ultimate impenetrability (1977a: 142). Its signified takes 'flight' down a chain of critical substitutions, signs substituting for and repeating previous signs. Thus *Mansfield Park* proves like *The Turn of the Screw* to be comparable to 'the unconscious [which] also governs an entire (hi)story . . . without ever letting itself be penetrated or understood' (1977a: 142).

Moreover, *Mansfield Park* is also, like *The Turn of the Screw*, a story *of* letters, letters which figure the figural status of the text itself. What sets the narrative going is after all, precisely, an exchange of letters between Mrs Price and her family which divides her from it, and her subsequent submissive letter, though it effects a reconciliation, does not overcome the separation. That letters separate, that they imply absence and loss, is repeatedly emphasized in the narrative. When Fanny, exiled from Mansfield at Portsmouth, receives a letter from Mary Crawford, the narrator remarks that 'it connected her with the absent' (*MP*, 387). Letters are reminders of what has been lost in separation but they fail to overcome separation itself. The *Nom-du-Père* bars what it signifies even as it holds out the promise of satisfaction. Thus when Mary writes a warning note about Henry's flirtation, 'it was impossible for Fanny to understand much of this strange letter' (*MP*, 426).

Most significant in this respect are the plays. Many plays are alluded to in the novel[22] but our knowledge of them, like knowledge of the unconscious, significantly remains indirect. *Lovers' Vows*, for example, for all its prominence, never appears directly as a text in the novel. Its effects, however, are manifest in the desires it excites, the discord, division, dissatisfaction, alienation it provokes, and the interference it constitutes in the peace of Mansfield. Critics such as Isobel Armstrong have pointed to its potential for 'radical critique' (Armstrong 1988: 99) of the world of Mansfield. She notes that 'the play speaks openly of what the novel can allude to only indirectly – illegitimacy, the sexual independence of women in marriage choice, the profligacy of the upper classes, the duties of fathers, the poor and the depredations of war' (Armstrong 1988: 67). Characters, we might argue, transfer onto the 'letter' of the play desires of which they remain quite unaware. As Armstrong also notes, for example, Henry's choice of the part of devoted son to Maria as his victimized mother is obviously a deliberate one, designed to allow close contact between them. Yet it has a further revealing appropriateness which neither he nor any of the other characters grasps. Henry acts out the seduction of his mother which, as Armstrong suggests, 'brings out the latent oedipal element in' the 'compulsive womanizing' of this orphaned son (1988: 71). *As You Like It*, which, Armstrong points out, forms a subtext to the Sotherton episode but is never directly mentioned in the novel (1988: 63), shows, yet more clearly, the characters unconsciously repeating a text which, as the very letter of their desire, remains incomprehensible to them, even as they act it out.

It is the way the novel thus foregrounds the unreadable nature of desire and the way it eludes the authority of the *Nom-du-Père*, the law of the absent father – so well figured by the absent Sir Thomas – that I want to focus on in my argument here. In unwittingly repeating *As You Like It* and in failing to grasp much of the potentially subversive force of their rehearsal of *Lovers' Vows*, the characters figure consciousness's relation to unconscious desire. The plays imply more about the characters than, consciously, they either can or want to understand. The illusion of mastery depends on *not* knowing, on repressing the castrating knowledge of desire, of the self-division that the *ex-istence* of the unconscious implies. Indeed, there is a danger in specifying what the characters unconsciously desire, as Armstrong does, because desire itself is ultimately not for any one thing in particular but a force of 'lacking' (Felman 1987: 83) fired by the inability of conscious knowledge to master an unconscious knowledge which can manifest itself only in letters which negate it – hence the mobility of desire in *Mansfield Park* as it transfers from one unsatisfactory letter to another, creating the story but eluding any final conscious meaning we try to assign to it. To aspire to mastery, then, is paradoxically an incitement to blindness.

Indeed, the young people's blindness to their own desires only repeats that of the 'master' (*MP*, 365) of Mansfield. Sir Thomas is shown to be a divided character, motivated by 'pride' in addition to 'principle' (*MP*, 41) in the very first paragraph of the novel. His pride makes him susceptible to the blandishments of Mrs Norris and blind to the passions of his children. The fact that his promised 'return' from Antigua is 'unwelcome' to his daughters (*MP*, 134) and that Mrs Norris sees a chance for her own increased importance in the possibility of his death (*MP*, 68) is a comic deflation (though significantly hidden from him) of his delusions of mastery.

Sir Thomas is blind to the effects of his own behaviour on his daughters, and thus unaware of the limited nature of their education. Significantly, he 'did not *know what was wanting*, because . . . the reserve of his manner repressed all the flow of their spirits before him' (*MP*, 55; emphasis added). When Sir Thomas leaves for Antigua we learn that since 'he had never seemed the friend of [his daughters'] pleasures' they feel on his departure 'relieved . . . from all restraint; and without aiming at one gratification that would probably have been forbidden by Sir Thomas, they felt themselves immediately at their own disposal' (*MP*, 66). His daughters are capable of feeling freed from 'restraint' but they are no more capable than he is of mastering or fully comprehending their own desire.

Instead of mastering desire Sir Thomas blindly acts it out. His actions when he returns from Antigua are significant in this respect. What particularly disturbs Sir Thomas about the play is that it implies that his family was not centred on him in his absence. His reaction to the castrating recognition that he has not been master in his own house is 'to try to . . . forget how much he had been forgotten himself as soon as he could, after the house had been cleared of every object enforcing the remembrance' (*MP*, 203). He hurries to 'wipe away every outward memento of what had been, even to the destruction of every unbound copy of "Lovers' Vows" in the house, for he was burning all that met his eye' (*MP*, 206). This foreshadows, of course, what he does at the end of the novel. It is not the specific desires of his family as much as the very *ex-istence* of desires of which he is not master that disturbs Sir Thomas and leads to his attempt to exclude what both excites and testifies to them. But to refuse to recognize the very ex-istence of desire is to be all the more powerfully affected – mastered – *by* it. Desire, repressed, breaks out again when Maria runs away with Crawford.

Freud refers to the insistence of desire manifested in the compulsion to repeat, as a 'spell' (Freud 1953–74, 10: 122) and, as we have seen, a reader of *Mansfield Park* writes of being 'spell-bound' by the book. When Yates speaks of the preparations for acting *Lovers' Vows* at Ecclesford we are told that the topic was 'bewitching' (*MP*, 147). Significantly, the characters' own self-division, unacknowledged, manifests itself in the very power that the signifier exercises over them. Letters exert a spell – a power to hold us beyond our conscious control – because they speak to the unconscious as a reader; they offer a chance for disguised representation of unconscious desire. Lady Bertram, for example, 'from want of other employment' and with Sir Thomas preoccupied with Parliamentary duties, has become 'addicted to letter writing' (*MP*, 415), virtually empty letters we are told, but that is the point. It is the insistence of desire whose ex-istence is not to be admitted which impels a resort to letters, however vacuous. Again, when Crawford reads parts of *Henry VIII*, Fanny is held by an 'attraction' in spite of herself, till 'the book was closed, and the charm was broken' (*MP*, 335). She is again held by his discussion of preaching with Edmund; yet, instead of exploring the implications of her own lack of self-possession in this episode, ironically all she can register consciously is *Henry*'s lack of self-knowledge and *his* inconstancy (*MP*, 340).

Fanny's education has taught her to believe in the wholeness of the sign, in proper meaning. 'I ought to believe you to be right' (*MP*, 61) she tells Edmund on an earlier occasion. When faced with self-division, with contrary desires, 'she was not left to weigh and decide between opposite inclinations . . . She had a rule to apply to, which settled every thing' (*MP*, 425). Fanny's belief in proper meaning makes her intolerant, like Sir Thomas, of that which attests to division and difference – in herself as well as others. Having learnt to read the world in Mansfield's terms she is alienated from her own home by its difference. Experiencing 'the ceaseless tumult' of Portsmouth, 'she could think of nothing but Mansfield' (*MP*, 384). Though Mansfield has confronted her with 'the pains of tyranny, of ridicule, and neglect' (*MP*, 173), she is capable by the end of the book of 'striking out' these 'other senses' (Felman 1977a: 173) so that it appears 'thoroughly perfect in her eyes' (*MP*, 457).

It is this inability to confront division, above all self-division, that makes for the strength of Edmund's rejection of Mary. She does not think like him; she sees as 'folly' (*MP*, 440) what he sees as 'crime' (*MP*, 443). Unable to countenance more than one reading of the situation, determined to fix signifer to signified in an assumption of mastery, Edmund can only hope 'that she might soon learn to think more justly' and acquire self-knowledge (*MP*, 444). Ironically, the very limits of his own self-knowledge – of his own self-mastery – are immediately evinced by his professed certainty that he will never be able to attach himself to another woman (*MP*, 447). We soon learn of the transfer of his affections to Fanny. She who, unlike Mary, shows no 'dissimilarity' (*MP*, 455) to himself, returns him an image of his own (imaginary) integrity. That the very opposite has been proved, that his lack of self-mastery has manifested itself in 'the cure of unconquerable passions, and the transfer of unchanging attachments' (*MP*, 454), is underlined by the textual irony here.

The return of difference in the text is marked in the last chapter. The 'conviction of his own errors' (*MP*, 447) does not affect the way Sir Thomas behaves. He rejoices at the departure of Mrs Norris, although 'she seemed a part of himself' (*MP*, 450). This is precisely what Edmund says earlier of the Crawfords, likewise excluded from Mansfield at the conclusion: 'they seem to be part of ourselves' (*MP*, 211). Sir Thomas deals with the difference which seems part of himself, like Edmund, by repressing it. Realizing that Mrs Norris thinks differently from himself, he is glad to lose sight of her.

But the very difference he seeks to exclude, for example by substituting Fanny for Maria as 'the daughter that he wanted' (*MP*, 456) and exiling the latter to 'another country – remote and private' (*MP*, 450), returns unnoticed in himself. 'Sick', we are told, 'of ambitious and mercenary connections, *prizing* more and more the *sterling* good of principle and temper, and chiefly anxious to bind by the strongest *securities* all that remained to him of domestic felicity . . .', he has 'the high sense of having realized a great *acquisition* in the promise of Fanny for a daughter' (*MP*, 455; emphasis added). The very sentence which tells us of Sir Thomas's rejection of 'mercenary' aims, exhibits their return in its language. Displaced onto virtuous intentions (and therefore 'covered' from conscious censorship like unconscious wishes in a dream), Sir Thomas's financial ambitions return to divide, from its own integrity, the very language of principle. All the words emphasized above show how blinded he is to the persistence of his own mercenary desires. His position as master is indeed but a fiction. Desire eludes conscious knowledge yet acts out its own return.

The ironic force of the textual performance, indeed, constantly outwits any attempt to master it in a statement. Like judgement *within* the story, any attempt to master the story as a whole, to 'demystify and judge it, locate it in the Other without oneself participating in it' (Felman 1977a: 200) proves fruitless; the 'error' of attempted mastery, as Felman points out, is to believe that 'the reader could indeed know *where* he is, what his place is and what his position is with respect to the literary language which itself, as such, does not know what it knows' (1977a: 201).

Yet the very elision of sexual difference in this sentence might prompt us to note that Felman's attempt to adopt what Lacan sees as Freud's 'new way of reading', with its attention to excluded differences, cannot itself avoid the exclusion of difference. When it comes to language Felman is as much analysand as analyst – blind to her own blindness. An argument which Felman would no doubt accept, since she suggests that the literary critic occupies precisely this divided position – at once analyst and patient – in relation to the literary text (Felman 1977b: 7). Nevertheless, her article on *The Turn of the Screw* omits consideration of the historical specificity both of the discourses in the story and of the critical discourses which attempt to master it. Highly significant differences are thus excluded.

A brief comparison with Isobel Armstrong's recent book on *Mansfield Park* brings this out. Armstrong, herself, like Felman, drawing on poststructuralist work, also opposes the idea of a single correct reading, (Armstrong 1988: 98). Rather, she shows how both the novel's historically specific discourses and the discourses to which they are intertextually related (for example, literary, political, religious discourses in play in the period) mutually reflect on, interrogate, and contest one another. Thus her reading, too, looks for questions not answers.

Yet Armstrong argues that 'simply to say that a text is fundamentally contradictory and leave it at that, [is] another form of mastery' (1988: 98). She calls instead for 'rational debate': 'There will always be contested areas in complex texts and that is why readings will always be contested. By clarifying the way in which problems are configured and exposed, however, one provides grounds for rational debate' (Armstrong, 1988: 99). Armstrong's historically specific reading practice is valuable and important, but does not, I think, invalidate Felman's practice as literary critic. Felman herself argues against a 'post-Nietzschean' philosophy 'which *believes it knows it does not know*', and argues instead that Freud's and Lacan's conception of the unconscious is indebted to 'literary knowledge' which '*knows it knows but does not know the meaning of its knowledge*, does not know *what* it knows' (Felman 1987: 92). Although Armstrong draws on psychoanalysis in her reading, her faith in 'rational debate' and the argument that 'contested areas' in 'texts' account for 'contested readings' seems to overlook the very radical nature of the reading lesson Freud derived from his discovery of the unconscious.

Felman defines 'what constitutes the radicality of the Freudian unconscious' as consisting in the conception of it as 'not simply *opposed* to consciousness' but as 'something other' which 'speaks . . . *from within* the speech of consciousness, which it subverts. It implies 'the radical castration of the mastery of consciousness, which turns out to be forever incomplete, illusory, and self-deceptive' (Felman 1987: 57). From this perspective, 'rational debate' itself can never be other than self-deluded; which, while it is not an argument for abandoning it, *is* an argument for recognizing its limitations. The acknowledgement of conscious meaning *or meanings*, can *never* master the performance of a text which, as a material process of differentiation, itself generates those meanings. The 'residue', the performative '*excess* of utterance with respect to statement' (1987: 79) negatively attests to the Real which meaning always 'misses' (1987: 82–3) and which has the effect of generating more performances.

By ignoring historical difference, Felman foregrounds both the persistence of critical attempts at mastering the meaning of *The Turn of the Screw* and the persistent return of repressed textual differences in this criticism. Thus she shows how our very conception of what we are doing when we read a text needs to be rethought. This has implications not only for how we read *Mansfield Park* but also for teaching. The teacher, like the psychoanalyst, far from being master of the knowledge she/he seeks to convey, is always partially blind, always also a 'student' (Felman 1987: 88) of what she/he teaches: 'passing on understanding that does not fully understand what it understands' (1987: 96).

In the dialogue between teacher and student, or between one critic and another, over a text such as *Mansfield Park*, a knowledge emerges in 'the Other' (1987: 56), in language, which is never fully in possession of itself, which can never be consciously, *rationally*, mastered. It is not simply that *Mansfield Park* is constituted out of contesting discourses but that these discourses have effects, have a force as linguistic performances which will always elude our interpretative grasp. Read in these terms, *Mansfield Park*, like any other text, teaches not just a specific lesson of contested historical meanings, but the more general and humbling lesson of our own perpetual self-division, of our own non-mastery – non-mastery, that is, of a textual performance which nevertheless has *effects*, 'governs' a critical or reading '(hi)story' (1977a: 142), and in doing so constantly returns our ex-centricity to ourselves.

Acknowledgements

I would like to take the opportunity to thank Maurice Biriotti and Nigel Wood for helpful discussion at a preliminary stage of writing this essay. I am also very grateful to Kate Ince for valuable suggestions.

SUPPLEMENT

NIGEL WOOD: Does it matter that *The Turn of the Screw* seems to be *about* very different narrated events to *Mansfield Park*?

BARBARA RASMUSSEN: No *and* yes. What seems striking, now that I have worked on both narratives in Felman's terms, is the way that we find the *same* story of a search for proper meaning – of a quest for mastery and the inevitable failure of that quest – being repeated in both narratives and in the narratives that their respective criticism has spawned. But the specificity of each story also matters. Felman constantly returns to the question of difference and constantly re-*turns* difference in 'Turning the Screw of Interpretation' but her emphasis does not fall, as I have noted in my essay, on the historical specificity of the discourses which constitute *The Turn of the Screw* and likewise of the criticism it has evoked. However, one cannot do everything! Focusing on one set of differences or similarities inevitably involves the exclusion of others. Moreover, what an analysis overlooks, what it misses, where it errs, is precisely what will generate more *acts*, in this case, more critical speech acts. Felman is interested in 'what *makes* history'. This is very much what she says (as I understand it!) in relation to the inevitable 'misunderstanding' of Austin's speech act theory (Felman 1983: 144).

NW: You mention in note 16 what seems to be an important point: the way Felman draws on very different areas of theory. Can you say a little more about this?

BR: Yes, I am glad to have the opportunity because it is a crucial part of her critical activity. For example, what Felman finds particularly seductive, enjoyable *and* significant in J.L. Austin is his *play* with ideas, his Don Juanism, and she in turn, plays with *his* ideas in 'Turning the Screw of Interpretation' and especially in her book on Austin, *The Literary Speech Act*. The way that Austin's terms – 'performative' and 'constative', 'utterance' and 'statement' – are linked allusively, though not explicitly, with Lacan's distinction between the ever elusive subject of the *enunciation* and the subject of the *enounced* in 'Turning the Screw of Interpretation' is very characteristic. The two pairs of terms are not conflated, it is important to note. Felman in her work seeks to 'play out both the *encounter* and the *interval* between' different 'cultural contexts' (1985: 20). As she says in *The Literary Speech Act* (significantly written in French and later translated into English), 'if Lacan and Austin . . . say (more or less, on certain points) the same thing . . . they say it in the specific ways in which English and French are . . . destined to *miss each other*, not to meet'. Felman suggests that this very 'nonmeeting' is an example of the way that the 'self-referentiality' of language always misses what language *does* – 'its performative functioning' as opposed to what it means or states (1987: 91). The gap that exists between Austin and Lacan is like the Lacanian concept of the Real which meaning fails to grasp but which nevertheless has effects – provokes, for example *acts of misunderstanding* but also productive encounters.

NW: Felman does not seem to engage with feminism at all in 'Turning the Screw'. Is this something she overlooks?

BR: I think Felman's 'Turning the Screw' does have feminist implications in its subversion of mastery and in its analysis of 'reading as a political project of sense-control' (1977a: 170). The way that a grasp of meaning is shown to involve the exclusion of difference, of Otherness, on which it nevertheless depends, and to which it, at some level, *wants* to remain blind, is important to feminism. The argument may seem a familiar one by now, but Felman's textual *performance* is what counts, and it is still very compelling, capable of powerful *effects*. Of course, for a more explicitly feminist text by Felman, one has only to turn to Catherine Belsey and Jane Moore's introductory anthology, *The Feminist Reader* (London, 1989), which reprints Felman's essay 'Women and Madness: the Critical Phallacy' (*Diacritics*, 5 (1975)). This short text performs a provocative feminist analysis of a realist short story by Balzac, of its criticism and also of different forms of feminist intervention.

Endpiece

NIGEL WOOD

Jane Austen's fiction is so much a part of the present canon that it is hard to *re*-encounter it with an awareness of historical difference or with an analytical eye. As Jonathan Culler has it, whether directly or not, we are 'competent' at reading her texts, in the sense that we have often been taught to recognize the 'set of conventions for reading texts' that signifies Literature (Culler 1975: 118). These usually involve the idea that, in literary criticism, we re-create the original intention that imbues/ imbued the text with significance – by isolating either the 'significant attitude' of the author or the metaphorical or thematic coherence that apparently gives it shape (Culler 1975: 115). Culler points out, however, that this comfortable 'fit' between deduced intention and consequent re-vision of the textual items that are presented to us in our reading, is little more than a *cultural* pattern. Literature, perhaps pre-eminently the pre-modernist novel, gives back to us the coherence we sense but cannot actually locate in reality.

A central concern of these essays has been the initial critical decision about Austen's context. For Mary Evans, 'context' does not spring from the work's contemporary history. If that were the case, we would have to conclude that there was no 'subconscious' or psychic repression before the mid-nineteenth century. Brean Hammond indicates that a text cannot render its full historical presence, that it is claimed by ideological restraints that are indeed necessary in order for a writer to communicate with any kind of shared focus with a reader. These 'competences' are questioned in Austen's case by Claudia Johnson, whose call for an alternative feminist reading of literary history involves an effort to locate sexual difference as productive of many varied (and not obviously related) cultural responses.

The difficulties posed by *Mansfield Park* are not pre-eminently those of immediate intelligibility, but rather those of unlearning what we think we 'know' of its author. At its extreme edge, such 'textual analysis impugns the idea of a final signified' according to Roland Barthes, because the work 'does not stop, does not close'. The 'play of signifiers' that Barbara Rasmussen enters in her reading, can only be brought to a synthesis or resolution by an arbitrary decision. We can then enumerate these signifiers, but not place them in a hierarchy that emerges from the considerations of common sense: 'textual analysis is pluralist', if this agenda is accepted ('Theory of the Text', trans. Ian McLeod, in Young 1981: 43).

When Ian Watt praised Austen's realism in his *The Rise of the Novel* (1957), it was enough to place her work as the zenith of the novel's advance as a serious art form:

> She was able to combine into a harmonious unity the advantages both of realism of presentation and realism of assessment, of the internal and of the external approaches to character; her novels have authenticity without diffuseness or trickery, wisdom of social comment without a garrulous essayist, and a sense of the social order which is not achieved at the expense of the individuality and autonomy of the characters.
>
> (Watt 1957: 297)

The realism that Watt has in mind shows a break with 'old-fashioned romances' for a 'more dispassionate and scientific scrutiny' (Watt 1957: 10–11), freed from generic formulations of experience, such as in the Traveller's Tale or Picaresque. 'Realism' can be a convention, if not immediately, then with time. For Barthes, the 'real' produces an effect rather than a likeness. In his short essay, 'L'Effet de réel' ('the reality effect') of 1968, details of narrative that would not *appear* instrumental and so redundant are regarded as stridently communicative, for they signify, not the content of reality, but rather 'the category of the "real" ' (Barthes 1986: 89). Our sense of the real is actually strongly literary, and these 'realisms' change much quicker than we realize (see Barthes 1967: 52–8).

However, there are strong voices raised against such a conversion of all representations to 'text', for it could be argued that a concentration on the signifier ignores important historical distinctions, details where accuracy of attention is crucial if we are to comprehend an alternative structure of thought. Consider this comment by Janet Todd on the Lacanian position: such an 'approach has replaced history with psycho-analysis and women writers with a mode called "feminine writing" which can be produced by either sex' (Todd 1988: 4; see also Walker's feminist defence of the 'author' as a critical as well as a historical con-cept). This lack of context

> is a manoeuvre that permits the critic a licence itself anything but critical, in the most useful sense of self-critical. It allows the original writer to evade meaningful challenges from her con-temporaries, and to take the colluding critic with her into an unsocial, unspecific, timeless zone called art. Art, an area set up by post-romantic intellectuals as a tax-free haven where there is nothing to pay.
>
> (Todd 1988: 102)

This distrust of unlocated semiosis has been shared by several recent commentators, including David Spring and Alistair Duckworth (in Todd 1983: 53–72, 39–52, respectively). The writing of all types of history, conceived of as an arena for victims and repression, needs some moral direction and commitment.

There is therefore often a fruitful synthesis between literary historians and feminists and non-feminists alike. As outlined in my Introduction, this has led to the exploration of new contexts, of necessary 'silences' and a renewed awareness of the politics of form, of realism and the sudden departures from it. For example, David Kaufmann's sharp obser-vations about Austen's act of closure at the end of *Mansfield Park* take issue with Alistair Duckworth's conclusion that the narrative is here twisted to fit a thesis (Duckworth 1971: 35–7). Kaufmann identifies a consistent ideological and rhetorical pattern, where the sanctity of the extended family must supersede the sanctity of the nuclear marriage (Kaufmann 1986: 227; see also Newman).

There are, however, other distinctions to make about narratives once we depart from the obligation to find them more or less obedient to the conventions of realism, where content is realized by form. In Peter Brooks's *Reading For The Plot* (1984) plot is taken to function typically as a clash between what in Russian formalism are known as *fabula* (the events of the plot in their linear, temporal, order) and *sjuzet* (the way that these events are ordered, for example, time-scheme, type of narra-tion). This 'double logic' is missed if we concentrate on *fabula*: 'Plot could be thought of as the interpretive activity elicited by the distinction between *sjuzet* and *fabula*, the way we *use* one against the other'. Thus, 'contradiction may be in the very nature of narrative' and supplies its fascination and (usually transitory) satisfaction of desire (Brooks 1984: 13, 29). Most recently, in the work of Jay Clayton, Susan Winnett and D.A. Miller, this dichotomy or tension has been built on to provide a new way of approaching the dynamics of our response to all narratives, including Austen's. At best, it aims to explain just why we may find *Mansfield Park* offensive or satisfying. For example, Miller's treatment of Henry Crawford's flirtation draws us to understand its textual satisfactions: 'What it threatens most directly in the novel is the possibility of fixing sexual attraction in love and marriage, but it is able to threaten this only on the basis of a semiological equivocation: its signs refuse to point straight' (Miller 1981: 21). But what might 'love' and 'marriage' actually be or mean, then or now? The fact that it is ambiguous, once established, might oblige us to account for these features, and our sympathetic or antagonistic decoding of them.

Notes

Introduction

1 Jocelyn Harris's study of the Richardson influence on Austen identifies several traces of *Sir Charles Grandison* (1753–54) in *Mansfield Park*, especially the implicit comparison between Sotherton ('the false, fallen, deceptive Paradise created by art') and Mansfield itself ('the true Paradise born naturally of time and tradition') (Harris 1989: 164). See also Moler (1968: 77–81, 105–7). For a fuller account of the amateur dramatics, see Tucker (1983: 100–5) and Honan (1987: 42–55). For an account of the pejorative view of the theatre, see Bevan, Jordan, and Litvak, but see also Fleishman (1967: 24–9) for the variety of motives behind the opposition.

2 See Chapman (1932, II: 267–79), for evidence of their friendship.

3 See the letter to James Stanier Clarke (1 April 1816), where Austen is flattered by his suggestion (as the Prince Regent's chaplain) that she dedicate one of her novels to the Prince and perhaps attempt a 'history of the august House of Cobourg' (Chapman 1932, II: 451). She refuses, as composition of such a 'historical romance' is, she now realizes, beyond her: 'No, I must keep to my own style and go on in my own way' (II: 453). See also Chapman (1932, II: 411, 483, 488).

4 See Gary Kelly's 'Jane Austen and the English Novel of the 1790s' in Schofield and Macheski (1986: 285–307); Kelly (1989: 111–16); Kelly (1976: 261–9); Johnson (1988: 1–27); Kirkham (1983: 13–26, 33–8); and Butler (1975: *passim*).

5 See Kelly (1976: 266–7); Kirkham (1983: 53–60); Butler (1975: 7–28) on the radical aspects of Sentimentalism.

6 For a detailed analysis of how Austen adapted Romance plots in her earlier fiction, see Brown (1979: 50–64), and Spencer (1986: 152–3, 167–77).

7 (On *Mansfield Park*.) 'Irony has been Jane Austen's only internal principle, her only method of suggesting impulse and response; and here she gives it up. The frame of reference is violated from without: Fanny and Edmund triumph, not through a development of will or vitality, . . . but because they represent a world which the author intrudes into her world of irony, and which she has engaged herself to affirm' (Mudrick 1968: 180).

8 See also Roberts (1979: 12–67, 155–202) and Fleishman (1967: 19–42) on *Mansfield Park*.

9 The Introduction to the second edition refuses to depart significantly from the history of ideas described in the first. See Butler (1975: xli–xlvi).

10 As Chapman discovered with his edition of the *Letters*. He comments in his Introduction how their 'enchantment' might be hard-won for some readers: 'To those who do not find these qualities [wisdom and humanity] in them, the letters may appear not merely trivial, but hard and cold. Even their professed admirers have deplored their occasional cynicism' (Chapman 1932, I: xliii). Deborah Kaplan has recently sketched in the ambiguous nature of this autobiographical evidence ('Representing Two Cultures: Jane Austen's Letters', in Benstock 1988: 211–29).

11 Lydia Languish uses her maid Lucy to ransack the Bath circulating library for works such as Smollett's *Peregrine Pickle* (1751), Mackenzie's *The Man of Feeling* (1771) and Sterne's *A Sentimental Journey Through France and Italy by Mr. Yorick* (1768). When visitors call, these are carefully hidden and Allestree's *The Whole Duty of Man* (1659), Hester Chapone's *Letters on the Improvement of the Mind* (1773) and Fordyce's *Sermons* (1765) carefully displayed (Sheridan 1975: 15–20).

12 See Browne (1987: 155–78) on the feminist debates of the 1790s and their influence on the novel form. These need not have affected novelists in radical ways (see Cole, and David Monaghan's 'Jane Austen and the Position of Women', in Monaghan 1981: 105–21).

13 The identification is made explicit when Catherine likens General Tilney to the dark villain of *Udolpho*, Montoni (*NA*, 190). Dorothy, the Northanger housekeeper, also brings to mind Dorothée from *Udolpho*.

14 The Austen family saw reading aloud in the family circle as a common entertainment. See Chapman (1932, I: 39, 89, 173, 197).

15 Its association with specifically female readers did not help. See Spencer (1986: 3–40) and Lovell (1987: 47–55).

16 See Pat Rogers, 'Classics and Chapbooks' in Rivers (1982: 27–45).

17 In the note to 'Crabbe's Tales' on p. 437 of the Oxford World's Classics edition, ed. James Kinsley, notes by John Lucas (1990).

18 *Mansfield Park* was written 'by the Author of "Sense and Sensibility," and "Pride and Prejudice" ', as was *Emma*. Before that, the author was 'A Lady' (*Sense and Sensibility*). Austen is known to have started to collect

together family or close friends' opinions of *Mansfield Park* and *Emma*. They are reproduced in Southam (1968, 1: 48–51, 55–7).

19 Austen's post-1790s approach to fiction is described succinctly by Paul Pickrel (1988).

20 'The degree of sympathy and inwardness of presentation of hero or heroine expresses an author's approach to human nature. The action through which the central character passes tends to reflect an ideal progress: either he is freed from social pressure, like Bage's heroes, and Maria Edgeworth's, or he is schooled in accepting it, like Jane West's and Jane Austen's' (Butler 1975: 293).

21 It is likely that this contemporary view of Austen's divided impulses derives from work by Patricia Meyer Spacks: Fanny Burney and Austen stood out from their peers because they perceived with particular intensity 'the dichotomy between public passivity and private energy that weakened those women unable to use their sense of division as material for strong images of female experience' (Spacks 1976: 89).

22 See Emsley (1979: 147–68) and Dickinson (1985: 62–77).

23 This is the point of Alison Sulloway's sympathetic reading of the Juvenilia and Austen's dialogue with conduct literature (Sulloway 1989).

24 See Angela Leighton, 'Sense and Silences: Reading Jane Austen Again', in Todd (1983: 128–41) and Marylea Meyersohn, 'What Fanny Knew: A Quiet Auditor of the Whole', in Todd (1983: 224–30).

25 For example, Maria's self-deception in 'favouring *something* which every body who shuts their eyes while they look, or their understandings while they reason, feels the comfort of' (*MP*, 134) or the pervasive satire on Mrs Norris: ' "I only wish I could be more useful; but you see I do all in my power. I am not one of those that spare their own trouble; and Nanny shall fetch her . . ." ' (*MP*, 46).

26 'In [Jane Austen's] novels the clichés of sentimental fiction are overturned: mothers are vulgar and limited, sentimental friends are a sham, and orphans prove not noble but lower middle class. Families exist not as images of harmonious society, infused with sentimental female values, but as constricting forces, embarrassments to the few sensible offspring they produce' (Todd 1986: 144). See also in this regard, Johnson (1989).

27 Austen's polemical characterization is comprehensively described in Smith (1983: 111–28).

28 See Spencer (1986: 161–2) for a pertinent treatment of Edgeworth's *Belinda* (one of Austen's favourite books) as a parody of this Rousseauistic ideal. Fanny is of *use* and so is central to the altered requirements for female accomplishment that were requested by the Evangelicals; see Linda C. Hunt, 'A Woman's Portion: Jane Austen and the Female Character', in Schofield and Macheski (1986: 8–28) and Judith Wilt, 'Jane Austen's Men: Inside/Outside "the Mystery" ', in Todd (1982: 59–76).

29 This is true of all characters but Edmund, and is the pattern for most of Austen's heroes: that they can 'read' female character successfully. Note Sir

Thomas's impercipience: 'She was always so gentle and retiring, that her emotions were beyond his discrimination. He did not understand her; he felt that he did not . . .' (MP, 361).

30 Fanny's conference with Sir Thomas in Chapter 32 about Crawford's proposal only emphasizes their quite alternative preconceptions about not just the matter at hand but also social life in general. Sir Thomas can mention Crawford's 'temper' whilst Fanny thinks of 'his principles'. She faces the 'appalling prospect of discussion, explanation, and probably non-conviction' (MP, 317). She therefore rests any case she has on 'the purity of her intentions' (MP, 323), whereas Sir Thomas forms his conclusions on the external appearances of social conduct. Fanny imagines that he thinks her 'self-willed, obstinate, selfish, and ungrateful' – which, given Sir Thomas's distrust of 'that independence of spirit, which prevails so much in modern days, even in young women', is, at the very least, a consistent conclusion (MP, 318–19).

31 See Kirkham (1983: 33–60), Johnson (1988: 14–16), and Cora Kaplan's 'Wild Nights: pleasure/sexuality/feminism' in Armstrong and Tennenhouse (1987: 160–84, especially 174–8).

32 A suggestive discussion of Austen's (and Byron's) own strain of irony can be found in Galperin (1990, especially 60–73).

1 Henry Crawford and the 'Sphere of Love'

1 These opinions have been catalogued by Jeffrey Weeks (amongst others) in Sex, Politics and Society (1981) pp. 38–56.

2 Freud, as Peter Gay points out, wrote about the Oedipus myth throughout his life. The first important account is in The Interpretation of Dreams (1900) but, as Gay notes, 'Freud's predilection for it steadily increased: he viewed it as an explanation of how neuroses originate, as a turning point in the developmental history of the child, as a marker differentiating male and female sexual maturation, even, in Totem and Taboo, as the deep motive for the founding of civilization and the creation of conscience' (Gay 1988: 113).

3 For example, Tanner, while admitting that the Crawfords 'are far from villains', still finds them 'spoilt and subtly corrupted by their prolonged immersion in the amoral fashionable London World' (Tanner 1986: 149).

4 For example: 'Too late he became aware how unfavourable to the character of any young people, must be the totally opposite treatment which Maria and Julia had been always experiencing at home, where the excessive indulgence and flattery of their aunt had been continually contrasted with his own severity. He saw how ill he had judged, in expecting to counteract what was wrong in Mrs Norris, by its reverse on himself, clearly saw that he had but increased the evil, by teaching them to repress their spirits in his presence, as to make their real disposition unknown to him . . .' (MP, 447–8).

5 Letter from Charlotte Brontë to George Lewes (1 January 1848) in Southam (1968, 1: 126).
6 See 'Some Psychical Consequences of the Anatomical Distinction between the Sexes' (1925; Freud, 1953–74, 19: 24–60).

2 The Political Unconscious

1 Naomi Royde Smith has written a follow-up to *Emma* entitled *Jane Fair-fax*. Constance Cox's dramatic version of *Mansfield Park: a Comedy in Three Acts* (1977), is set entirely in the drawing-room at Mansfield.
2 Edwin Muir, 'Burns and Popular Poetry' in *Uncollected Scottish Criticism*, ed. and intro. Andrew Noble (1982: 193).
3 'And where lies the real difficulty of creating that taste by which a truly original poet is to be relished? Is it in breaking the bonds of custom, in overcoming the prejudices of false refinement, and displacing the aversions of inexperience?' ('Essay, Supplementary to the Preface' (1815), in *The Prose Works of William Wordsworth*, ed. W.J.B. Owen and Jane Worthington Smyser, 3 vols (Oxford, 1974), III: 80) – a formulation first tried out in his letter to Lady Beaumont of 21 May 1807.
4 Fanny is said to have 'all the heroism of principle' when she accepts a self-denying ordinance against loving Edmund.
5 The generalization made in this paragraph about Jane Austen criticism can be sustained over many of the major critical studies produced in the 1960s and 1970s. Even into the 1980s, some critics were content to raise issues wholly internal to the novels concerned. John Hardy's discussion, in *Jane Austen's Heroines: Intimacy in Human Relationships* (1984), revolves around the 'suitability' of Mary Crawford as a partner for Edmund Bertram: 'how confident are we invited to be of their future "happiness"?' (p. 58). John Halperin asserts that '*Mansfield Park* is largely about true and false values, right and wrong ways of looking at things – how to live, in short' (1984: 234). Even critics who perceive that the novel treats a society under threat and deals with the collision of the individual and society, sometimes fail to open the work up properly to history. Thus Leroy W. Smith's feminist-inspired reading, in *Jane Austen and the Drama of Woman*, is happy to blame 'patriarchalism' for all the evils of Mansfield society and leave it at that. There have been, however, some important attempts to contextualize the novel in terms of contemporary historical events and broader historical changes, which are influential on the present reading (see Fleishman, 1967: 19–42; Duckworth; Butler; Brown, 1979; and Tanner).
6 Some of the best recent studies of Jane Austen are inspired by feminism, but feminist readings do not usually produce 'metacommentaries' as defined above. Books like Kirkham's situate the characters' conduct in terms of Jane Austen's gender politics. But the critical approach remains ethical, although the burden is transferred to the reader, who is put under some

moral pressure to judge those aright. Mary Poovey's extremely intelligent and subtle study, *The Proper Lady and the Woman Writer*, impressively elucidates the ideological contradictions facing Jane Austen, but Poovey sees those as in Austen's conscious capacity to resolve and indeed sees *Mansfield Park* as offering such a resolution in terms of the Austenian notion of 'heroism of principle' (Poovey 1984: 172–224).

7 Raymond Williams complains that 'according to its opponents, Marxism is a necessarily reductive and determinist kind of theory: no cultural activity is allowed to be real and significant in itself, but is always reduced to a direct or indirect expression of some preceding and controlling economic content, or of a political content determined by an economic position or situation' (Williams 1977: 83). Williams is forced to admit, however, that there is some substance behind this attack. Some Marxist literary critics have indeed written as if the economic 'base' of a society is entirely separable from its forms of consciousness (the 'superstructure'), so that ideas and thought are not considered to be part of material production. This often leads to a simple reflection theory according to which art 'reflects' reality in some direct way, and the prescriptive consequence is that art is only valuable if it is seen to be doing this. C.S.J. Sprigg [Christopher Caudwell]'s *Illusion and Reality: a Study of the Sources of Poetry* (1937) might offer an example of the criticism that equates evolution of literary art with evolution of social and political forms in a very direct, unmediated way. The collection *Aesthetics and Politics*, ed. Ronald Taylor, afterword Fredric Jameson (1977), is a convenient anthology in which to study the debates between leading Marxist critics, where the accusation of 'vulgar' Marxism is made in particular against the thinking of Georg Lukács. His political views sometimes resulted in a preference for what might be termed (unkindly) 'boy meets tractor' literature over more complex works.

8 For a discussion of Charlotte Smith's influence on Jane Austen, see F.W. Bradbrook, *Jane Austen and Her Predecessors* (Cambridge, 1967), pp. 103–5. Anne Henry Ehrenpreis, in her edition of *The Old Manor House* (London, New York, Toronto, 1969), makes clear that Austen had read all of Smith's novels by the time she was seventeen (p. vii).

9 See Butler, ch. 1. Butler argues that the 1790s were the high-water mark of reaction against sentimental writing, which had become associated with political radicalism in its espousal of feeling and sympathy.

10 A summary of social change in the period can be found in John Steven Watson, *The Reign of George III, 1760–1815* (Oxford, 1960) *passim*. See also Ian R. Christie, *Stress and Stability in Late Eighteenth-Century Britain* (Oxford, 1984).

11 The point about the fluidity of woman's class position is brilliantly made by Catherine A. Mackinnon in her *Towards a Feminist Theory of the State* (Cambridge, MA, 1989): 'from a feminist perspective, a woman's class position, whether or not she works for wages, is as much or more set

through her relation first to her father, then to her husband. It changes through changes in these relations, such as marriage, divorce, or aging. It is more open to change, both up and down, than is a man's in similar material circumstances. Through relations with men, women have considerable class mobility, down as well as up. A favorable marriage can rocket a woman into the ruling class, while her own skills, training, work experience, wage scales, and attitudes, were she on her own, would command few requisites for economic independence or mobility' (pp. 34–5).

12 Many commentators make the point that the novel is virulently antimetropolitan in its bias. Julia Prewitt Brown even sees a symbolic correspondence between London–Portsmouth–Mansfield and hell–purgatory–heaven as operative in the novel's structure (Brown 1979: 3 ff.).

13 Tony Tanner points out that exchange of social identity is fundamental to plot and characterization in the novel as a form (Tanner 1986: 142 ff.). Even so, in *Mansfield Park* the extent to which Fanny's selfhood is emancipated from her social status is remarkable. Tanner's distinction between 'guardians', 'inheritors' and 'interlopers' is a suggestive alternative way of plotting social status against moral worth in the novel.

14 Rack studies the mid-eighteenth-century religious Revival and its manifestations in Anglican Evangelism, in various forms of Dissent and in Methodism (Rack 1989: 1–42, 158–80, 314–29).

15 Avrom Fleishman conjectures a biography for Sir Thomas as a sugar planter whose interests have been harmed by the Napoleonic blockade, and who may have been in contact with enlightened thinking about slavery (Fleishman 1967: 36–9). Margaret Kirkham also makes suggestive remarks on the 'Mansfield Judgement' of 1772, Lord Mansfield's decision that slaves taken to England could not be considered as enslaved *in* England. I am less persuaded by her argument that Jane Austen would have perceived an analogy between treatment of women and treatment of slaves (Kirkham 1983: 116–19). Many women poets of the 1780s and 1790s expressed abolitionist sentiments; one in particular, Hannah More, was well known to Jane Austen. Though her ideology was conservative, her *Slavery, A Poem* (1788) is liberal on this issue:

> Perish th'illiberal thought which would debase
> The Native genius of the sable race!
> Perish the proud philosophy, which sought
> To rob them of the powers of equal thought!
>
> (Lonsdale 1990: 330)

16 Several discussions are available of the play staged at Mansfield, *Lovers' Vows*. Mrs Inchbald's version of the German Kotzebue's *Das Kind der Liebe* (1798) is not only objectionable on the grounds that its content is bound to put Mansfield characters into compromising positions, and on the old Puritan grounds that acting is immoral, but also on the grounds that it was seen as an expression of Continental radicalism and revolutionary fervour

in its anti-aristocratic bias. Honan makes the point that *in propria persona*, Austen did not object to plays and enjoyed first-rate acting very much – see his account of her theatre-going in 1813 (Honan 1987: 326–7). Irrespective of that, in *this* novel, acting – being an 'actor' – is a psychological 'index' of insincerity, superficiality, even of diabolism. Thus, while Henry Crawford is a superb 'actor', Edmund finds it very difficult and, of course, Fanny cannot and will not act at all. Here, acting is part of a binary opposition that counterpoints acting: being oneself.

17 The lines Fanny is referring to are those beginning 'Ye fallen avenues! Once more I mourn/Your fate unmerited' (William Cowper, *The Task* (1785), 1: 338–9). The poem 'Yardley Oak', written in the early 1790s, is an even better example of the melancholy sensibility Fanny here manifests. The sole surviving oak tree celebrated in this poem is invested with ancient religious sanctity as a tree consecrated in Druid worship. It becomes symbolic of endurance, of pastness, of history, of the poet's own selfhood. Another poem written around 1790 by the almost forgotten poet Susanna Blamire, entitled 'When Home We Return', includes the following stanza that almost exactly expresses Fanny's sentiment:

Should we miss but a tree where we used to be playing,
Or find the wood cut where we sauntered a-Maying, –
If the yew-seat's away, or the ivy's a-wanting,
We hate the fine lawn and the new-fashioned planting.
When I found them all gone, 'twas like dear friends departed,
And I walked where they used to be, half broken-hearted.

(Lonsdale 1990: 289)

18 Fanny Price is here alluding to the description of Melrose Abbey given in Sir Walter Scott's *The Lay of the Last Minstrel* (1805), Canto II, stanzas 10, 12. The opening lines of the Canto give an idea of how her imagination has been working:

If thou would view fair Melrose aright,
Go visit it by the pale moonlight;
For the gay beams of lightsome day
Gild, but to flout, the ruins grey.
When the broken arches are black in night,
And each shafted oriel glimmers white;
When the cold light's uncertain shower
Streams on the ruined central tower;
When buttress and buttress, alternately,
Seem framed of ebon and ivory;
When silver edges the imagery,
And the scrolls that teach thee to live and die;
When distant Tweed is heard to rave,

And the owlet to hoot o'er the dead man's grave,
Then go –

(II.1: 1–15)

What a disappointment Sotherton must have been to her! Henry Rack points out (Rack 1989: 19) that during the eighteenth century, the prevailing taste in church interiors 'moved in favour of light, plainness and enlightenment rather than darkness, ornament and mystery'.

19 In Crabbe's poem *The Parish Register*, II. 500–73 (published in *Poems, 1807*), the story is told of a virtuous bailiff's daughter called Fanny Price who resists the blandishments of the 'amorous Knight' Sir Edward Archer and reconciles him to the simple lad she later loves (George Crabbe, *Complete Poetical Works*, eds. Norma Dalrymple-Champneys and Arthur Pollard, 3 vols (Oxford, 1988), 1: 251–3). Crabbe's preface to *Poems, 1807* provides a wider context to Austen's admiration of his work: he praises the conservative anti-revolutionary Edmund Burke in extravagant terms, and explains his own desire not to write on topical or patriotic themes, distancing himself from the 'hyperbolical or hypocritical expressions of universal philanthropy' to be found in radical writings (1: 207).

20 Tony Tanner graphically illustrates the extent to which Fanny is associated with images of stillness in opposition to images of violent motion and noise (Tanner 1986: 145 ff.).

21 Lionel Trilling, 'Why We Read Jane Austen', *Times Literary Supplement*, 5 March 1976, pp. 250, 251.

3 Gender, Theory and Jane Austen Culture

1 It is worth noting that Austen's detractors shared many of the same outlooks as her idolators: between the gentle Janeites and the 'nasty' Janeites, there was much in common. See Southam's superb overview of Austenian commentary from the mid-nineteenth century until the 1930s, in Southam (1985, 2: 1–158).

2 For the proceedings of The Jane Austen Society of North America, see its journal *Persuasions*, published annually.

3 Note that D.A. Miller's superb readings of Austen (in *Narrative and Its Discontents*) as well as his essay 'The Late Jane Austen' in *Raritan*, 10 (1990), 55–79, presuppose a Janeite placidity and orthodoxy (if only then deconstructively to unsettle and complicate them).

4 This discussion rehearses arguments I have already made in Johnson (1988: xvi–xvii).

5 See, for example, Mary Evans's remarks on Tory Janeism (Evans 1987: 1–2); and James Thompson's observation that Austenian commentary consists more of 'appreciation' than of criticism (Thompson 1988: 5–6). For other discussions of the conservative nature of Austenian criticism, see Joel Weinsheimer, '*Emma* and its Critics, The Value of

Tact', in Todd (1983: 257–72); and ' "Misreading" *Emma*: The Powers of Perfidies of Interpretive History,' *Journal of English Literary History*, 51 (1984), pp. 315–42. Finally, new right conservatives hostile to critical theory, feminism, and gay studies have gleefully pointed to Eve Kosofsky Sedgwick's discussion of the auto- and homoerotic elements in Austen's novels as though the supposedly self-evident absurdity of such an enterprise in Austen's case pointed to the ridiculousness of critical theory in general. See Eve Kosofsky Sedgwick, 'Jane Austen and the Masturbating Girl', *Critical Inquiry*, 17 (1991), 818–37.

6   For the most recent instance of this kind of criticism, see Roger Gard, *Jane Austen's Novels: The Art of Clarity* (New Haven, CT, 1992).

7   See also Kay's study of eighteenth-century fiction, *Political Constructions: Defoe, Richardson and Sterne in Relations to Hobbes, Hume, and Burke* (Ithaca, NY, 1988).

8   'Introduction' to *Emma* (Cambridge, MA, 1957), p. v. Cf. Trilling's argument that Emma has the 'moral life' of a man – a transgression which, however singular and fascinating, requires Austen's punishment and Knightley's disciplinary presence.

9   For discussions of *Mansfield Park*, see *Sincerity and Authenticity*, (Cambridge, MA, 1971), and his last, unfinished essay, evidently drafted in 1975, 'Why We Read Jane Austen', *Times Literary Supplement*, 5 March 1976 (no. 3, 860), pp. 250–2. In so far as this last seems to be moving towards Austen's alleged preference of stasis, it appears to be rearticulating the preoccupations of his earlier pieces on *Mansfield Park* within a context (the aftermath of unrest at campuses across the USA, especially Columbia University) markedly more reactionary. For a discussion of Trilling's views on *Mansfield Park*, see Pickrel (1987).

10   For a Foucauldian argument reaching precisely the opposite conclusion, exploring the politically motivated construction of the domestic as intrinsically non-political, see Armstrong (1987).

11   Harrison's letter to Thomas Hardy is dated 10 November 1913, quoted in Southam (1985, 2: 87–8).

12   Christopher Kent, 'Learning History with, and from, Jane Austen', in J. David Grey (ed.), *Jane Austen's Beginnings* (Ann Arbor, MI, 1989), p. 59. I am much indebted to this fine essay.

13   For a discussion of the impact which the male experience of shell-shock had on theories of gender during the same period, see Elaine Showalter, *The Female Malady: Women, Madness, and English Culture, 1830–1980* (New York, 1985), pp. 167–94.

14   Edward Said argues that *Mansfield Park* anticipates Conrad and later theorists of empire in 'Jane Austen and Empire', in Terry Eagleton (ed.), *Raymond Williams: Critical Perspectives* (Boston, MA, 1989), pp. 150–75.

15   It should be pointed out that the very productive and influential way of studying ideology that Poovey and Kay propose has a complex theoretical provenance, reaching from Jameson (whom Poovey cites), to Althusser's

theories of relative autonomy, and to Gramsci's theories of hegemony (see Headnote).

16 For an extremely clear analysis of the tension between post-modernist theory (which contends that feminist theory is disabled by foundationalism and essentialism in its insistence on the extralinguistic dimension of the very category 'woman') and feminist theory (which holds that post-modernist theory is androcentric, and politically naive in its insistence that gender is exclusively linguistic), see Nancy Fraser and Linda J. Nicholson, 'Social Criticism without Philosophy', in Linda J. Nicholson (ed.), *Feminism/Postmodernism* (New York, 1990), pp. 19–38.

17 The interpretative weight variously accorded the concluding marriage in love plots is incisively analysed in Joseph Allen Boone, *Tradition Counter Tradition* (Chicago, IL, 1987).

18 One of the most virulent attacks on Austen from the left is David C. Aers, 'Community and Morality: Towards Reading Jane Austen', in Aers *et al.* (1981).

19 The pagination here refers to the new introduction Butler wrote when the book was reissued in 1987.

20 For discussions of Austen's relation to Johnson, see my ' "The operations of time and the changes of the human mind": Jane Austen and Dr. Johnson Again', *Modern Language Quarterly*, 44 (1983), 23–38; and Peter L. De Rose, *Jane Austen and Samuel Johnson* (Washington, DC, 1980).

21 See Johnson (1988: 1–27, 94–120). Much of my discussion here emerges from this material.

22 I believe I am describing what is still the majority opinion here, as forcefully argued by critics as diverse as Duckworth, Butler, and Trilling.

23 Gina Luria has edited a massive facsimile collection of primary material on this subject. See *The Feminist Controversy in England, 1788–1810* (New York, 1974), 43 vols.

24 See also Ronald Paulson, *Representations of Revolution (1789–1820)* (New Haven, CT, 1983); Bernadette Fort (ed.), *Fictions of the French Revolution* (Evanston, IL, 1991); Lynn Hunt (ed.), *Eroticism and the Body Politic* (Baltimore, MD, 1991).

25 'From . . . sleep the queen was first startled by the voice of the centinel at her door, who cried out to her, to save herself by flight . . . A band of cruel ruffians and assassains, reeking with his blood, rushed into the chamber of the queen, and pierced with an hundred strokes . . . the bed, from whence this persecuted woman had but just time to fly almost naked . . . to seek refuge at the feet of a King and husband . . .' (Burke 1968: 164).

26 That is, economic power, not some psychic repression.

27 For informative and provocative discussions of Austen's treatment of contemporary notions of womanhood, see Sulloway (1989) and Kirkham.

28 This story vindicates the paternalism of Mr Edwards, a model slaveowner, over his slaves by figuring his dominion as enlightened and kind. In it, an uprising of slaves is foiled by a 'grateful negro' who loyally refuses to

betray his master. For a discussion of Maria Edgeworth's uses of patriarchal ideology as a way of maintaining her own authority, see Elizabeth Kowaleski-Wallace, *Their Father's Daughters: Hannah More, Maria Edgeworth, and Patriarchal Complicity* (New York, 1991).

29 The fact that Austen's novels end with traditionally comic marriage is very commonly taken as evidence of their intrinsic conservatism. See for example, Armstrong (1987: 29); Brown (1990). In my view, more nuanced – are I say, even belletristic – reading practices must have a place in literary studies of ideology, for they help determine the terms on which various narrative outcomes can be taken. Precisely because Patricia Meyer Spacks, for example, pays much more attention to the moods of Austen's representations, she is able to make a crucial distinction between the institutions the novel *describes* and those it *affirms*, in *Desire and Truth: Functions of Plot in Eighteenth-Century English Novels* (Chicago, IL, 1990), p. 224. Terry Lovell's discussion of feminism and the possibilities for subversion in popular texts is relevant here (see Lovell 1987: 55–72).

30 Ruth Yeazell argues that Austen recuperates conventional notions of modesty and thus shores up Sir Thomas's authority in *Fictions of Modesty: Women and Courtship in the English Novel* (Chicago, IL, 1991), pp. 143–68.

31 Joan B. Landes discusses the misogynist agendas of republican ideology as they surface in Rousseau and Wollstonecraft, in *Women and the Public Sphere in the Age of the French Revolution* (Ithaca, NY, 1988). See also G. Barker Benfield's 'Mary Wollstonecraft: Eighteenth Century Commonwealthwoman', *Journal of the History of Ideas*, 50 (1989), 95–115, and his *The Culture of Sensibility: Sex and Society in Eighteenth-Century Britain* (Chicago, IL, 1992).

32 Christine L. Krueger discusses More's uses of religious discourse as a means of negotiating her own authority in *The Reader's Repentance: Women Preachers, Women Writers in Nineteenth-Century Discourse* (Chicago, IL, 1992).

4 Discovering 'A New Way of Reading'

1 F. Nietzsche, *The Will to Power*; quoted in Felman (1977a: 203).

2 'Transcribed from a recording of J. Lacan's talk at the "Kanzer Seminar" (Yale University, 24 November 1975), which has been translated into English by Barbara Johnson' (Felman's footnote 22, 1977a: 118). Quoted in 'Turning the Screw' (1977a: 118).

3 'A Difficulty in the Path of Psycho-Analysis' (1917) in Freud (1953–74, 17: 142–3). Quoted in Felman (1987: 75–6).

4 Edmund Wilson, 'The Ambiguity of Henry James', *Hound and Horn*, VII (April–May 1934), pp. 385–406.

5 Felman quotes here at some length from *The Interpretation of Dreams* (1977a: 136–7).

6 Jacques Lacan, *The Four Fundamental Concepts of Psycho-analysis*, ed.

J-A. Miller, trans. Alan Sheridan (Harmondsworth, 1979), 139. Antony Easthope discusses this example in his lucid account of Lacan to which I am indebted in my argument here. See Easthope (1983: 30–47, especially 44).

7 See Wright (1984: 107–32) for a particularly helpful short account of the *Nom-du-Père* and subsequent discussion of 'Turning the Screw' to which I am indebted in my argument here.

8 See Lacan's 'Seminar on "The Purloined Letter" ' in *Ecrits* (Paris, 1966), English translation by Jeffrey Mehlman, *Yale French Studies*, 48 (1972), 39–72. Felman (1987), Chapter 2 is a useful discussion of this Seminar.

9 J. Lacan, 'Introduction à l'édition allemande des *Ecrits*,' *Scilicet* no. 5 (Paris: Seuil, 1975), 16. (Felman 1977a: 159, n. 37). Quoted, in Felman's translation (1977a: 159).

10 J. Lacan, *Le Séminaire – Livre XI: Les Quatres concepts fondamentaux de la psychanalyse* (Paris, 1973), 158. (Felman 1977a: 133, n. 26). Quoted in Felman's translation (1977a: 133).

11 J. Lacan, *Encore* (Paris, 1975), 23. Quoted in Felman 1983: 83.

12 Sigmund Freud, ' "Wild" Psycho-Analysis' in Freud (1953–74, 11: 223).

13 Jacqueline Rose, 'Introduction – II', in J. Mitchell and J. Rose (eds), *Feminine Sexuality: Jacques Lacan and the école freudienne* (1982), p. 42.

14 Oliver Evans, 'James's Air of Evil: *The Turn of the Screw*', in Gerald Willen (ed.), *A Casebook on Henry James's 'The Turn of the Screw'* (New York, 1969), p. 211. Quoted in Felman (1977a: 114).

15 My summary of Austin's theory is based on Felman's reading of him in Felman (1983). For Austin's own account, see, for example, J.L. Austin, *How to do Things with Words* (Oxford, 1962). It is important to note that in 'Turning the screw of interpretation', Felman always uses the Austinian terms 'utterance' and 'statement' (see, for example, 1977a: 200) and never uses 'enunciation' and 'enounced'. This latter pair relate directly to the French terms *énonciation* and *énoncé*. These are used in a very specific way by Lacan (in the wake of work by R. Jakobson and E. Benveniste among others (see Easthope 1983: 40–3)) in insisting on the difference between, and the privileging of, the 'subject of the enunciation' over the 'subject of the enounced'. However, given the overall Lacanian bent of her argument in 'Turning the Screw', one can say that the terms 'enunciation' and 'enounced', with all their specifically Lacanian connotations, are constantly in 'play' on the level of allusion. I have therefore explicitly used both sets of terms in my commentary on 'Turning the Screw'; partly to make the allusion more explicit, partly because I agree with Easthope that there are distinct reasons for preferring 'enunciation/enounced' over 'enunciation/statement' (see Easthope 1983: 43). It is crucial however, to note that the two sets of terms come from very different contexts.

16 Lacan, *Encore*, 81. Quoted in Felman's translation (1977a: 157).

17 Felman does not explicitly refer to the philosopher C.S. Peirce in 'Turning the Screw' but in the Introduction to her book *Writing and Madness*, in which it is reprinted, she does. There she quotes Paul de Man who argues,

for example, that 'The interpretation of the sign is not, for Peirce, a meaning, but another sign: it is reading not a decodage, and this reading has, in its turn, to be interpreted into another sign, and so on *ad infinitum*'. See de Man (1979) 9. Quoted in Felman (1985: 24).

18 Felman's own 'frame' of reference in examining the prologue is Derridean as well as Lacanian. The reader new to Derrida might find Gayatri Spivak's 'Translator's Preface' to Jacques Derrida's *Of Grammatology* (Baltimore, MD, 1976), particularly useful here. See especially xvi–xviii.

19 Henry James referred to it as 'an *amusette* to catch those not easily caught' (see the Norton Critical Edition of Henry James, *The Turn of the Screw*, ed. R. Kimbrough (New York 1966), p. 120). Quoted in Felman (1977a: 101–2).

20 Reginald Farrer, 'Jane Austen's *Gran Rifiuto*', *Quarterly Review*, July 1917. Reprinted in Southam (1985, 2: 264). For this quotation see Southam (1976: 211).

21 See, for example, *MP*, 368 and 454. Claudia L. Johnson discusses incestuous relations in 'Mansfield Park' in Johnson (1988: 116–19).

22 Apart from Kotzebue's *Lovers' Vows* and Shakespeare's *Henry VIII* which feature explicitly in the novel, critics have noted significant allusions to, among others, Shakespeare's *As You Like It* (see Armstrong 1988: 58–66) and *King Lear* (see Fleishman 1967: 62–3). A number of other plays are cited in the novel (see, for example, *MP*, 155).

References

Unless otherwise stated, place of publication is London.

Aers, David C., Cook, Jon and Punter, David (eds) (1981) *Romanticism and Ideology: Studies in English Writing, 1765–1830*.

Althusser, Louis (1977) *Lenin and Philosophy and Other Essays*, trans. Ben Brewster.

Amis, Kingsley (1957) 'What became of Jane Austen?' *Mansfield Park, Spectator*, 4 October: 33–40.

Armstrong, Isobel (1988) *Jane Austen: Mansfield Park*. Harmondsworth: Penguin Critical Studies.

Armstrong, Nancy (1987) *Desire and Domestic Fiction*. New York.

Armstrong, Nancy and Tennenhouse, Leonard (eds) (1987) *The Ideology of Conduct: Essays in Literature and the History of Sexuality*. New York.

Austen, Jane (1965) *Persuasion*, ed. D.W. Harding. Harmondsworth.

Austen, Jane (1966a) *Emma*, ed. Ronald Blythe. Harmondsworth.

Austen, Jane (1966b) *Mansfield Park*, ed. Tony Tanner. Harmondsworth.

Austen, Jane (1966c) *Pride and Prejudice*, ed. Tony Tanner. Harmondsworth.

Austen, Jane (1969) *Sense and Sensibility*, ed. Tony Tanner. Harmondsworth.

Austen, Jane (1971) *Lady Susan/The Watsons/Sanditon*, ed. Margaret Drabble. Harmondsworth.

Austen, Jane (1972) *Northanger Abbey*, ed. Anne H. Ehrenpreis. Harmondsworth.

Barker, Francis *et al.* (eds) (1977) *1848: The Sociology of Literature. Proceedings of the Essex Conference on the Sociology of Literature, July, 1977*. Colchester.

Barthes, Roland (1967) *Writing Degree Zero and Elements of Semiology*, trans. Annette Lavers and Colin Smith.

Barthes, Roland (1977) *Image – Music – Text*, trans. Stephen Heath.

Barthes, Roland (1986) *The Rustle of Language (Le Bruissement de la Langue)*, trans. Richard Howard. Oxford.

Beer, Frances (ed.) (1986) *The Juvenilia of Charlotte Brontë and Jane Austen*. Harmondsworth.

Belsey, Catherine (1980) *Critical Practice*.

Belsey, Catherine and Moore, Jane (eds) (1989) *The Feminist Reader: Essays in Gender and the Politics of Literary Criticism*.

Benstock, Shari (ed.) (1988) *The Private Self: Theory and Practice of Women's Autobiographical Writings*. Chapel Hill, NC.

Bevan, C. Knatchbull (1987) Personal identity in *Mansfield Park*: Forms, fictions, role-play, and reality, *Studies in English Literature*, 27: 595–608.

Brooks, Peter (1984) *Reading for the Plot*. New York.

Brown, Julia Prewitt (1979) *Jane Austen's Novels: Social Change and Literary Form*. Cambridge, MA.

Brown, Julia Prewitt (1990) The feminist depreciation of Jane Austen, *Novel*, 22: 303–13.

Browne, Alice (1987) *The Eighteenth-Century Feminist Mind*. Brighton.

Burke, Edmund (1968) *Reflections on the Revolution in France and on the Proceedings in London Relative to that Event*, ed. Conor Cruise O'Brien. Harmondsworth.

Butler, Marilyn (1975) *Jane Austen and the War of Ideas*. Oxford.

Cecil, Lord David (1978) *A Portrait of Jane Austen*.

Chapman, R.W. (ed.) (1932) *Jane Austen's Letters to her Sister Cassandra and Others*, 2 vols. Oxford.

Chapman, R.W. (ed.) (1953) *Jane Austen: A Critical Bibliography*. Oxford.

Clayton, Jay (1989) Narrative and theories of desire, *Critical Inquiry*, 16: 33–53.

Cole, Lucinda (1991) (Anti) feminist sympathies: The politics of relationship in Smith, Wollstonecraft, and More, *Journal of English Literary History*, 58: 107–40.

Copley, Stephen and Whale, John (eds) (1992) *Beyond Romanticism: New Approaches to Texts and Contexts, 1780–1832*.

Culler, Jonathan (1975) *Structuralist Poetics*. Ithaca, NY.

de Man, Paul (1979) *Allegories of Reading: Figural Language in Rousseau, Nietzsche, Rilke, and Proust*. New Haven, CT.

Dickinson, H.T. (1985) *British Radicalism and the French Revolution, 1789–1815*. Oxford.

Dowling, William (1984) *Jameson, Althusser, Marx: an Introduction to 'The Political Unconscious'*.

Drakakis, John (ed.) (1985) *Alternative Shakespeares*.

Duckworth, Alistair (1971) *The Improvement of the Estate*. Baltimore, MD.

Eagleton, Terry (1976) *Criticism and Ideology: A Study in Marxist Literary Theory*.

Eagleton, Terry (1991) *Ideology: An Introduction.*

Easthope, Antony (1983) *Poetry as Discourse.*

Emsley, Clive (1979) *British Society and the French Wars, 1793–1815.*

Evans, Mary (1987) *Jane Austen and the State.*

Felman, Shoshana (1977a) Turning the screw of interpretation, in Shoshana Felman (ed.), *Literature and Psychoanalysis: The Question of Reading: Otherwise.* Yale French Studies, 55/56.

Felman, Shoshana (ed.) (1977b) *Literature and Psychoanalysis: The Question of Reading: Otherwise.* Yale French Studies, 55/56.

Felman, Shoshana (1983) *The Literary Speech Act: Don Juan with J.L. Austin, or Seduction in Two Languages.* Ithaca, NY.

Felman, Shoshana (1985) *Writing and Madness.* Ithaca, New York.

Felman, Shoshana (1987) *Jacques Lacan and the Adventure of Insight.* Cambridge, MA.

Feuer, Lewis S. (ed.) (1959) *Marx and Engels: Basic Writings on Politics and Philosophy.* New York.

Fleishman, Avrom (1967) *A Reading of Mansfield Park: An Essay in Critical Synthesis.* Baltimore, MD.

Foucault, Michel (1972) *The Archaeology of Knowledge*, trans. A.M. Sheridan Smith.

Freud, Sigmund (1953–74) *The Standard Edition of the Complete Psychological Works*, ed. J. Strachey, 24 vols.

Galperin, William (1990) Byron, Austen and the 'revolution' of irony, *Criticism*, 32: 51–80.

Gay, Peter (1988) *Freud: A Life for Our Time.* Harmondsworth.

Gilbert, Sandra and Gubar, Susan (1979) *The Madwoman in the Attic.* New Haven, CT.

Grey, J. David (ed.) (1986) *The Jane Austen Handbook.*

Grosz, Elizabeth (1990) *Jacques Lacan: A Feminist Introduction.*

Gubar, Susan (1975) Sane Jane and the critics: 'Professions and falsehood', *Novel*, 8: 246–59.

Halperin, John (1983) The novelist as heroine in *Mansfield Park*: A study In Autobiography, *Modern Language Quarterly*, 44: 136–56.

Halperin, John (1984) *The Life of Jane Austen.* Baltimore, MD.

Harding, D.W. (1939–40) Regulated hatred: An aspect of the work of Jane Austen, *Scrutiny*, 8: 346–62.

Harris, Jocelyn (1989) *Jane Austen's Art of Memory.* Cambridge.

Hays, Mary (1796) *Memoirs of Emma Courtney*, 2 vols.

Honan, Park (1987) *Jane Austen: Her Life.*

Jameson, Fredric (1972) *The Prison-House of Language: A Critical Account of Structuralism and Russian Formalism.* Princeton, NJ.

Jameson, Fredric (1981) *The Political Unconscious: Narrative As A Socially Symbolic Act.* Ithaca, NY.

Jameson, Fredric (1988) *The Ideologies of Theory: Essays 1971–1986*, 2 vols.

Johnson, Claudia L. (1988) *Jane Austen: Women, Politics, and the Novel.* Chicago.

Johnson, Claudia L. (1989) A 'Sweet face as white as death': Jane Austen and the politics of female sensibility, *Novel*, 22: 159–74.

Jones, Vivien (ed.) (1990) *Women in the Eighteenth Century: Constructions of Femininity*.

Jordan, Elaine (1987) Pulpit, stage, and novel: 'Mansfield Park' and Mrs Inchbald's 'Lovers' Vows', *Novel*, 20: 138–48.

Kaufmann, David (1986) Closure in *Mansfield Park* and the sanctity of the family, *Philological Quarterly*, 65: 211–29.

Kay, Carol (1986) Canon, ideology, and gender: Mary Wollstonecraft's critique of Adam Smith, *New Political Science*, 15, Summer, 63–76.

Kelly, Gary (1976) *The English Jacobin Novel, 1780–1805*. Oxford.

Kelly, Gary (1989) *English Fiction of the Romantic Period, 1789–1830*.

Kirkham, Margaret (1983) *Jane Austen: Feminism and Fiction*. Brighton.

Koppel, Gene (1988) *The Religious Dimension of Jane Austen's Novels*. Ann Arbor, MI.

Leavis, F.R. (1948) *The Great Tradition: George Eliot, Henry James, Joseph Conrad*.

Lewes, George H. (1847) Recent novels: French and English, *Fraser's Magazine*, 36: 686–95.

Litvak, Joseph (1986) The infection of acting: Theatricals and theatricality in *Mansfield Park*, *Journal of English Literary History*, 53: 331–55.

Lodge, David (1966) *Language and Fiction: Essays in Criticism and Verbal Analysis of the English Novel*.

Lodge, David (ed.) (1988) *Modern Criticism and Theory*.

Lonsdale, Roger (ed.) (1990) *Eighteenth-Century Women Poets*. Oxford.

Lovell, Terry (1987) *Consuming Fiction*.

MacCabe, Colin (1979) *James Joyce and The Revolution of the Word*.

McDonnell, Diane (1986) *Theories of Discourse: An Introduction*. Oxford.

Macherey, Pierre (1978) *A Theory of Literary Production*, trans. Geoffrey Wall.

Miller, D.A. (1981) *Narrative and its Discontents: Problems of Closure in the Traditional Novel*. Princeton, NJ.

Mitchell, Juliet (1974) *Psychoanalysis and Feminism*.

Moler, Kenneth L. (1968) *Jane Austen's Art of Allusion*. Lincoln, NB.

Monaghan, David (ed.) (1981) *Jane Austen in a Social Context*.

Mudrick, Marvin (1968) *Jane Austen: Irony as Defense and Discovery*. Berkeley, CA.

Newman, Karen (1983) Can this marriage be saved? Jane Austen makes sense of an ending, *Journal of English Literary History*, 50: 693–710.

Newton, Judith Lowder (1985) *Women, Power, and Subversion: Social Strategies in British Fiction, 1778–1860*. New York.

Pickrel, Paul (1987) Lionel Trilling and *Mansfield Park*, *Studies in English Literature*, 27: 609–21.

Pickrel, Paul (1988) 'The Watsons' and the other Jane Austen, *Journal of English Literary History*, 55: 443–67.

Poovey, Mary (1984) *The Proper Lady and Woman Writer: Ideology as Style in the Works of Mary Wollstonecraft, Mary Shelley, and Jane Austen*. Chicago.

Rack, Henry D. (1989) *The Reasonable Enthusiast: John Wesley and the Rise of Methodism*.

Reeve, Clara (1785) *The Progress of Romance*, 2 vols. Colchester and London.

Rivers, Isabel (ed.) (1982) *Books and their Readers in Eighteenth-Century England*. Leicester.

Roberts, Warren (1979) *Jane Austen and the French Revolution*. New York.

Ruoff, Gene (1992) *Jane Austen's Sense and Sensibility*.

Schofield, Mary Anne and Macheski, Cecilia (eds) (1986) *Fetter'd or Free? British Women Novelists, 1670–1815*. Athens, GA.

Selden, Raman (ed.) (1988) *The Theory of Criticism: From Plato to the Present*.

Sheridan, Robert Brinsley (1975) *Sheridan's Plays*, ed. Cecil Price. Oxford.

Smith, Barbara Herrnstein (1968) *Poetic Closure: A Study of How Poems End*. Chicago.

Smith, Charlotte (1969) *The Old Manor House*, ed. Anne Henry Ehrenpreis.

Smith, Leroy W. (1983) *Jane Austen and the Drama of Woman*.

Southam, B.C. (1968; 1985) *Jane Austen: The Critical Heritage*, 2 vols.

Southam, B.C. (ed.) (1976) *Jane Austen: Casebook on 'Sense and Sensibility', 'Pride and Prejudice' and 'Mansfield Park'*.

Spacks, Patricia Meyer (1976) *Imagining a Self: Autobiography and Novel in Eighteenth-Century England*. Cambridge, MA.

Spencer, Jane (1986) *The Rise of the Woman Novelist: From Aphra Behn To Jane Austen*. Oxford.

Sulloway, Alison (1989) *Jane Austen and the Province of Womanhood*. Philadelphia, PA.

Tanner, Tony (1986) *Jane Austen*. Basingstoke.

Thompson, James (1988) *Between Self and World: The Novels of Jane Austen*. University Park, PA.

Todd, Janet (ed.) (1982) *Men By Women*. New York, Women in Literature, n.s., 2.

Todd, Janet (ed.) (1983) *Jane Austen: New Perspectives*. New York, Women in Literature, n.s., 3.

Todd, Janet (1986) *Sensibility: An Introduction*.

Todd, Janet (1988) *Feminist Literary History: A Defence*. Oxford.

Trilling, Lionel (1955) *The Opposing Self*. New York.

Trollope, Anthony (1938) On English prose fiction as a rational amusement, in Morris L. Parrish (ed.), *Four Lectures*.

Tucker, George H. (1983) *A Goodly Heritage: A History of Jane Austen's Family*. Manchester.

Walker, Cheryl (1990) Feminist literary criticism and the author, *Critical Inquiry*, 16: 551–71.

Watt, Ian (1957) *The Rise of the Novel: Studies in Defoe, Richardson and Fielding*.

Watt, Ian (ed.) (1963) *Jane Austen: A Collection of Critical Essays*. Englewood Cliffs, NJ.

Weedon, Chris (1987) *Feminist Practice and Poststructuralist Theory*. Oxford.

Williams, Raymond (1977) *Marxism and Literature*. Oxford.

Winnett, Susan (1990) 'Coming unstrung: Women, men, narrative, and principles of pleasure, *Publications of the Modern Language Association of America*, 105: 505–18.

Wollstonecraft, Mary (1976) *Mary, A Fiction*, in James Kinsley and Gary Kelly (eds), *Mary, and The Wrongs of Woman*. Oxford.

Wollstonecraft, Mary (1989) *The Works of Mary Wollstonecraft*, ed. Janet Todd and Marilyn Butler, 7 vols.

Wright, Elizabeth (1984) *Psychoanalytic Criticism: Theory in Practice*.

Young, Robert (ed.) (1981) *Untying the Text: A Post-Structuralist Reader*.

Further Reading

1 Henry Crawford and the 'Sphere of Love'

Marilyn Butler, *Jane Austen and the War of Ideas* (Oxford, 1975)
 A study that is of lasting significance, not least because of its interest in some of the social theories I examine in my essay.

Mary Evans, *Jane Austen and the State* (1987)
 Examines the difficulties in assessing Austen's political loyalties and her particular view of community.

Sandra Gilbert and Susan Gubar, *The Madwoman in the Attic* (New Haven, CT, 1979)
 Not exclusively on Austen. It deals with the pressures felt by nineteenth-century women novelists in a patriarchal society and the fictional strategies they took up both to conform to and challenge it.

Margaret Kirkham, *Jane Austen, Feminism and Fiction* (Brighton, 1983)
 Tackles a range of issues, but is excellent on the cultural debates on women's rights and place in society that provides a significantly fresh context for Austen's fiction.

Terry Lovell, Jane Austen and the gentry, in Diana Laurenson (ed.) *The Sociology of Literature: Applied Studies* (Keele Sociological Review Monographs, no. 26, 1978)
 Concentrates on Austen's references to class, and is particularly illuminating on the rather careful treatment of gentry figures.

2 The Political Unconscious

Alistair Duckworth, *The Improvement of the Estate* (Baltimore, MD, 1971)
The title suggests emphases on landscape gardening or country-house architecture. There are such references, but Duckworth's central concern is with the ideology of 'improvement' and consequently Austen's perspective and what it entailed.

Terry Eagleton, *Ideology: An Introduction* (1991)
A wide-ranging and accessible review of the various uses of the term.

Avrom Fleishman, *A Reading of Mansfield Park: An Essay in Critical Synthesis* (Baltimore, MD, 1967)
As the title suggests, the approach is an eclectic one, and Fleishman is perceptive and resists premature judgements on Austen's values in the novel.

Raymond Geuss, *The Idea of a Critical Theory* (Cambridge, 1981)
An excellent guide to the various usages of the term, 'ideology'.

Mary Poovey, *The Proper Lady and Woman Writer: Ideology as Style in the Works of Mary Wollstonecraft, Mary Shelley and Jane Austen* (Chicago, 1984)
Difficult to describe economically. Poovey accomplishes the difficult task of linking form with prior ideological assumptions with ease and also detailed commentary.

Tony Tanner, *Jane Austen* (Basingstoke, 1986)
Seems mainstream and orthodox, and yet Tanner is an acute critic of Austen, who is excellent on *Mansfield Park*.

Raymond Williams, *Marxism and Literature* (Oxford, 1977)
Not only concentrates on the main tenets of Marxism, but also dwells valuably on how they bear on literary and cultural study.

3 Gender, Theory and Jane Austen Culture

Nancy Armstrong, *Desire and Domestic Fiction: A Political History of the Novel* (New York, 1987)
A Foucauldian study of the political role fiction played in establishing the structure of the middle-class family and the boundary between public and private life.

Teresa de Lauretis, *Technologies of Gender: Essays on Theory, Film, and Fiction* (Bloomington, IN, 1987)
A brilliant critique of the heterosexism and/or gender blindness of post-structuralist theory, demonstrating how 'woman' remains both inside as well as outside representation.

Joan B. Landes, *Women and the Public Sphere in the Age of the French Revolution* (Ithaca, NY, 1988)

Drawing on the work of Habermas, Landes contrasts the role of gender in the old regime with the more repressive and rigidly gendered bourgeois public sphere associated with the French Revolution.

Terry Lovell, *Consuming Fiction* (1987)

Placing sex and gender along with class at the centre of materialist analysis, this persuasive study examines the history of the novel from the standpoint of consumption.

Nancy K. Miller, *Subject to Change: Reading Feminist Writing* (New York, 1988)

Illuminating the strategies women authors use to resist dominant discourses about femininity (such as contesting and revising conventional plots for female development, representing other modes of female subjectivity, and exposing the status of femininity itself as a social construction), these influential essays have been particularly helpful to readers of eighteenth- and nineteenth-century texts.

Mary Poovey, *The Proper Lady and the Woman Writer: Ideology as Style in the Works of Mary Wollstonecraft, Mary Shelley, and Jane Austen* (Chicago, 1984)

Integrating Marxist and feminist theory, this landmark study explores the ways in which women writers accommodated as well as resisted ideologies of female propriety.

Denise Riley, *'Am I That Name?': Feminism and the Category of 'Women' in History* (Minneapolis, MN, 1988)

Combining deconstructive strategies with historical scholarship, this important study traces the ambiguous and oscillating constructions of 'women' as a collective category distinct across other categories of personhood from the late seventeenth to the nineteenth centuries.

Alison G. Sulloway, *Jane Austen and the Province of Womanhood* (Philadelphia, PA, 1989)

Placing Austen's representations of gender within the context of diverse contemporary debates about women, this study argues that Austen is a moderate feminist.

4 Discovering 'A New Way of Reading'

Isobel Armstrong, *Mansfield Park* (Harmondsworth, 1988)
This little Penguin Critical Studies volume takes an interrogative and provocative stance in relation to *MP*. Very aware of both current critical theory and of debates and issues contemporary with the writing of the novel. Armstrong draws on the work of, among others, Fredric Jameson in *The Political Unconscious* (1981).

Peter Brooks, *Reading for the Plot: Design and Intention in Narrative* (New York, 1984)
This book, like much of Shoshana Felman's work, explores questions of reading and psychoanalysis and rethinks the relations between literature and psychoanalysis, Brooks is particularly interested in relations between plot and desire, and in the repetition compulsion and transference.

Terry Eagleton, *Literary Theory: An Introduction* (Oxford, 1983)
This includes a useful chapter on psychoanalysis, Freudian and Lacanian. It is a good starting point for a reader new to either, or both.

Antony Easthope, *Poetry as Discourse* (1983)
The chapter on 'Discourse as Subjectivity' offers a most helpful introduction to aspects of Lacan's work which are of particular relevance to Felman's practice.

Shoshana Felman, *Jacques Lacan and the Adventure of Insight: Psychoanalysis in Contemporary Culture* (Cambridge, MA, 1987)
A very provocative set of essays exploring the implications of Lacan's work for reading, for psychoanalysis, and for other areas of cultural activity.

Shoshana Felman (ed.), *Literature and Psychoanalysis: The Question of Reading: Otherwise* (Yale French Studies 55/56, 1977)
This contains the essay 'Turning the screw of interpretation' and a range of other essays by, among others, Lacan, Barbara Johnson, Fredric Jameson and Peter Brooks. All the essays are concerned with rethinking the relations between literature and psychoanalysis.

Shoshana Felman, *The Literary Speech Act: Don Juan with J.L. Austin, or Seduction in Two Languages* (Ithaca, NY, 1983)
This book attempts to articulate Austin's speech act theory with Lacanian psychoanalysis and to explore the misunderstandings that arise between English and French modes and traditions of thought.

Shoshana Felman, *Writing and Madness: Literature/Philosophy/Psychoanalysis* (Ithaca, New York, 1985)
This book reprints 'Turning the screw of interpretation' and explores the interimplication of madness and literature in a number of other essays. Her

Introduction provides a useful, if difficult, starting point for reading 'Turning the screw'.

Elizabeth Wright, *Psychoanalytic Criticism: Theory in Practice* (London, 1984)

A useful, though highly condensed, introduction to the subject; the chapter on 'Structural Psychoanalysis' discusses both the work of Lacan and, more briefly, Felman's 'Turning the screw'.

Index

A CRITICAL AND CULTURAL THEORY READER

Antony Easthope and Kate McGowan (eds)

The 'death of literature' and the rise of post-structuralist theory has breached the traditional opposition between the literary canon and popular culture, both in principle and in academic practice. There is therefore a growing need for a collection of essays and extracts required for the study of both high and popular culture together. Covering 'Semiology', 'Ideology', 'Subjectivity', 'Difference', 'Gender' and 'Postmodernism', this reader contains essential writing by Saussure, Barthes, Lacan, Kristeva, Foucault, Derrida and Cixous, as well as material for the study of popular culture. It concludes with a section of 'Cultural Documents' with extracts from Leavis, Adorno, Williams and Tzara. With the concerns of students in mind, each section is fully introduced and each piece of writing summarized in the notes.

Contents

288pp   0 335 09944 0 (Paperback)   0 335 09945 9 (Hardback)

ENGLISH ROMANTIC POETRY
AN INTRODUCTION TO THE HISTORICAL
CONTEXT AND THE LITERARY SCENE

Kelvin Everest

This new study presents a concise but comprehensive introduction to the political, social and literary contexts of English Romantic poetry. The significant movements and events of the momentous historical epoch in which the major English Romantic poets lived and worked – which stretched from the American War of Independence to the Great Reform Bill – are presented in careful outline. The life and career of each of these poets – Blake, Wordsworth, Coleridge, Shelley, Keats and Byron – is then described and placed in detailed relation to the larger historical forces and circumstances of the period, and to the literary culture within and against which they worked and published.

The book includes a detailed historical and literary chronology of the period and bibliograhpies on the historical and literary context and on works by and about the six poets featured.

Contents
Part 1: The historical context – Years of revolution: 1775–93 – Years of reaction: 1793–1815 – The post-war period: after 1815 – Part 2: The social relations of the Romantic poets – Blake, Wordsworth, Coleridge – Keats, Shelley, Byron – Part 3: The literary scene – Conclusion – Chronology – Bibliography – Index.

128pp   0 335 09297 7 (Paperback)   0 335 09298 5 (Hardback)

REVOLUTION IN WRITING
BRITISH LITERARY RESPONSES TO THE
FRENCH REVOLUTION

Kelvin Everest (ed.)

The bicentenary of the French Revolution gave rise to immense interest, both popular and academic, into the historical, political and cultural legacies of the events of 1789. This innovative volume forms a broad-ranging investigation into the British literary reponses to this monumental upheaval. Mary Wollstonecraft, Edmund Burke, and Tom Paine of course provide a recurring central focus of attention, but there are also searching considerations of the impact of the Revolution on the romantic poets, and on such relatively neglected figures as Hannah More, who here for the first time receives constructive analysis a feminist perspective. Theoretical issues are also a major interest in this volume, including both the Revolutionary period's own attempts to theorize its experience, and our contemporary struggle to establish a mode of literary-historical analysis which can mediate between text, history, and theory.

Contents
Introduction – Romanticism, history, hitoricisms – Hannah More's counter-revolutionary feminism – Gender in revolution: Edmund Burke and Mary Wollstonecraft – 'The cool eye of observation': Mary Wollstonecraft and the French Revolution – The limits of Paine's revolutionary literalism – Shelley, The Cenci *and the French Revolution – Index.*

Contributors
Kelvin Everest, Tom Furniss, Harriet Devine Jump, Philip W. Martin, Michael Rossington, Kathryn Sutherland, John Whale.

176pp   0 335 09756 1 (Paperback)

BYRON

Angus Calder

Perhaps the most remarkable truth about Byron is that his verse has remained continuously controversial since his first 'slim volume' to the present day. His was a literary personality which overwhelmed his contemporaries. They read him fast, for pleasure. Whether or not they 'understood' what they read (and like many writers, Byron often complained of being misunderstood), they reacted strongly to it, for or against, sometimes for *AND* against at once. Angus Calder invites us in this Guide to do likewise, and to test our own reactions against the texts and against the arguments he advances. His aims are: firstly, to help us to enjoy Byron's poetry; secondly, to assist us in placing Byron within the context of the British and European Romantic movements, of the history of Europe in his lifetime, and of British literary history; and ultimately to encourage us to take our own part in the hitherto ceaseless controversy.

Contents

Contexts – Byronic narrative: The Siege of Corinth *and* The Prisoner of Chillon – *'Personality' and convention: from* Childe Harold *to* Don Juan – The Vision of Judgement – Don Juan – *Notes and references – Further reading – Index.*

112pp   0 335 15086 1 (Paperback)   0 335 15095 0 (Hardback)